A Lesson in Scandal

Tales from The Burnished Jade
Book 1

ADELE CLEE

This is a work of fiction. All names, characters, places and incidents are products of the author's imagination. All characters are fictitious and any resemblance to real persons, living or dead, is purely coincidental.

No part of this book may be copied or reproduced in any manner without the author's permission.

Cover by Dar Albert at Wicked Smart Designs
Dragonfly motif by Vika Glitter via Pixababy

Chapter One

The Burnished Jade
Aldgate Street, London

Miss Sofia Moorland occupied a front-row seat in The Jade's elegant music room, listening to the doctor's lecture. She gripped her pencil tightly and made notes in her leather-bound journal, the implement dancing across the page as swiftly as fire in a hay barn. The other ladies sat in rapt attention, staring at the enigmatic Mr Gentry as he spoke about the importance of a healthy mind.

"A simple walk in the park can calm the senses," he said, the seductive lilt of his voice wrapping around the audience like a warm blanket. "Taking time to absorb the natural world reaps rewards."

The handsome doctor shifted his weight to his other foot, the fabric of his trousers tightening around the curve of his muscular thigh.

"Have you ever seen such a virile specimen of masculinity?" Mrs Reagan whispered to Sofia. "I may feign hysteria in the hope Mr Gentry will loosen my clothing. With such skilled hands, I imagine he could cure any ailment."

Sofia straightened her spectacles and considered Mr Gentry's fine physique. How fast did one's heart need to pump to ensure blood filled those powerful muscles? The man must exert himself frequently. No doubt he rode his mount hard and fast until they were both slick with sweat and panting. People said he was an excellent pugilist, or perhaps lunges with a rapier explained those robust thighs.

"A fluttering pulse can be an early sign of agitation," he added.

"Mr Gentry has more than my pulse fluttering," Mrs Reagan uttered, fanning her face with her hand.

Being versed in medical literature, Sofia knew the widow spoke about arousal and the convulsions a lady felt deep in her core—the cure suggested by men to reduce the effects of hysteria.

"I cannot afford such a luxury," Sofia whispered back.

It's why she took notes at Mr Gentry's lectures and rarely looked his way. She absorbed every word, every minute detail. Knowledge was a lifeline to a brighter future, and Mr Gentry was the one person who could save her from a wretched fate.

"A slight rise in temperature soon follows," Mr Gentry continued with such poise Sofia doubted he ever lost control of his faculties.

Like a rock against the tide, he stood firm, his emotions guarded. His calm facade left women intrigued and drawn to his unreachable allure.

"I'm on fire," Mrs Reagan purred.

Keen to focus on the lecture and not the charismatic gentleman, Sofia thrust her hand in the air and wiggled her fingers, forcing Mr Gentry to fix her with his intelligent blue gaze.

"Yes, Miss Moorland?"

Despite his smooth tone, she sensed his annoyance.

"I believe there is a difference between agitation and nervous disorder, sir."

Sofia's stepmother suffered from the latter, from bouts of violence and terrible changes in mood. Judith's comments left a sting sharper than her back-handed slaps.

"Agitation is a temporary state," Sofia continued, trying to impress him. "A walk in the park may give a lady perspective, but what if nothing helps? What if you're dealing with a chronic condition?" One made worse by the excessive consumption of gin.

Mr Gentry smiled, but as a chorus of soft sighs whispered through the room, Sofia noted the strain behind his feigned expression. He wanted rid of her. He wanted her to button her lips and stare at his broad chest like the other ladies in the room.

"Such conditions are beyond my realms of expertise," he said with the eloquence befitting a viscount's grandson. Yet she had heard him curse men to the devil and regale bawdy tales to his friends.

While the wallflowers, widows and bluestockings saw a distinguished gentleman, Sofia heard murmurs of a darker side to Mr Gentry's character. There was a reason he scoured the alleys of Whitechapel at night. A reason he rode a black beast of a horse out onto the Barking Road and did not return home until dawn.

A reason that eluded her.

That's the man she must appeal to: the reckless rogue, the lone crusader hiding beneath a breathtaking smile and an expensive blue coat.

"Would you consider female hysteria a temporary malady or something more complex?" Sofia asked, her heart pounding. A tight coil of anxiety twisted in her gut, but she held his gaze, refusing to falter. "Are women not more expressive by nature? Is the release of pent-up emotions an adequate cure or the abuse of a naive mind?"

She referred to the unscrupulous doctors who pleasured ladies as an excuse to calm their restless spirits.

While Mr Gentry stared at her, Mrs Reagan uttered, "I pray he deals with the condition. I suddenly find my emotions in a terrible tangle. Perhaps he might unravel the knot."

Mr Gentry's blue eyes turned glacial. "May I speak to you outside for a moment, Miss Moorland?"

Good Lord!

Sofia could converse in medical terms and argue her point but would struggle if he did anything but berate her. "Certainly."

Mrs Reagan tugged Sofia's sleeve and mumbled, "Swoon, and he'll be forced to carry you to a private room." Then she gave an encouraging nod.

While Mr Gentry silenced the muffled protests and assured the ladies he would return to continue the lecture, Sofia rose demurely and let him escort her into The Burnished Jade's elegant pale blue hall.

"How many times must we have this conversation?" he whispered, closing the music room door behind him. "Will you stop interrupting my lectures with your relentless questions? This isn't a lesson at King's College."

"If it was King's College, they'd usher me from the building merely because I am wearing a dress."

Mr Gentry's gaze slid over the dull grey garment. "Is it a dress, Miss Moorland? You wear it like a shroud. I suggest you return your medical books to the library and meet with Lady Berridge's modiste."

Mr Gentry was often blunt to prove a point. He made it clear few women could stomach broken limbs, gruesome diseases, or the trauma of losing a patient.

"Believe me, sir, I have more urgent matters to attend to than my wardrobe." Sofia hugged her journal to her chest, her hands trembling with the weight of her challenge. If she couldn't find a way to support herself before her stepmother returned from Edinburgh, she would be forced to marry Mr Harrop. "I challenge you to find fault with my argument. Most men would label me hysterical for having a firm opinion."

Mr Gentry did not disagree.

"I'll admit you understand the mind better than most." He bent his head. A rakish lock of golden-brown hair fell over his brow, offering a glimpse of the untamed man beneath his facade. "You're out of your depth. What you've learnt in those old tomes is of no practical use."

"How do you know?" It was now or never. Persuading Mr Gentry to hire her would be the answer to her prayers. "Why not put me to the test? You have two employees; why not hire a third?"

Mr Gentry jerked his head. "I cannot employ a woman."

"Yet people claim you're a modern man."

Why else would he lecture at a ladies' club owned by the Countess of Berridge? He supported her charitable work and was an advocate of social reform. He cared about people and the plight of the poor.

"My patients will ignore your advice." His striking blue eyes met hers, his disappointment evident as he considered her dowdy day dress. "Despite your efforts to make yourself unappealing, I'll have men lining the streets, eager to drop their trousers and have you *tend* to their ailments."

Sofia felt a blush rise to her cheeks.

Like a hound scenting blood, Mr Gentry pounced at the first sign of weakness. "Have you ever touched a man, Miss Moorland?" He cupped her elbow and drew her deeper into the hall. "Have you ever wrapped your dainty fingers around his manhood and given the task your full attention? Because that's what you'll be expected to do."

Her traitorous mind conjured an image of the doctor slowly peeling off his clothes, every movement revealing the power lurking beneath his polished exterior. Yet amid the thrill of the fantasy lay a nagging doubt. If Mr Gentry made her nervous, how would she deal with other men?

Sofia gulped and bit her inner lip, the metallic taste of blood a sign of defeat, but she refused to surrender without a fight.

"The study of anatomy includes all bodily parts," she said, trying not to stutter. "I see no difference between them and would approach the task in a professional manner."

It was the biggest lie she had ever told.

The mere thought gave her the jitters.

A glimmer of intrigue flashed in his eyes. "And when the touch of your hand arouses the patient, and his manhood hardens beneath your fingers, what then, Miss Moorland?"

Based on the husky notes in his voice, Mr Gentry could

add acting to his repertoire. He certainly knew how to play the libertine and highlight her inexperience.

"I would make a diagnosis and ask him to dress."

Mr Gentry stepped closer, his presence enveloping her as he drew her into his orbit. The air shifted between them, a crackle of electric tension. This was a lesson in scandal. Another test of her resolve.

Good.

Then he might see she was serious in her endeavour.

"How will you fare when he puts his filthy hands on you, Miss Moorland? When you're alone in a room and you arouse him to the point of madness?" A darkness passed over his features as his gaze dipped to her bodice, a heated look that spoke of hidden danger. "What happens when having you is the only cure for his malady?"

Sofia snapped her spine straight and avoided inhaling too deeply. Mr Gentry smelled as good as he looked. His cologne was like a drug, an addictive mix of spice and musk that clouded the senses.

She gritted her teeth for dramatic effect. "I shall grab him between the legs and squeeze hard." The Countess of Berridge had ensured the ladies who visited The Jade were tutored in self-defence. "I shall remind him what it means to be a gentleman."

Mr Gentry threw back his head and laughed.

"Do you find something amusing, sir?"

"Yes, you, Miss Moorland. Like everything else about you, you lack real experience when it comes to … anything. I could have you pinned to the wall in a heartbeat. You'd struggle to move your hands, let alone grab me by the proverbials."

The thought of tussling with him sparked a fire in her

blood. She wanted to wipe the smug grin off his face and show him she wasn't afraid. She wanted him to pin her to the wall and pretend his desire for her had driven him mad.

"Do it," she said in open challenge, daring him to make a move and strangely hoping he would.

"I would never hurt a woman. I would never hurt you."

The devil!

Anyone deprived of affection would falter under the weight of his kind words. In truth, the comment was designed to suggest he cared when all he wanted was her submission.

"You hurt me every time you dismiss my ambitions as folly." He treated her like an annoying spider that reappeared after being tossed out. "You profess to save people, yet I die a little when you treat me like a child. Let me accompany you for a week. I promise you will not regret your decision."

A weary sigh left his lips. "I cannot employ a woman," he reiterated. "Doubtless your parents would drag me over hot coals for—"

"The Merricks are not my parents." The mere mention of their names roused an inner fury, an anger born from resentment. Her stepmother had recently remarried, and the couple planned to get rid of Sofia when they returned from their sojourn in Scotland. "I assure you, they don't care about my welfare."

"Nevertheless, I do."

Again, his simple statement caught her off guard.

"No, you don't. You're worried about how your patients and colleagues will receive me. You're afraid I might prove to be a valuable asset, and you'll suffer the ridicule of your peers."

"I'm afraid of nothing and no one," he said, his tone

suddenly sharp, a rare crack in his composure. "But I will not be held accountable for your reckless ambitions."

A tense silence descended.

A moment of stark reflection.

In her desperation, she had pushed him too hard. He was not to blame for her predicament. Everything he'd said was true. She was a foolish, inexperienced woman clinging to the last vestiges of hope.

"Forgive me." Though tears pricked her eyes, she found the courage to look at him. "Sometimes my passion overwhelms me. The truth is, I'm in desperate need of work. There are few options open to gently bred women, and you're my last hope. I have nowhere else to turn."

He studied her, his piercing cobalt eyes fixed on her face, holding the gaze for what felt like forever.

"May I see your journal?" He motioned to the blue book she gripped like the survivor of a sinking ship did a piece of wreckage. "You write in it whenever I give a lecture here. I saw you in Pickins coffeehouse, absorbed by the contents of the pages."

Her pulse quickened.

He had sat watching her?

The sudden creak of the music room door stole their attention, and Mrs Reagan appeared. "Are you returning to finish the lecture, Mr Gentry, or shall I gather the ladies for refreshments?"

"Remain in your seats," he said in the commanding tone that always made the widow sigh. "I'll be with you shortly."

Mrs Reagan smiled and made to close the door, but not before winking at Sofia and pretending to swoon.

Sofia gave Mr Gentry the journal, opening it on a specific page. "You may read anything except for my research on hysteria." She'd been a fool to document her findings and should tear out the pages and throw them in the grate.

"I thought you wished to impress me with your study of the female mind. That is the topic of the day."

"Those particular notes are personal." Heat filled her cheeks, but a brief blush was better than lifelong mortification. "My experiments are of a confidential nature."

"I see."

She prayed he didn't see. How could a lady understand the cure for hysteria without experiencing the remedy firsthand?

"My mother was a skilled herbalist," she said, keen to change the subject. "I make remedies, too. Amongst her many books, she kept a copy of *The Female Physician* by Maubray. I managed to study and sketch parts of the anatomy before my stepmother sold the volume."

Judith had gutted the library and converted it into a gaming room for her dissolute friends. Mr Harrop, a wealthy merchant nearing sixty, came to drink and play whist every Monday evening. The vile creature watched Sofia as she poured his claret, the predatory gleam in his eyes making her flesh creep.

"You surprise me," Mr Gentry said, drawing Sofia from her reverie. "You admire Maubray, yet he suggested men should be midwives." He glanced at the book, his brows rising when he saw her detailed drawing of the heart. "Hmm." He repeated the sound as he flicked through the pages. "Can you name three symptoms of pleurisy?"

Sofia blinked, surprised he'd not slammed her book shut. "A sharp pain in the chest that worsens with breathing. Perhaps a dry cough, and sometimes a fever."

"And a cure?" he asked, scanning her notes.

"Willow bark can help with pain and inflammation. The apothecary in Covent Garden stocks a wide range of herbs and exotic ingredients. I know how to make herbal teas, tinctures and poultices."

Mr Gentry glanced up at her with a glimmer of admiration. "How would you determine the patient is not suffering from pneumonia?"

She knew the answer because her mother had perished from the illness when Sofia was fifteen. "Pneumonia causes a feeling of malaise. The cough is not dry but produces sputum."

He closed the book. "What is your view of bloodletting?"

She hesitated.

What if their opinions differed and it ruined her prospects?

"I believe the loss of blood weakens the patient. I have seen evidence of this personally." As her father lay dying, she had argued with Judith, insisting bloodletting would aggravate his symptoms.

"Some might say that's modern thinking, Miss Moorland."

"Is it modern to learn from past mistakes?"

A slow smile warmed his face, one that had a strange heat coiling in her belly. "I cannot employ you to tend to my patients, but I may be able to help in other ways." He studied her before asking her to remove her spectacles.

A frisson of alarm shot through her.

Why should her appearance matter?

"Remove my spectacles? For what purpose?"

"So I might look at you properly." He returned her journal and folded his arms across his broad chest. "If I'm to pay for your services, I need to know you'll obey my instructions."

Shocked, Sofia stepped back and hit the wall. "I'm not sure what type of services you have in mind, sir, but I am not a woman—"

"Your spectacles, Miss Moorland. I'll not ask again."

With muttered protests, Sofia removed her spectacles.

Mr Gentry snatched them and peered through the lenses. "It's as I suspected. You don't really need these. It explains why you can write and look at me while wearing them."

"They help a little with distance," she admitted, somewhat unnerved as he gazed at her face, "but as you say, the magnification is so mild, I can read and write without removing them."

"How old are you?"

"Three and twenty, sir."

He nodded like that was important. "May I take down your hair?"

"I beg your pardon?"

Clearly she had misheard.

"Your hair. May I see it when it's not scraped back so severely?"

Sofia glanced left and right as her heartbeat thumped in her ears. It was as she feared. The service he wanted her to perform had nothing to do with treating ailments, though why he was interested in her remained a mystery.

"Mr Gentry, you should know I am seeking honest employment." She had no intention of selling herself, even to a man she admired. "I intend to open my own practice one day, and cannot do that if people think I'm a harlot."

Mr Gentry's low chuckle stirred the hairs at her nape. "Removing a few pins does not make you a harlot, Miss Moorland."

"What does it make me, sir?" A simpleton who hung on

his every word? A slave to this man's odd whims? A doe being hunted by a wolf?

He heard the implicit meaning behind her question and quickly offered every reassurance. "I don't need a mistress if that's your fear."

Of course he didn't. The long list of ladies vying for the position would cover the length of Pall Mall.

"If I needed a woman to warm my bed, I would choose one who didn't persist in asking probing questions."

So, this was a means to test her mettle.

Hoping she'd fall at the first hurdle.

He wanted an excuse to refuse giving her a position.

Sofia lifted her chin, ready to prove nothing fazed her. "Now we understand one another, you may remove the pins, but I demand an explanation as you do."

Mischief danced in his eyes as he stepped too close and his elegant fingers slipped into her hair. "Would you care to hear my motive, Miss Moorland?"

"Please."

One after another, he pulled the pins free, a slow, agonising attack on her senses. Her breath caught in her throat, her pulse quickening as his fingertips caressed her scalp.

"I must be sure your disguise is satisfactory."

"My disguise?"

"Hold out your hand," he uttered, gasping as her dark brown hair tumbled around her shoulders. "You might want to keep the pins."

He dropped them into her palm, then brushed his fingers through her hair. The gentle caress created an intimacy that left her knees shaking and her heart pounding. If the job of mistress was available, she might be tempted to apply.

Mr Gentry stepped back and perused her from head to toe. "Report to my practice tomorrow at noon. Wear the monstrosity you call a dress. I expect all your garments to be just as poorly fitted. Tie your hair so tightly not a single strand escapes. And never, never remove your spectacles. Is that understood?"

He was going to employ her?

A wave of gratitude almost knocked her off her feet.

Sofia was so stunned she could barely form a word.

"Miss Moorland? Do you want to work for me or not?"

She nodded profusely. "Yes. I do. Thank you, sir." Daring to be bold out of necessity, she asked, "Might the position come with lodgings? A small, simple room would suffice. You might deduct the rent from my wages. I shall be no trouble."

Mr Gentry frowned, the lines on his brow deepening the longer he considered her. "Who are you running from, Miss Moorland? I'll not have your personal troubles affecting your work."

Sofia couldn't bring herself to answer.

It wasn't the image of Mr Harrop's wobbling jowls or the memory of his wandering hands that sent her pulse soaring. It wasn't the evil glint in her new stepfather's eyes that crushed the air from her lungs.

Judith Merrick had a secret plan for Sofia, one that beggared belief. If the letter she'd found was proof of her stepmother's intention, it painted a terrifying picture, a scene worse than a chilling nightmare.

Chapter Two

Gentry's Private Practice
Leadenhall Street, London

"You have a three o'clock appointment in Highgate with Mr Dennison," Turner said, scanning the diary. "The gout in his foot shows no improvement and he suggests leeches to balance the humours."

"Leeches won't reduce the swelling." Reid Gentry relaxed in the leather chair behind his desk and considered his colleague. "If Dennison stopped drinking port for a month, he'd be pain-free in no time."

Every man had a vice—some turned to drink, some to women; Reid chased danger. That said, he had little choice but to spend his nights in a tavern teeming with footpads and thieves.

"On a diet of wine and laudanum, is it any wonder the man struggles to haul himself out of bed?" Turner's sigh echoed Reid's frustration. "Let me visit Dennison and remind him of his failings. When it comes to awkward patients, my father always said persistence pays."

Reid heard the thread of grief in the younger man's voice. Losing one's parent and mentor struck a double blow. "Your father would be proud of the work you do here. Another year, and you can afford to open your own practice."

Turner's smile barely reached his eyes. "I'm in no hurry to leave. My father worked himself to the bone, and I have no intention of doing the same."

"Your father was a brilliant surgeon and physician. We all feel his loss deeply. You'll have a position here until you're ready to pursue your own venture." Which might be anytime within the next hour when Turner met the new female employee.

Reid glanced at the mantel clock as it chimed a quarter to the hour.

Miss Moorland would arrive soon. She was bound to cause a stir, precisely for the reasons one would expect. Few people would trust a woman's diagnosis, hence Reid had no choice but to hire her as a herbalist. A fact he failed to make clear during their heated discussion yesterday.

Who are you running from, Miss Moorland?

The brief flash of terror in her eyes and her refusal to answer a simple question intrigued him. It's why he made a concession and offered her a room upstairs. The gesture went against his better judgement. There was a killer on the loose, one targeting his patients. Indeed, how could he leave Miss Moorland alone in the building and still sleep soundly?

A knock on the study door brought Reid's secretary, John Hickman. Despite being thirty-three and completing his medical training at St Bartholomew's, Hickman suffered from a nervous disposition and lacked the stomach to carry out painful procedures. His vibrant mop of red hair did nothing to brighten his tight expression.

"There's a lady here to see you, sir." The slight tremble in Hickman's voice mimicked the tremor in his hands. "A Miss Moorland. She claims she has an appointment, but there's no record in the diary."

For no sensible reason, Reid smiled.

He couldn't help but admire the lady's determination despite the obstacles thrown in her path. He'd met women desperate to lure him into bed, never one desperate to make use of his credentials.

Reid stood and rounded the desk, quick to banish the thrum of excitement. He had placed bets with his friends last night, wagering ten pounds Miss Moorland would find subtle ways to challenge his strict instructions.

"Show the lady in." Reid straightened his coat sleeves and combed his fingers through his hair. "You'll both remain here while I introduce her."

Confusion lined Turner's brow. "I assume Miss Moorland is a new patient and not a society lady your grandfather is forcing you to marry."

The innocent remark struck a nerve.

"My grandfather would never trade my happiness for wealth and status." Not after the unforgivable mistake the viscount had made thirty years ago. "Miss Moorland is …"

He couldn't quite find the right word to describe her. Those sumptuous pink lips prevented him from naming her a bluestocking. Her waves of lustrous dark hair meant he couldn't call her a wallflower, either. The term spinster might suffice, but her passionate nature could grant her a place in many a man's bed.

"A relative?" Hickman offered.

"No, she's our new herbalist."

"Our herbalist?" both men said in unison, their chins hitting their chests.

"I would prefer to know what's in the tinctures we prescribe." Reid spoke as if hiring Miss Moorland was part of a clever business strategy, not a reckless decision based on her tears and the detailed notes in her journal.

A muscle ticked in Hickman's cheek. "She looks quite young."

"She's three and twenty."

Being three years older, Turner appeared intrigued. "And she's not married?"

Reid was quick to squash any romantic notions his colleague might have. "No, Miss Moorland is dedicated to her work." Keen to settle their fears, he added, "She's here on a trial basis. As always, our patients' needs are a priority, and I expect you to support her appointment."

Both men nodded.

Before Hickman went to fetch Miss Moorland, Reid thought to make an important point clear. "You're to treat her with the respect one affords a lady, but you will not undermine her opinion. Discuss theories, by all means, question her knowledge, call her out for her mistakes, but do not treat her like an imbecile because of her sex."

He thought about adding another caveat.

Don't ask her to remove her spectacles and take down her hair. Not unless you want those intelligent green eyes haunting your dreams. Not if you want to lie in bed without imagining her hair splayed over your pillow.

Damn the woman.

She had no idea she was even remotely attractive, which

only added to her allure. The air of mystery surrounding her had awakened something strange inside him. It was easily explained. Men liked solving puzzles, and Miss Moorland was a fascinating enigma.

Don't ask to read her notes on hysteria, he added silently. Because he'd spent restless hours wondering what secrets she kept hidden within the pages of her sacred journal. The fact he thought he knew only added to the torment.

Hickman withdrew and returned with Miss Moorland.

She entered the room in her usual unassuming manner. "Good afternoon, Mr Gentry." She curtsied and then offered Mr Turner a warm smile.

"Good *morning*, Miss Moorland. You're ten minutes early, though I'm glad to see you followed my instructions."

There wasn't a stray hair visible beneath her dark blue bonnet. Her spectacles remained firmly in place. But by God, if her lips weren't the most desirable pink he'd ever seen. He couldn't see much of her dress hidden beneath the black silk pelisse. The coat was outdated, but it cinched at her waist, forcing his attention to the soft curve of her breasts.

"One must satisfy one's employer," she said.

Hell! Now his thoughts were running amok.

"Allow me to introduce Mr Turner." Reid gestured to the handsome physician who struggled to keep his mouth closed. "His father, Ambrose Turner, was my mentor and taught me everything I know about amputation."

Miss Moorland did not wrinkle her nose at the mention of lost limbs. "I read your father's papers on the subject, Mr Turner," she said, her countenance brightening. "The success of an amputation hinges on swift precision."

Turner gawped at her like she belonged to the world of the fae. "Y-yes, although the proper use of ligatures is vital."

"Indeed. I imagine a quart of brandy helps, too." She shifted her attention back to Reid. "I'm told you conduct some surgeries on the premises."

If she expected to stand at his shoulder while he operated, she was sorely mistaken. "Yes, and also at Guy's Hospital. My expertise covers a wide range of fields."

He had the steady hands of a surgeon and the sharp instincts of a physician. Whether diagnosing ailments or making precise cuts with his scalpel, he had mastered both skills. What a shame he wasn't as proficient in solving crimes.

Hickman cleared his throat and introduced himself. "I will be responsible for ordering your supplies, Miss Moorland."

"My supplies?"

"Your herbs and tinctures. The apothecary requires a week's notice for the less common ingredients. He stocks a wide range from exotic sources. I can accompany you there later today if you'd like to place an order."

"Miss Moorland starts work tomorrow," Reid said, though he feared his men would be as useful as rotten turnips when she was on the premises. "She will need a few days to become familiar with the practice."

"A day should suffice," she said confidently.

Reid inclined his head. "Allow me to show you the treatment rooms and answer any questions you may have. Hickman will take your outdoor apparel."

While Turner hurried away to tidy his cluttered consulting room, Hickman jumped at the chance to play footman.

Reid perched on the edge of his desk, arms folded, and watched his secretary help Miss Moorland undress. She untied the ribbons on her bonnet and quickly flattened the stray curl of dark hair behind her ear.

Wary eyes met his, but she said nothing.

Her gloves followed, each innocent tug on the fingers holding Reid's attention. Her hands were soft and small and slender. Too delicate to dig deep into a leg wound and remove wooden splinters and fragments of lead. Too pure to be stained crimson with blood.

Her fumble with the buttons on her pelisse betrayed her calm facade. "It's a little cold out. My fingers are still numb."

Liar! I make you nervous, he wanted to say. It was a mild March day, filled with the promise of spring.

"You walked here?"

"Yes, from Dean Street near Soho Square."

Reid stood abruptly. "Through Seven Dials and Holborn?"

"Yes."

"Carrying luggage?"

Miss Moorland removed her pelisse and gave it to Hickman. The dress she wore sagged around the waist and hips, the deep shade of midnight blue draping her figure like night itself, concealing the secrets hidden beneath.

"I have no luggage today," she said, thanking Hickman. "I will explain why during the tour."

As a man constantly searching for the truth, Reid dismissed Hickman and closed the door. "Sit down, Miss Moorland, while we discuss the details of your employment. Do your step-parents know you're here?"

The lady sat and clasped her hands in her lap. "Mr and Mrs Merrick are in Scotland visiting family." The sudden strain in her voice was unmistakable. "They left a month ago and plan to return home soon, though didn't state when."

He perched on the desk, hoping the close proximity unnerved her because she needed to get used to being surrounded by men. "Am I right in saying you don't want the Merricks to return?"

"Yes."

"Because ..." He waved his hand, prompting her to continue.

"They will force me to marry."

She averted her gaze for a few seconds, a clear sign she was hiding a crucial part of the story. While Reid had his own secrets, he couldn't offer a woman sanctuary without knowing her history.

"Force you?" He didn't like the image those words conveyed. "You mean coerce? You're of an age to make your own decisions."

The light in her eyes died. "It doesn't matter."

He required more information but would not distress her today.

"If you want to work here, honesty is a requirement." He raised a silencing hand before she interrupted. "I will employ you as a herbalist, pay for all supplies, provide lodgings and a salary of eighty pounds per annum. It's far more than you would earn elsewhere."

A frown marred her brow. "A herbalist?"

"Allow me to explain." He inhaled deeply and wished he hadn't. The unique aroma of ... what? ... he had no clue ... stirred something primal in him. "What is that perfume?" It was unlike anything he had smelled before.

"Just something I made in the stillroom at home." She stretched out her arm, baring her wrist. Her pale, porcelain skin reminded him she was delicate, feminine, and nowhere near as strong as she professed. "The apothecary in Covent Garden supplies me with various ingredients—vetiver, patchouli, orris root—in exchange for herbal remedies."

While every instinct warned him not to touch her, he captured her dainty wrist. Amongst the sweet note of iris, lay the darkly exotic scent of musk. The fragrance was complex yet simple. It embodied the essence of the woman, a contradiction he found intriguing.

Reid would be wise to maintain some distance.

If he was to catch a killer, he could not afford distractions.

"If I employ you as a herbalist," he said, returning to the matter at hand, "you will be met with less prejudice. You can make notes and observe medical procedures. In time, you may accompany Mr Turner on his visits, but it's important to gain the men's trust first."

Disappointment radiated from every fibre of her being. "Can I not accompany you? People may take me seriously if I am your student."

No one would.

Surely she knew she'd be dragged through the mire and hung out to dry. Some patients would consider an unmarried working woman to be one step up from a bawd.

"I work alone," he said, referring to his clandestine investigations, too. "If the terms are not to your liking—"

Her brows shot up. "No, I'm sure Mr Turner is a gentleman, and I'm hardly marriageable material. I thought it would be easier if we worked together since there'd be no risk of a romantic entanglement."

The comment pricked his masculine pride.

"And how did you draw that sconclusion?"

Her gaze trailed over him like she knew they were incompatible, like his secret was a badge of dishonour emblazoned on his lapel. "Isn't it obvious?"

"Not to me."

She looked at him like he was a simpleton. "You'll marry

a lady of your grandfather's choosing. The daughter of some lord or other."

"Do I look like a man who enjoys recitals and reels?"

She scanned the breadth of his chest. "No, sir. You look like a man who enjoys vigorous activities." A pink blush touched her cheeks, and she mumbled as she fought her embarrassment. "I speak of riding and the boxing bouts you attend in the basement of Fortune's Den."

How much did this woman know about him?

As The Burnished Jade was across the street from the gaming hell, he supposed his attendance was common knowledge.

"I'm paid to tend to the injured—broken noses and sprained limbs—and gain no satisfaction from watching men pummel each other senseless."

Miss Moorland decided to trawl her mind and find another reason why the thought of them kissing proved abhorrent. "You're confident; I'm reserved. Opposites rarely attract."

"Reserved?" He scoffed. She aired her opinions without needing a prompt. "You're one of the most forthright women I know."

"It's taken a lot of training to ask for what I want without reservation," she admitted proudly. "I used to chatter nervously until Lord and Lady Berridge offered their counsel."

Reid recalled a time three months ago when Miss Moorland asked if she could examine his implements. He'd almost choked on his brandy. Yet the memory had lived with him ever since.

"A lady must be seen as strong," she continued, "if she's

to make her way in a man's world. Do you not agree, Mr Gentry?"

Reid pictured the body he had identified in the mortuary a month ago, his patient Mrs Aspall. The coroner recorded her death as an accidental overdose of opium, ignoring the bruise on the widow's wrist. No matter how strong a woman might be, she could not overpower a male attacker.

"One must never lose sight of their limitations," he warned, dread a tight knot in his chest. What chance would she stand against a man twice her size?

A mocking snort escaped her. "My stepmother often reminds me what it means to be weak. Many times lately, I have felt utterly helpless."

Reid did not wish to dwell on her personal problems. "I know the position here is not what you hoped, but I'm sure you'll prove your worth in no time." He stood and gestured to the door. "Let me show you where you'll be working."

She smiled, though remained silent as he escorted her across the hall to Hickman's office. Reid's secretary was a stickler for tidiness, with everything stored neatly in its place. He stood in the middle of the sparse room, wringing his hands so they wouldn't shake.

"Liaise with Mr Hickman if you have any questions or need supplies. He will tell you what herbal remedies are most popular."

"Am I permitted to make my own formulas?" she asked.

Reid nodded. "I'll want a written card detailing the contents of each bottle." He turned to Hickman. "Have all medicines moved to the stillroom. Miss Moorland will run the dispensary."

Hickman's mouth parted, wordless and wide.

Before his secretary objected, Reid said, "With Miss

Moorland's appointment, you will have a few hours free to tackle those patients with minor ailments. Nothing too taxing. You can deal with Mr Dennison's gout."

He didn't give Hickman a chance to protest and led Miss Moorland down the corridor to Turner's office. Reid knocked and entered without waiting, only to find the physician shoving a messy stack of papers into the desk drawer.

Miss Moorland scanned the piles of books and the shelves sagging under the weight of the heavy tomes, her eyes sparkling like polished emeralds. Had Turner been wearing a jester's hat, she would not have noticed.

"What an impressive selection of books, Mr Turner."

"They belonged to my father," he said, quickly hiding the jar of alcohol with the severed finger preserved inside. "There are some rare volumes amongst the collection. You're welcome to borrow them as long as they remain on the premises."

The way she gasped and clutched her chest, one would think the King had proposed marriage.

"That's extremely kind of you, Mr Turner."

Turner's cheeks burned like coals in the grate. "If you tell me what topics interest you, I can recommend something suitable." He glanced at Reid like one would an older brother, seeking his permission.

"Once Miss Moorland has organised the stillroom and prepared enough tinctures, she may spend an hour a day reading."

Miss Moorland glanced at Reid, her smile brimming with gratitude. That's when he realised her mouth had the power to disarm a man. It didn't matter if she wore a grain sack, mob cap and thick spectacles. The sensual curve of her lips blinded him to her lacklustre attire.

"Then I must begin work at once," she said with an eagerness rarely seen in the practice these days. "May I see the stillroom?"

As Reid escorted her to the rear of the house, he asked the question that bothered him most—not why the hell he felt a pang of jealousy at the thought of her spending time with Joseph Turner.

"Am I to assume you no longer need lodgings? You said you would explain the lack of luggage."

Miss Moorland entered the stillroom, her breath a faint mist against the cold, stale air. Ignoring his question, she ran her fingers over the dusty shelves and mentioned the absence of herbs and distilling apparatus.

"Now I see why you had no objection to me reading," she said, opening the drawers in the apothecary cabinet. "It will take weeks to get this room in order."

"Surely that's a pleasing prospect for someone who's desperate for work."

She rubbed her hands together to chase away the chill. "I'll need coal for the stove. I can't begin until I've cleaned every surface. I must purchase muslin to make poultices, new bottles and equipment."

"I'll have Hickman fill the scuttle. Charge whatever provisions you need to my account. I'll give you a note for the apothecary ... once you've answered my question about lodgings."

The tension in her posture returned, and taut lines appeared on her brow. "I still need a room, but not until the Merricks return from Edinburgh. Until then, I must give the illusion all is well and would be grateful if we kept our arrangement between ourselves."

He inclined his head. "Of course."

He'd get the truth out of her soon enough, though was somewhat relieved he didn't have to think about her sleeping alone in the dark.

"Before I start work, may I see the room?" She shifted her feet. "I would like to bring a few items from home and must do so without alerting the servants, though Mrs Pugh spends most of the time in a drunken stupor."

An image of her dragging a valise across town filled his head, her barely making it through Seven Dials before a thug wrestled it from her grasp.

"You'll take a hackney cab to and from work," he insisted. "It's not open to negotiation. I'll cover the cost until you're able to rent the room upstairs. Hickman will hail one for you when you're ready to leave today."

Her eyes softened, a glimmer of curiosity mingling with quiet surprise. "You needn't feel responsible for me, Mr Gentry. This must seem strange, but I expect you to treat me as you do Mr Turner. Otherwise, I shall be more of a hindrance than a help."

He sometimes got drunk with Turner and visited bathhouses for the elite.

"You cannot erase years of patriarchal breeding in the space of a day," he said, amused. "I cannot treat you like Turner. Not unless you want to accompany me to Porretta's Bathhouse in St James' tonight and lounge naked in a mineral pool. Now, permit me to pay for a hackney."

Miss Moorland gulped and fussed with her dress. After a brief tussle with her nerves, she said, "Only a certain type of lady may attend men in bathhouses."

"Some men take their wives and hire a private room."

"I doubt any take female colleagues."

Why the devil had she said that?

Now he imagined her standing at the edge of the pool, slipping off that hideous dress to reveal soft curves and luscious breasts. Amid the intimate candlelit setting and the smell of exotic oils, she would enter the water, moving gracefully towards him, the fire of desire in her eyes.

"I thought you were a modern woman, Miss Moorland."

She snorted. "We both know I walk a dangerous line."

He thought of Mrs Aspall cold on the slab and the three women who had lost their lives in similar suspicious circumstances.

"Which is why you will take a hackney to and from work. I'll ensure it's the same jarvey. We'll keep your appointment here quiet for the time being. Just as a precaution."

There was no reason to suspect the villain would target her. Miss Moorland was not his patient. She was young and healthy, not an ailing widow in her fifties. He had not prescribed her opium for pain. She bore no comparison to the deceased women.

Miss Moorland nodded. "I don't want to cause problems, and will take a hackney if it eases your conscience."

Reid might have breathed easily again, but as he led Miss Moorland upstairs to view her room, she paused at the locked door on the landing.

"Are all the chambers empty?" She tried the door, much to his horror.

"That room is out of bounds." He ushered her away before she sensed his rising panic. "I keep important documents there: deceased patients' records and coroners' reports." That was true. "I'm the only person with a key."

"I see." Her voice carried a strange cadence that spoke of a thousand unasked questions.

Anyone who peeked inside would think he was mad, a

loon fit for Bedlam. They'd believe the pressure of work had taken its toll. That he was suffering from the lack of mental clarity he cautioned others about.

But Reid was gathering evidence of a crime. Sooner or later, he would find the clue to catching the villain. Time was a tightening noose, every wasted day drawing the knot closer to his throat. If he didn't find answers soon, he might be the next victim.

Chapter Three

The letter Sofia had been dreading arrived on a dreary April morning, three weeks into her employment at Mr Gentry's practice. She knew her stepmother's handwriting. It betrayed Judith's humble beginnings, and her impatience was evident in the ink smudges on the first line of the address.

Sofia tore open the missive, her heart stuttering as she peeled back the folds and read the only words that mattered.

The Merricks would return home in four days.

Four days!

Lord have mercy!

The news sucked the air from her lungs. It forced her to question her actions and the foolish plan to escape. What made her think she could hide from the Merricks in London? A wise woman would take what little money she'd saved, board the stagecoach to Southampton, then buy a ticket to sail … anywhere.

It wasn't too late.

She could leave London tonight.

But an inner tug of resistance said escape was impossible.

Mr Gentry was in trouble. Call it a woman's intuition, but the truth lived in the dark circles beneath his eyes and the curt tone that was so unlike him. He disappeared for hours, leaving Mr Turner to tend to his patients. He missed an important dinner with his friends, causing them to call at the practice, fearing something was dreadfully wrong.

It shouldn't matter to her.

Mr Gentry was merely her employer, yet he'd helped her when no one else had. He paid for a hackney to collect her from the corner of Dean Street every morning. He bought furniture for her room above the practice: a chest of drawers, a French armoire and a carved wooden bed.

A friend is moving abroad and needs to empty his house.

Mr Gentry implied someone had given him the furniture, yet she had seen an invoice from Ingrams stating the items were new.

Then there was the locked room, which he insisted was out of bounds. If Sofia had the skill to pick the lock, she might discover his secret. Something sinister kept him working long into the night.

And so, she had four days to help Mr Gentry before she boarded a boat from Southampton and sailed far from England's shores.

Sofia studied the letter in her hand.

Judith had compiled a list of jobs for the housekeeper, Mrs Pugh, in preparation for a soiree to celebrate the couple's nuptials. Cook was to organise a feast and order cases of burgundy from Rudd's wine merchant. Unbeknownst to Sofia, invitations were sent weeks ago, though there was no mention of the names on the guest list.

Anger surfaced.

This was no longer her beloved family home. Her

father's favourite chair had disappeared one night, along with his portrait, clothes and the trinkets in his study, every cherished memory eradicated like footprints washed away by the tide.

Judith had moved Mr Merrick into the house mere weeks into her widowhood, making excuses for his presence.

"Your father left us penniless," Judith had complained. "I've no choice but to take a lodger. And Mr Merrick is handy around the house."

A week later, the couple were sleeping in the same chamber. Mr Merrick wasn't so handy because Judith's bed developed a persistent creak.

Upon hearing the patter of approaching footsteps, Sofia slipped her hand beneath the folds of her skirt and shoved the letter into the concealed pocket.

"Was that the postman?" Mrs Pugh entered the hall, redeyed and ruddy-cheeked, swaying like she was aboard *The Mayweather* during a violent storm. "I heard you talking to someone."

"No. I stubbed my toe on the chair leg and muttered a curse," Sofia lied. When Mrs Pugh learned of the Merricks' impending return, she would demand Sofia stay at home to help tidy the house.

The housekeeper ambled closer. The smell of gin clung to her like a second skin. "Happen you're spending too much time trudging around museums and libraries," she slurred. The foul woman burped and almost knocked Sofia out with the toxic fumes. "That'll all change when your mother comes home."

Judith is not my mother, Sofia silently screamed.

"She'll have you entertaining gents here." Mrs Pugh cackled like a hag. "There'll be no more flitting about town like a restless sparrow." She flapped her hands as if they were a fledgling's fragile wings.

"And you'll have to wear clean clothes and rise with the larks," Sofia countered before reminding the housekeeper of their pact. "Just like you won't mention my outings, I won't mention your complete disregard for the rules."

Mrs Pugh's bloodshot eyes narrowed. "Best you don't go out today. I have a nasty feeling the mistress will arrive without notice. You'll help me straighten the house. We agreed that's the price for your gallivanting."

Sofia pasted a smile, yet her pulse fluttered in her throat. "I'll rise at dawn tomorrow and assist you then. I promised the Countess of Berridge I would help plan for next month's recital." Before Mrs Pugh could protest, she added, "And you're hardly in a fit state to work at present."

Mrs Pugh went to brace her hands on her bony hips, but her arms slipped, and she stumbled forward. "You'll start now. I need you to fetch—"

"I'll begin in the morning." Sofia was late to meet the hackney cab, though Mr Gentry always paid the jarvey to wait. "We'll compile a list of jobs when I return this evening."

She would not return this evening.

She would never come home again.

The thought tightened her throat as she snatched her pelisse off the coat stand in the hall. There was no time to race upstairs to fetch a bonnet and the last of her belongings.

Amid Mrs Pugh's drunken protests, Sofia darted from the house, slamming the door shut and leaving the past behind. Tears blurred her eyes as she hurried along Dean Street, wearing her sad memories like a heavy shroud.

How could her father have been so foolish?

How had Judith persuaded him to leave Sofia out of his will? She could find no documents, nothing in writing that expressed her father's dying wishes. The ten solicitors she had visited were no help. All refused to check their records, insisting their clients' names were confidential.

Relief washed over her when she saw the parked hackney and the usual jarvey waiting patiently atop the box.

He tipped his hat. "Morning, miss."

"Good morning, Mr Peters. Sorry I'm late."

"I've instructions to wait an hour before informing Mr Gentry."

A subtle warmth settled in Sofia's chest. Mr Gentry's quiet presence made her feel oddly comforted. What would he do if she failed to show? That posed an interesting question.

She had barely settled inside the cab when it lurched forward and picked up speed. The clopping of the horse's hooves sounded like the rapid ticking of a clock. Time stood still for no one. Change was the only certainty in life, yet she feared it most. She didn't need strength to start anew and do the job she loved. She needed strength to sever the ties to the past.

"Empty-handed today?" Mr Hickman glanced up from his ledger as if expecting to carry her valise upstairs.

"I was running a little late."

Half an hour late, to be precise. There had been no time to wear extra layers or sneak ribbons and stockings into her concealed pockets.

Mr Hickman's warning gaze shifted briefly to the door. "Mr Gentry is inspecting the new dispensary. He asked to see you when you arrived. Best hurry, as he's leaving for Guy's Hospital in half an hour."

The mere mention of the doctor had butterflies dancing in her stomach. She had not expected to see Mr Gentry today. Perhaps fate had granted her a boon, aware she had but a few days to help him.

Sofia found Mr Gentry examining the labels on a row of brown bottles. He took one, removed the stopper and inhaled the contents.

Her gaze moved over him. His dark blue waistcoat clung to his torso like a second skin. His broad shoulders narrowed to a lean waist, a striking testament to strength and grace. In his shirt sleeves, he looked relaxed and utterly masculine. The cut on his knuckle was new.

Sofia cleared her throat. "You wished to see me, sir."

Her heart lurched when he turned to face her. This little infatuation she had developed sent heat spreading through her body like wildfire.

Mr Gentry's swift observation of her caused him to frown. "You're wearing your hair in a different style, and we agreed you would start work at nine. There are rules for a reason, Miss Moorland."

His voice carried an air of cool detachment, yet he seemed distracted by the soft wisp of hair stroking her cheek.

She straightened her shoulders. "A letter arrived. The letter I've been dreading for weeks. Forgive my tardiness, but the news sent me into a panic."

"A letter from the Merricks?" He returned the bottle to the shelf before giving her his full attention. "I presume they're due home soon."

Sofia nodded, afraid to speak in case he heard the thread of fear in her voice.

He closed the gap between them. "Do you intend to move into the room upstairs when they do?"

"I had hoped to stay here tonight." Her throat tightened at the thought of sleeping in an empty house alone, one with a human skull on a shelf and eyeballs floating in glass jars, but reminded herself the situation was temporary. "I cannot let the Merricks find me, not until I decide if it's safer to leave England."

"Leave England?" His voice rose a notch. "Where the devil would you go? Are you unhappy here?" He gestured to the rows of medicines and tinctures lining the shelves, to the polished distilling apparatus and the baskets of dried herbs on the oak table. "You've achieved miracles in three weeks. Imagine what you could achieve in months."

A wave of sadness washed over her.

While Judith was hundreds of miles away in Scotland, Sofia had allowed herself to dream. But the chilling reality of her situation sank in.

Tell him!

Tell him what they plan to do to you!

Tell him what's at stake!

How could she? Mr Gentry had his own demons. If she was to help him, she couldn't add to his burdens.

"I have a few days to decide," she said, praying Judith wouldn't find her and Mrs Pugh had been too drunk to remember anything useful. "I love my work here. Mr Turner taught me how to tie a ligature to stem a bleeding wound. He said I can sew minor cuts as I'm skilled with a needle and thread."

Mr Gentry smiled, the sight like a blessing from heaven. "Sewing flesh is not like sewing muslin."

Sofia managed a smile, too. "Yes, it's not like I can work on a sample piece. Not unless you have a mummified cadaver hidden in that room upstairs."

The light in his eyes died. That's when she knew his odd behaviour had something to do with what he kept in his inner sanctum.

"As a woman with no medical training, they'll not permit me to work at Guy's Hospital," she added to avoid an awkward silence.

"Leave me to consider the matter." Faint creases appeared between his brows as if his thoughts lingered miles away. "I have a patient or two who won't mind that you're a woman."

Is everything all right? she wanted to say.

She suspected a walk in the park would not lift his spirits. Mr Gentry was a complex case, but not because of any mental disorder. The weight of his problem was taking its toll.

"Thank you." Her heart brimmed with gratitude. "I pray I won't be a disappointment."

His gaze flicked over her body. "I'm sure you'll rise to the challenge. Just like you have here."

A sudden spark in the air made her stomach flip.

"Is there a reason you wanted to see me, sir?"

He blinked like he had forgotten. "You're never late. You refuse to discuss your fears, and I wondered if they were the reason for your tardiness." He muttered under his breath. "I need to know you're well."

"I'm quite well."

Knowing it was a lie, he gave a solemn nod. "If you need help, Miss Moorland, all you need do is ask."

"You once said talking could ease a troubled mind. I hope you've followed your own advice, sir, and discussed your worries with someone."

He stared at her for the longest time.

She thought she glimpsed the prisoner behind the bars,

but he quickly closed the cell door. "Medical men never practise what they preach. I assumed you knew that."

"And ladies often find themselves in hot water as they scramble to break free of their shackles. Perhaps we both need help, but fear confiding in someone will only add to the problem."

"Perhaps I'm prepared to risk *my* life but draw the line at hurting someone else," he agreed. "The less you know about me, the better."

She didn't demand an explanation, but whatever he did on the Barking Road had nothing to do with healing the sick. Yet Mr Gentry was a gentleman, not a criminal. Perhaps he was being blackmailed.

"I shall leave you to your work," he said, desperate to retreat. "Draw all the bolts tonight. A rowdy bunch often gathers outside the King's Arms, and men visit the East India House round the clock."

"If I can't sleep, I can come to the dispensary and grind herbs." She could read or take a bath. However, bathing without Mrs Pugh's help would be an arduous task. "In the absence of servants to lug the water, may I bring the hip bath to the dispensary?" It was another item Mr Gentry had been kind enough to purchase. "I can ask Mr Turner to carry it down from upstairs."

Talk of tending to her ablutions seemed to unsettle him. The reason became apparent when he said, "Ensure you keep the door locked, including the one to the yard. I may have cause to return to collect some *papers* and wouldn't want to cause any embarrassment."

Sofia bit back a smile. "There's no reason why anyone should be embarrassed. If I've drawn the bolts, you cannot enter."

"True." He pursed his lips while considering the dilemma. "If you decide to stay, I shall hire a housekeeper. Then we can move freely, without restriction." The chime of the hall clock had him excusing himself. "I'll fetch the hip bath before I leave for Guy's. Avoid having this discussion with Turner. He might find it hard to concentrate on his patients."

"And you won't?" she teased.

His eyes brightened for the first time in days. "As you said, we're unlikely to form a romantic attachment."

He left her to begin work, returning with the hip bath minutes later—his tense muscles straining against the fine lawn of his shirt as he positioned it near the fire—then he bid her a good day.

With a list of tasks longer than Oxford Street, there was no time to consider the letter hidden inside her pocket. No time to dread her first night in a strange house all alone.

Mr Turner visited the dispensary at seven o'clock to see if she needed anything before he left for the evening. "Perhaps you'd like to catch a bite of supper at the King's Arms."

"Thank you, but I bought a steak pie from Martin's Bakery and plan to eat supper while I work." Sofia glanced at the list on the table. "Mr Hickman asked for a batch of digestive remedies, and the peppermint from the apothecary only just arrived."

As the herb needed weeks to seep, time was of the essence.

Mr Turner lingered in the doorway. "Will you be all right here alone?"

She pasted a smile. "Of course."

He stared for a moment before remembering he held a folio of papers in his hand. "The coroner delivered a report for Mr Gentry, but the study is locked. Might I leave it with you?" His cheeks reddened. "I often misplace things, and I know Mr Gentry will want to examine the report tomorrow."

"I shall keep it safe in the drawer."

Sofia took the folio, wondering if it would give her an insight into Mr Gentry's problems. She followed Mr Turner into the hall, bid him good evening and secured the door behind him.

The sudden silence sent a prickle of awareness chasing up her spine. The next four or five hours would pass slowly. She prayed Mrs Pugh was sotted and didn't notice her absence until morning.

Sofia returned to the dispensary, placed the report on her wooden workbench and gathered the ingredients to make the digestive remedies. Though she crushed the dry peppermint with her pestle, her gaze kept flitting to the documents in the folio.

Would it hurt to scan a page or two?

Mr Gentry knew she had a curious mind, and a feeling deep in her gut said the notes were part of his pressing problem.

She tipped the crushed leaves into a large brown bottle along with ginger and cardamon, then added ethanol. As soon as she pushed the cork stopper into the neck, she set the bottle aside and took the coroner's notes.

The coroner was adamant Mrs Beckman's heart had given out, and it accounted for her fall. There was a sketch of the woman's injuries: a broken wrist, numerous bruises, and a wound to the left temple where she hit the newel post with blunt force.

Absorbed by the information, Sofia continued reading until she stumbled on the comments that sent her heart thundering.

I can find nothing to link the deaths you mentioned, nothing to suggest foul play. It may be that Mrs Beckman stumbled on a burglar, but I spoke with the sergeant, and nothing was taken. I'll reiterate: you're not to blame for the series of explainable deaths.

Sofia reread the last line.

So, that was the cause of Mr Gentry's disquiet. He believed he was responsible for this lady's ill fate. Surely all doctors felt a moral duty to their patients. Preventable things like falls must be harder to bear.

Sofia glanced at the ceiling. So what did he keep locked away upstairs? He'd mentioned patients' records and must be searching for clues. Who better to help him than a woman with an inquisitive mind?

Gathering the folio and the lit oil lamp, she hurried upstairs to Mr Gentry's concealed chamber. A quick peer through the keyhole revealed nothing but darkness. It was pointless trying to pick the lock. Hairpins bent too easily. Three snapped yesterday when her attempt to force the mechanism failed. If only she had the proper implements.

The sudden bang on the front door made her jump.

Sofia hurried to the window, a relieved sigh escaping her when she saw Lady Berridge's elegant equipage. However, it soon became clear the countess wanted to question her, not offer assistance.

"Mr Gentry said you were sleeping here tonight." Joanna swept into the hall, her golden hair framing a look of concern, the jaunty pillbox hat hinting at her unconventional spirit. "Has something happened at home? Has Judith returned? If you needed help, you should have come to The Jade."

"So you've seen Mr Gentry this evening?" Sofia said, keen to learn of his current whereabouts.

Joanna frowned. "Yes, he called to cancel next week's lecture and wants you to speak on his behalf. He said you're more than capable."

Mr Gentry had chosen her to act in his stead?

The burst of pride was short-lived. It was a ploy to stop her leaving London—a dangling carrot of hope for someone who craved a better life.

"He suggested I offer you a room at The Jade," Joanna continued, "but I explained that's the first place Judith will look." She moved farther into the gloomy hall, her gaze scanning the corridor like it was a passageway to hell. "Mr Gentry dislikes the idea of you staying here alone at night, and I quite agree. It feels like the troubled spirits of the sick lurk in the shadows."

"There's no need for concern," Sofia assured the countess before mentioning her plan to move abroad. "I appreciate you calling, but I'm a little busy with work at present."

Joanna was undeterred. "When did you decide to move abroad? What's happened? I'm not leaving until you tell me." She called to her husband, who stood outside, leaning against the parked carriage with his arms folded across his chest.

The gentleman entered the house. No matter how often Sofia spoke to Mr Chance—now the Earl of Berridge—his presence proved unnerving.

"Close the door," Joanna said, touching his muscular arm. "Miss Moorland is about to explain why she feels it necessary to leave London."

The man fixed Sofia with his intense stare. "Allow me to save you the trouble, Miss Moorland. Your stepmother is due home and wants rid of you. The Merricks need money—more money than you could earn working as a herbalist. Word is, there's to be an auction. I don't need to explain the one thing you have that's of any value."

Tears pricked the backs of Sofia's eyes. So it was true. "I found a letter suggesting as much, though have no notion which men will attend."

"I have a list." He reached into his pocket, removed a slip of paper and handed it to her. "It's remarkable what you can learn when a man owes you a debt and you hold his proverbials in a vice."

Nausea roiled in her stomach as she scanned the names, noting Mr Harrop topped the list of degenerates. Many of the others were unknown to her.

"I'm so afraid," she confessed, allowing the tears to fall. "Judith is cunning. It was foolish of me to think I could hide here."

"I'll not mince words," the handsome lord said. "Hell is a better prospect than marrying any of those men. I'm willing to help you, but I advise you to marry a man of your own choosing and do so quickly."

A strained snort escaped her. "I'm not exactly inundated with offers, not from anyone decent." And where would she find someone kind who supported her work? "My only hope of evading Judith is to leave town."

The thought dragged another sob from her throat. She loved working in the dispensary. It was the first time she had felt true joy since her father passed a year ago.

Joanna reached for Sofia's hand and clasped it tightly. "I'm surprised you're still here. If you need money for your fare, I will give it to you. But I think you should stay and fight."

An image of Mr Gentry formed in her mind. He was the

reason she had not fled. Her mild infatuation for him would pass, yet she would never forget his generosity or the soft caress of his fingers in her hair.

"I'm here because I'm worried about Mr Gentry."

"Worried?" Joanna seemed unsurprised and shared a knowing look with her husband. "Do you have a reason to be anxious about his welfare?"

Not wanting to break a confidence or admit she had read the coroner's letter, she said, "He's troubled and barely sleeps. I hoped to help him before Judith returns but I don't know where to begin. I know he lives in Mayfair with his grandfather but stays out most nights."

"I know where you can find him," Lord Berridge said, drawing his pocket watch and inspecting the time. "I had him followed when he left The Burnished Jade earlier. We can take you there if you're serious about helping him. Perhaps you might help each other."

Sofia didn't need to give the matter any consideration. "Let me fetch my coat and gloves." Heaven knows what she would say when she got there. Maybe the time had finally come for them to share their secrets. "Where is he, my lord?"

She held her breath, praying she didn't have to storm the bathhouse.

"You'll call me Mr Chance, Miss Moorland. It's my preferred form of address. As for Gentry, you can find him at the Hare and Hounds coaching inn on the Barking Road, playing at being a highway robber."

Chapter Four

The Hare and Hounds
Barking Road, London

Dressed head to toe in black, Reid sat at a table in a dark corner of the taproom, supping ale from a tankard and listening to Pete the Piper play a lively tune on his penny whistle. Punters gathered around the huge stone hearth, warming their hands and tapping their feet in time to the music.

To the untrained eye, those enjoying the festivities were local labourers, farmhands and weary travellers, but it was easy to spot the crooks. Not because their worn shoes were at odds with their silver pocket watches or because they kept their eyes trained on the door, often slipping the innkeeper, Weaver, a shilling to use the rear exit.

Criminals befriended criminals.

Hence Reid shared a table with two such men, Slater and

Doyle, one a dim-witted poacher, the other a fence peddling stolen wares, when he wasn't sneaking outside to make clandestine deals with petty thieves.

"The merchant from Brentford upped his price for that fine mount of yours," Doyle said, his gaze drifting from Reid to the buxom serving wench who'd gone to refill their tankards. "I could sell him for a tidy profit. You could buy yourself a cheaper horse. Save you hanging about in here tonight."

Keen to show he was no easy target, Reid whipped a blade from his boot and plunged it into the crude oak table. "Touch my horse and I'll have your fingers."

Doyle jumped, clutching the oversized coat that concealed his ill-gotten gains. "It was just an idea, gov'nor. I know how fond you are of the beast, but a hefty sum in your purse saves you risking your neck on the road."

Slater, a scrawny fellow who smelled of fish and damp fur, added his two pennyworth. "If you're caught with a loaded pistol, they'll haul you straight to Chelmsford gaol and have you tried at the quarterly assizes."

"I'm not robbing coaches. I'm looking for someone. When I find him, there'll be the devil to pay."

The four women who'd met a tragic end had one thing in common, other than their widowed status and being Reid's patients. They were acquainted with a gentleman from Barking.

The maid's confession entered his mind.

They met when Mrs Aspall visited her brother, and she stopped at the Hare and Hounds on the Barking Road.

Mrs Nelson's sister made a similar statement.

Agnes' new gentleman friend travels from Barking into the city three times a week. I warned her he was married.

Why else insist they meet in secret and spend a night at the Hare and Hounds inn?

So Reid started stalking the yard and taproom, hoping to spot another widowed patient and prevent the next murder.

Was it murder? The coroner thought not.

Reid's friends failed to see the connection. Patients died. It was an unfortunate aspect of the job.

So why did visions of a faceless assailant haunt his dreams? Why did he scour the obituaries, expecting to find the names of more victims?

Finding answers had become a compulsion, a burning obsession. The quest for the truth was a constant itch he had to scratch.

The thud of the tankards on the table snapped Reid from his reverie. The wench winked at him and bent low enough to flash her wares, though he suspected the valley between her breasts was a well-worn path.

Doyle watched her like a hawk did a field mouse and only spoke when she left to serve the next punter. "How will you find the cove if you've never met him? It will be like searching for a pearl in a bed of clams."

Careful not to disclose more details than necessary, Reid said, "Worry about your affairs, and I'll worry about mine. I pay you for information. All I need are the names of women in their fifties who stay here."

To keep the fellow sweet, Reid took a leather purse full of crowns from his pocket and pushed it across the table.

Doyle snatched it before he exhaled his next breath. "I'd ask what the gent's done but reckon you'll dispose of any witnesses."

Reid pinned the crook to the seat with a hard stare. "The

less you know, the better. Let's not spoil this cosy arrangement."

Eager to please, Doyle pulled a crumpled piece of paper from his shabby coat pocket. "Weaver said three older women rented a room here last week. All widows visiting friends in Barking. One gave a false name. Weaver knew it was false because the groom heard her talking to her coachman."

Reid straightened the paper and read the pencilled words. The name Mrs Jones was crossed through and replaced with Mrs Ludgrove.

Mother of all saints!

His heart lurched.

He had a patient of that name who fitted the profile.

"Did any of those listed meet anyone?" He feigned indifference, firming his grip on the paper to stop his hand shaking.

Doyle shrugged. "Not that I know. There was a fair on in Upminster. The taproom was teaming with drunken nabobs."

"I can speak to O'Connor in the stables once I've checked all my traps," Slater said, reminding Reid he was sitting at the table, too. "He knows every bit of skirt from here to London Bridge. Says a woman alone is like a lamb straying from the flock."

Reid flicked Slater a coin, hoping he'd take the lingering smell of animal carcasses with him, and insisted he report back within the hour.

Doyle released a leery chuckle before swigging his ale. "Happen I'll leave you to dream about older ladies, gov'nor. I've set my sights on a young bit of muslin."

"The serving wench hates you. A sovereign says you'll get nothing but a kick in the ballocks."

Doyle gave the side of his nose a sly tap. "Why have the

wench when I can have a fancy bit of totty, one fresh as a daisy?" He gestured to the lady pushing her way to the bar, uttering a string of "Excuse me's". "You know what they say about the prim ones? Beneath them spectacles there's a fire needing a proper poke." He grabbed his loins as if preparing for the challenge.

Reid might have laughed had he not recognised the woman squeezing past burly labourers and excusing herself politely.

Curse Lucifer to Hades!

Why the hell was Miss Moorland at the Hare and Hounds? She should be at home mixing potions or sleeping in the new French bed he'd bought her.

A frisson of fear shot through him.

Had the killer lured her here?

Good God. Was *she* the next victim?

Doyle downed the last of his ale and wiped his mouth with his grimy fingers. "I reckon I can have my hand up her skirts in no time. Care to make a wager?"

Touch her and you're a dead man.

Reid imagined driving his hard fist into Doyle's face and splitting his nose, the miscreant's blood coating his knuckles. "You'll remain in your damn seat. That lady is my mistress. I don't need to tell you what I'll do if you lay your grubby hands on her porcelain skin."

Doyle froze, then gave a sharp bark of laughter. "Now I know you're having a lark. I doubt she's parted her legs for any man."

Reid rubbed his thigh, resisting the urge to lunge across the crude table and throttle the fool. "I can prove she's mine."

Doyle eyed him warily. "I'll stake a crown you're lying

through them nice white teeth. You've a minute to prove me wrong and claim your winnings."

With his blood pumping too fast in his veins, Reid stood. He should curse Doyle to hell, but if he hoped to catch the culprit, he couldn't afford trouble at the inn.

"No forcing her, mind," Doyle said, adding another caveat. "That's against the rules. If she's your mistress, happen she'll be happy to kiss you madly."

Bloody hell!

Reid hoped his confident grin hid his panic. Luring a cobra into a basket would be easier than bending Miss Moorland to his will. Well, without a detailed explanation, at least. "I suggest you root through your purse and have a crown ready."

"The clock's ticking," Doyle teased.

Reid rolled his shoulders and cricked his neck before marching through the drunken throng, keeping Miss Moorland in his sights.

He reached the lady just as she reached the bar.

"Good evening, madam," he said above the din.

Miss Moorland whirled around, clutching her chest in surprise. "Mr Gentry. Thank heavens. I hoped to find—"

Reid pressed his finger to her luscious lips. "Don't utter my name here. I'll tell you why later, but for now I need you to do something if we're to avoid rousing suspicion."

Her eyes widened behind her spectacles, the flare of intrigue unmistakable. Doyle was right. A passion for life simmered beyond her prim facade.

"I shall escort you to a table in the corner," Reid continued. "As soon as we sit down, you're to wrap your arms around my neck and kiss me like you've been aching to do it for days."

Her pillow lips parted beneath the soft press of his finger, her warm breath like a lover's caress on his skin.

"Be bold. The man at the table thinks you're my mistress. You will play the part until we're alone. My life depends on it. Do you understand?"

She blinked rapidly. "But I'm not—"

"It's too late to plead innocence. All hell will break loose if you fail."

Doyle would think her fair game, leaving Reid no option but to brawl with the fellow in the taproom. He'd be barred from the premises, all hope of stopping a killer lost.

He called to Weaver and ordered wine, then cupped Miss Moorland's elbow and led her to the table where Doyle sat flipping a crown between his fingers.

"This is Doyle," Reid said as they slid onto the bench.

She straightened her skirts before finding the courage to look at the crook. "Good evening, Mr Doyle. I trust you don't embarrass easily. They say patience is a virtue, but it won't sate the craving that's tormented me for days."

By God, she excelled at this game. Months ago, she would have stuttered and stumbled. Work had clearly given her a newfound confidence.

"I've missed you desperately, too, love." Reid smoothed his hand over her upper arm, aware the frisson of excitement felt surprisingly real.

Miss Moorland removed her spectacles. "I know you like it when I look nervous and innocent," she said, the excuse accounting for her trembling lips.

Reid was staring at her mouth now, everything else blurring into the background. Doyle deserved a barrow of sovereigns for suggesting the wager. One taste and Reid could forget about his herbalist and concentrate on catching the devil killing his patients.

"Do you remember that wild night at the Adelphi?" she whispered, threading her arms around his neck and curling her fingers in his hair.

The muscles in his abdomen hardened.

There was no night at the Adelphi, but he conjured a vision of them writhing naked in bed, a sheen of perspiration coating his back, her gripping his buttocks as he took her hard and deep.

"How could I forget?" The fictitious memory would leave him with a throbbing cockstand until dawn.

"Let me give you a gentle reminder," she whispered, her warm breath breezing over his lips as she closed her eyes and pressed her innocent mouth to his.

He felt her nerves in that first tender touch.

It was obvious she had never kissed a man.

But Miss Moorland conquered every obstacle fate placed before her.

She leaned into him, her breasts brushing his chest, her fingers tugging his hair. Curiosity lived in every hot slide of her mouth.

He needed more.

A need that grew insistent.

He coaxed her moist lips apart—like he would her legs if they were at the Adelphi—the desire to drive into her fierce and wildly primal.

That's it, love.

She opened for him, almost begging him to enter her.

He did.

Slipping his tongue inside her mouth. Groaning when she stroked him back, the first touch sending a bolt of pleasure to his groin. The throbbing pulse between his legs left him near mindless. The raw masculine need to possess her became a frantic mating of mouths.

Devour me.

He needed more of her.

Heat twisted in his stomach, coiling tighter, the tension drawing every muscle taut like strings about to snap.

This was something new.

Something unexpected.

Something that reached beneath his crafted veneer.

This was more than a kiss.

It was a revelation.

"Happen I'll go for a stroll in the yard." Doyle's comment dragged Reid from the pleasurable abyss, but Miss Moorland broke contact first, the baffled look in her eyes at odds with her moist mouth and ragged breathing.

"If only we were at the Adelphi," Reid groaned, unable to ignore the heavy ache between his legs. He wished she was his mistress, just for tonight. What he'd give to lose himself in her and forget his troubles for a few hours.

Doyle slapped the crown on the table. "A bit more stoking and you'll be battling an inferno." He stood, laughing to himself as he sauntered away.

Miss Moorland watched Doyle before whipping back to face Reid, the earlier signs of arousal dissipating. "You owe me an explanation, sir. It's one thing to take down my hair in an empty hallway, but to kiss me … in public … well … it's downright scandalous."

Reid bit back a smile. No more scandalous than an unmarried woman entering an inn at night. "You kissed me, Miss Moorland."

By God, he'd never experienced anything like it.

She lowered her voice. "Because you claimed it was a matter of life or death. I may have pressed my mouth to yours first, but then you did that *thing* and …" Knotting her brows, she waved her hand back and forth between them.

"*Thing*?"

She leant closer, filling his head with her captivating perfume. "You know what you did. You moved your mouth in a teasing way. Like the gentle tug of a soft current pulling me into deeper water."

Yes, kissing her had felt like sinking into a sea of warmth. He hadn't meant it to go that far, but this woman undid him with her witty banter and plump lips.

"What will people think?" She snatched her spectacles and shoved them on like they were a shield with the power of protection.

"No one saw us." Except for Doyle. "It's dark. The punters here don't care what goes on in shadowy corners of the room. People are more interested in getting Pete the Piper to play another tune."

Weaver appeared with the wine.

Reid paid, pushing a goblet towards Miss Moorland.

She took a fortifying sip, waiting for Weaver to leave them. "Are you going to explain why I had to pretend to be your mistress?"

"Are you going to explain how you knew to find me here?" Suspicion flared. He had not mentioned his late-night outings to anyone.

Was she involved in the plot to frame him for murder?

Because that had to be the villain's motive. Like a salmon nibbling the bait, Reid was being reeled in slowly. But why? Who despised him enough to kill four innocent women? No one, except for his Uncle Edmund, heir to his grandfather's estate. None of it made sense. Which begged the question: How would he explain the problem to Miss Moorland?

"Perhaps it's time we stopped playing games," she said.

Reid snorted. "Believe me, this is no game."

She considered him like he was a complex puzzle. Being sharp-minded, it didn't take her long to offer a solution. "Trust must be earned. I haven't been entirely honest with you, either. Perhaps it's time to rectify that."

Reid held his breath.

Had he been a fool to hire her?

"The Merricks plan to do more than force me to marry." She removed her spectacles, her green eyes revealing the truth she no longer wished to hide. "They mean to auction me off to the highest bidder. Mr Harrop will take a front-row seat." She shivered at the mention of the man's name. "He's a lechery old fool, though there's something terribly sinister in his gaze."

The men who paid for a young woman's virginity were deviants who got a thrill from overpowering someone half their size and age. Miss Moorland would command a high price. More so because she would fight for her freedom, her struggle feeding her husband's perverse desires.

"Then why the devil are you still in London?"

She hung her head. "I thought I could outwit them, that they would fail to find me, but gossip spreads like wildfire. It's only a matter of time before someone spots me at the apothecary."

As she hugged herself, it struck him how utterly alone she was and that this simple embrace was her only comfort. The sight hit like a bolt to Reid's heart. Was this how his mother looked when she arrived at his grandfather's door pleading for help? Had she hugged her swollen stomach and trudged two miles back to the pokey room above the milliner's shop?

"I've heard talk of such auctions," he said, unable to shake the memory of his mother from his mind. "The women are drugged and remain that way until the devils who've bought them have had their fill. Running is your only safeguard against being kidnapped off the street and sold like cattle at Smithfield Market."

She raised her eyes to his. "There is another option."

One did not need a sage's wisdom to understand her meaning. "You could marry before the Merricks find you."

"I could marry you, Mr Gentry."

"Me?" If he'd been drinking, he would have choked.

What the hell had given her that idea?

"You're married to your work," she sputtered. "Everyone says so. And you're unlikely to fall in love, what with your busy schedule and lack of social engagements."

A chuckle burst from his lips. "Have you been snooping in my diary, Miss Moorland? I confess work is my priority, but I could marry the *ton*'s prettiest debutant if I so wished."

Her gaze moved over his face, and she gave a resigned sigh. "Of course you could. One need only listen to your lectures at The Jade to know ladies come for the pleasure of watching you."

The fact had not escaped his notice.

He doubted they listened to a word he said.

"But not you, Miss Moorland. You're not there to glimpse my solid thighs."

"No, I'm more intrigued by the quality of your mind." A slow smile tugged at her mouth. "That was before you did that arousing thing with your tongue and lured me into uncharted waters. I wasn't thinking about hysteria at all then."

Reid laughed. "Are you sure you weren't thinking about the *cure* for hysteria? The one you've documented in your journal?"

Her cheeks turned the shade of ripe cherries. "If I was, it's of no consequence. You won't have cause to kiss me again."

"Not even if we marry?"

The lady sat bolt upright, hope a blossoming light in her eyes. "You're considering my proposal? I would be no trouble. I could continue working in the dispensary. We wouldn't even have to live together. You'd hardly know I exist."

Reid smiled to himself.

After such a passionate kiss, did she honestly think he wouldn't entertain her in bed? Doyle was right. Miss Moorland came alive when lust pumped through her veins. She was no diamond of the first water. Her beauty lay buried like a precious stone waiting to be unearthed.

"I cannot marry you," he said. After watching his mother perish from the weight of his father's betrayal, trust would always be an issue.

"You refused to employ me, yet I've worked miracles in the dispensary. You cannot deny I've made your professional life easier."

"Turner's room has never been tidier," he admitted. "And you're more than proficient at mixing herbal remedies."

"But you could never love me, is that it?"

He felt like she deserved some semblance of the truth. "I've seen the damage love can do. Love is nothing more than an obsession that wanes with time."

Miss Moorland shook her head. "Try sitting in a carriage with Lord and Lady Berridge for half an hour. I defy you to say love is a madness of the mind. It radiates from every fibre of their being."

"There is always an exception to the rule," he said.

Miss Moorland's expression turned quizzical. "There's more you're not telling me, which is deeply disappointing when I have been honest with you."

He admired her candour.

Yet he couldn't tell her the truth.

"All the more reason you shouldn't marry a man with questionable morals." Despite forgiving his grandfather for his spiteful actions all those years ago, Reid still bore the secret stain. But secrets rarely stayed buried forever. They lay dormant, waiting for someone to disturb the earth so they might see daylight again.

"I'd rather marry you than Mr Harrop," Miss Moorland said with a sad sigh, "but perhaps a fresh start is what's needed."

"A fresh start abroad?" She'd be wise to flee.

She gave a half shrug. "Perhaps. Presently, nothing matters but the reason I find myself at the Hare and Hounds tonight."

Ah, now for an answer to the question burning in his mind. "You were obviously looking for me. You indicated as much upon our greeting at the bar."

The lady reached for her wine, shivering visibly upon taking a large gulp. "I received the coroner's report regarding Mrs Beckman's fall. I'm eager to learn, and the coroner mentioned your suspicions about—"

Reid pressed a chaste kiss to her lips, to silence her while maintaining a facade. "Not here," he said. "We'll talk outside."

He planned to lie and put her mind at ease, though how

would he explain why he'd insisted she kiss him and pretend to be his mistress?

Fate saw fit to delay the inevitable.

Slater came bursting into the inn, tripping over his feet, his face ghostly pale. The poacher forced a smile and danced a little jig for the piper before heading towards Reid.

"I need a word." Slater rested his palms on the table, drawing Reid's attention to the fresh blood beneath his fingernails. "It can't wait."

Reid slid out from the bench, a gnawing dread settling in his stomach. He gripped the scrawny fellow by the arm and pulled him away from inquisitive ears. "What is it?"

Slater let his mask slip and craned his neck, as if anticipating the burn of the noose. "I went to speak to O'Connor in the stables like we agreed, to see what he knew about that woman who used a false name, except he wasn't there."

"And?"

Slater put a shaky hand to his mouth to calm himself. "I found him slumped behind the stables and thought he'd been guzzling mother's ruin."

"If you found him sotted, you wouldn't be quivering like a doe in a trap." Reid knew the haunted look of someone who'd gazed into the bowels of hell and couldn't quite pull himself back. "Are you trying to tell me O'Connor is dead?"

Slater drew his finger across his neck to show how the groom met a gruesome end. "He ain't just dead. The blade sliced through him like a knife does butter. O'Connor had something in his hand."

Reid braced himself, a sense of dread settling over him. An optimist might hope it was something to tie O'Connor to the spate of murders. "A strand of hair or a scrap of clothing?"

"No. A calling card for a doctor named Mr Gentry."

Chapter Five

Sofia noticed the furrows on Mr Gentry's brow from her vantage point in the dim taproom. His shoulders slumped as he fought to maintain his composure. Something weighed heavily on his heart and mind.

How much longer could he keep up the pretence?

How might she persuade him to confide in her?

His scruffy companion trembled as if an army of marauders were about to storm the inn. He continued to shake his head, even when Mr Gentry grabbed him by the upper arms and whispered through gritted teeth.

The messenger pointed to the yard.

The doctor's gaze snapped to Sofia, tension hardening his chiselled features. Suspicion crept into his eyes like a shadow at dusk.

Mr Gentry marched towards her, closing the gap between them and looming over the table. "You neglected to mention who brought you to the inn." His blade-sharp tone failed to hide a trace of panic. "Why the devil didn't you tell me Aaron Chance was outside?"

Sofia gathered her nerve and rose to her feet. "When was I supposed to mention it? When you demanded we kiss? When I bared my soul and confessed my worst fears?"

"You should have told me before we left the bar."

"When you pressed your finger to my lips and refused to let me speak?" When he'd whispered to her like they were lovers and his gaze lingered longer than it should?

He stepped back, dragging his hands through his hair as if anger and desperation battled inside him and he didn't know which side to choose. "I should have known you would interfere. I should never have hired you."

The words cut deep.

A civil war erupted inside her, too.

Women were supposed to be quiet and obedient, not voice their opinions or pry into a man's affairs. Sofia had always been different. An inner defiance simmered beneath the surface.

A passion for life is a potent aphrodisiac.

Lady Berridge's words entered Sofia's mind.

Never be afraid to fight for your beliefs.

Sofia swallowed her nerves and rounded the table. Laying her hand on Mr Gentry's arm caused a wave of warmth to flood her body. "Let me help you. You need a friend to confide in. This burden is too great to carry alone."

His eyes met hers, the artic blue irises thawing. "I have friends."

"Men think differently from women. They often fail to notice emotional cues and subtle details. I've already proven I'm a help, not a hindrance."

He stared at her but said nothing.

"You coming here is not a secret," she informed him. "Aaron Chance had you followed. Mr Daventry mentioned your nightly antics to him three months ago. As the owner of London's best enquiry agency, I suspect Mr Daventry has spoken to the coroner and read the files."

The veins in Mr Gentry's temples bulged.

He bent his head, his mouth an inch from her ear. "You need to leave here now," he whispered. "You need to find Lady Berridge and have her coachman drive like the devil is at his heels."

Sofia turned her head to look at him, panic rising. Not because his mouth was so close or because she ached at the thought of never feeling such pleasure again. "You're in trouble. What's happened?"

"The less you know, the better."

She dared to lay her hand on his chest. "That's the worst thing you could say to a lady with an inquisitive mind. I mean to help you, whether or not you agree."

He wrapped his fingers around her upper arm, the gentle pressure a warning. "The man who's out to hurt me may hurt you, too."

Sofia gave a faint snort. "Many men want to hurt me, and they're willing to pay a high price for the pleasure. Besides, I might be forced to leave England in a few days. At least let me help you until then."

He hesitated but did not release his hold on her arm.

She pressed her case by offering her own opinion of the evidence. "The coroner's report into Mrs Beckman's death suggests a fall from the lower steps, which is why the victim hit the newel post. Yet the bruise on the bridge of the foot suggests someone dragged her down the stairs by her arms. Livor mortis may have masked the bruises on her abdomen."

Mr Gentry stared at her, the subtle arch of his brow a sign of respect. "I see you've given the matter much thought."

"We should visit the coroner and demand a more thorough examination," she added. "Having suffered similar bruises in the past, I could present a convincing argument."

"Someone hurt you?" he growled.

"It's not important." When Judith's bed wasn't creaking like a ship in a storm, she sobbed for hours or flew into a violent rage.

After a few tense seconds, he said, "Follow me, Miss Moorland. It seems you'll get to examine a cadaver after all."

"Someone is dead?"

"Say nothing more until we're in the yard."

With his hand pressed to her back, Mr Gentry led her through the taproom, beckoning his lean friend to follow.

Outside, clear skies brought a biting nip to the air. Stars glittered like silvery pinpricks. The night was serene, yet it had borne witness to a heinous crime. Mr Gentry hadn't mentioned a cause of death, but the messenger had swiped his finger across his throat like a blade.

Aaron Chance's elegant black coach stood in the yard, facing the Barking Road. The coachman sat bolt upright, gripping the reins as if anticipating trouble. Sensing the tension, the horses pawed the ground, their breath fogging the crisp night air.

"This way." Mr Gentry guided her to the stables.

They passed the rows of stalls lining each side of the cobbled walkway, the smell of hay and leather and damp earth flooding her nostrils.

An ostler nodded to Mr Gentry, asking if he wanted his horse saddled and brought into the yard.

Mr Gentry flicked the man a coin. "Settle him down for the night."

Aaron Chance appeared like a wraith in the darkness, his

clothes black like his hair and expression. He jerked his head towards the path leading to the rear of the stables and the coppice beyond.

"Leave the lady here if you're looking for O'Connor," one groom cautioned. "He often takes his exercise against the oak tree, if you get my meaning."

An image of a bare behind entered Sofia's mind. She'd likely heave, reminded of Mr Merrick's habit of dropping his trousers whenever she passed the open door of his chamber.

"Did you see O'Connor's companion?" Mr Gentry asked, avoiding words that might offend a lady.

The groom chuckled. "He has a different partner most nights and never asks their names."

"Have you seen Doyle?"

"Last I saw, he was walking along the Barking Road. Probably meeting a man about a dog, though he'll be quick to sell it on."

Mr Gentry laughed, the hollow sound so unlike the warm, husky chuckle he gave when Sofia had asked to see his implements. "One day, the dog will bite him." He snatched a lit lantern from a hook outside the end stall and held it aloft to light the way.

They found Aaron and Joanna looming over the body of a man slumped against the wall of a stall like a half sack of grain.

"I believe this belongs to you." Aaron thrust a blood-stained calling card at Mr Gentry. "Sadly, your man isn't entirely illiterate and read your name. I had the pleasure of prising the card from his hand."

Mr Gentry snatched the card and cursed under his breath. "Later, you'll have the pleasure of explaining why the hell you had me followed."

"You're lucky I did. Miss Moorland is your alibi." Mr Chance gestured to the dead man. "The lout was breathing half an hour ago. We heard his bawdy banter in the yard."

Blood soaked the upper half of the victim's clothing, which might have looked like a claret chemisette were it not for the red rivulets running down his waistcoat.

Mr Gentry placed the lantern on the ground and crouched beside the body. He grabbed O'Connor's lank hair and raised the man's head a fraction. "It's a clean cut. A determined strike made with some force."

The gory sight had Sofia inhaling sharply. "The killer must have surprised him, or the stable workers would have heard his cries."

"Or they thought O'Connor was up to no good in the woods." Mr Gentry rifled through the deceased's pockets yet found nothing but a few coins, a bit of twine, a knife and a small pot of wax. "What made you search for O'Connor here?" he said, his tone accusatory as he beckoned the messenger forward.

The lean fellow averted his gaze. "I—I can't say in present company."

"Oh, for heaven's sake," the countess said. "We're women of the world. I suspect you thought O'Connor was in the woods and thought to spy."

"It ain't a crime to look. Besides, I set a trap and came to see if I'd caught a rabbit. I thought O'Connor was napping, till I saw the blood."

For a few silent seconds, everyone gaped at the body.

"Mr Rowe is the local justice of the peace," Aaron informed them, "but based on the nature of the crime, we should alert the magistrate at Bow Street. The area falls under his jurisdiction."

The messenger went into a panic. "I'll not speak to the magistrate. They're still hunting for the poacher who made off with Lord Carstairs' prized stag." He raised his calloused hands and backed away. "It weren't me, but I reckon they'll blame anyone to keep his lordship happy."

"The magistrate needs to know you were here," Sofia said, wishing he'd not found the calling card. "You discovered the body."

The poacher hardened his tone and stance. "Listen here. You ain't pinning this on me. What about Doyle? He fought with O'Connor last night over that serving wench with the big—" He paused, his hands making round shapes in the air. "Annie. That's her name."

"There's not a speck of blood on your clothes. I'm confident that confirms your innocence," Aaron Chance reassured him. "Perhaps you should make yourself scarce. If you want to keep your tongue, you'll not discuss what you've seen with anyone."

The poacher edged closer to the woodland path. "Happen I need to check the trap before the magistrate and his men are crawling all over this place." With that, he slunk into the blackness and disappeared into the woods.

"As a peer, I'll act in the magistrate's stead until he arrives." Mr Chance spoke in his usual commanding tone. "Gentry, examine the body while I alert the innkeeper. I'll send my coachman to report the crime. He'll summon Daventry first, of course. We need a man we can trust."

Joanna spoke up. "I'll remain here and witness the examination. Heaven forbid the coroner accuses Mr Gentry of tampering with evidence."

"I swear, when I find the devil who did this, I'll make

sure he rots in hell." The tremor in Mr Gentry's voice was a barely contained storm.

"Had we not arrived when we did, you could be facing a murder charge," Joanna said, watching her husband leave. "Does Rothley know you're out playing the vigilante? I assume that's what you're doing here. I cannot believe a surgeon of your standing would risk his reputation."

"Rothley is my friend, not my keeper."

"He's your dearest friend. One wonders why you haven't confided in him. I doubt he would let you risk your neck for —What is it you're doing out here, sir? I suggest you tell me now so my husband can persuade the authorities you're on the right side of the law."

"You've known me for ten years," he argued, avoiding her question. "Have I given you cause to believe I'm anything but a gentleman?"

The countess narrowed her gaze. "Only once."

She spoke of the time her brother, Justin, went missing from Cambridge a decade ago, and his friends—Rothley, Gentry, Rutland and Dalton—had to provide an alibi. They found the body, but no one was charged.

"You know I would never hurt Justin," he said, his plea carrying the weight of a past pain. "We were like brothers. All of us were."

Joanna's eyes softened "If I thought you were responsible for his death, I wouldn't be here."

"Why are you here?"

Joanna looked at Sofia and smiled. "Because I care about Miss Moorland, and she cares about you. Because my brother would want me to assist you in his absence. You're a good man and don't deserve to hang for this."

Mr Gentry released a slow breath. "I made a mistake hiring Miss Moorland." He turned to Sofia, knowing the comment would hurt her. "I've placed you in danger, and that's the last thing I wanted to do. Were it not for your desperate plea …"

One could not undo the past.

Finding a way forward was all that mattered.

"Perhaps you were meant to hire me, and I was destined to help you." Surely none of this was a coincidence. "The person who left your card in Mr O'Connor's hand won't stop until you're charged with murder. I'm sure you've asked yourself who despises you that much. But often outsiders have a clearer picture of the situation."

Mr Gentry's head fell back. He gazed at the scattering of stars in the night sky. Whatever he saw there gave him the courage to speak.

"Four of my patients died suddenly, one a month since early December, though their ailments were not life-threatening. They were all widows of the same age, which suggests their deaths are not random."

He spoke in the detached way he did when giving a lecture to ladies who preferred to watch, not listen. Yet the fact he had neglected his work and befriended criminals said he was deeply troubled.

"What has their deaths got to do with this coaching inn?" Sofia asked.

He explained two victims met a man from Barking at the Hare and Hounds. "Another one of my patients used a false name when she visited the inn last week. I only pray she's still alive."

"And you have no idea why the villain is targeting you?" Sofia asked, doubting he would confess to past mistakes, and she was right.

"No reason I can think of." He turned to Joanna. "Unless this has something to do with Justin's death and I'm the next target." He dismissed the notion as soon as the words left his lips. "It makes no sense. Why wait a decade?"

Few people were patient enough to wait a year to exact revenge.

Now was not the time to debate the issue.

"We can draw up a list of suspects later." Sofia swallowed past her nerves and crouched beside Mr O'Connor to examine his hands. "Once we've studied the body, we must question the witnesses and look for clues."

Suppressing a shiver, Sofia gathered the victim's hand. The chill of death was already upon him. His hand felt unnaturally heavy like it was made of unfired clay. She pushed up his coat sleeves and examined his wrists.

"There are no defensive wounds," she said.

Mr Gentry crouched beside her. "I see no signs of a struggle."

The hairs on her nape stirred, his presence charging the air with an excitable energy. Her pulse quickened. The quiet ache returned, the one she fought to ignore whenever he was near.

"The murderer positioned the body like this," he said, forcing her to focus on the dead man. "Based on the sudden slash to his neck, I would have expected O'Connor to fall forward."

"Someone added your card after staging the scene."

Mr Gentry raised the man's eyelids, smelled his mouth and clothes. "Someone fed O'Connor laudanum to subdue him, though the motive is unclear. I barely know the devil."

Joanna moved towards the woodland path and peered into the eerie blackness. "Whoever killed O'Connor came through these woods. We'll know for sure once we've questioned the ostlers."

Mr Gentry rifled through Mr O'Connor's coat again but found nothing. "He must have consumed laudanum an hour ago, though I see no flask or bottle."

A sudden commotion brought Mr Chance and the barrel-bellied innkeeper. The latter looked at his deceased employee and swore until the air was blue.

"I've told the fool a hundred times. The married ones might be willing, but you'll have a fight on your hands when their husbands find out."

Mr Chance was quick to agree. "O'Connor is renowned for his amorous antics. It will be impossible to narrow down the investigation to one suspect."

That's when the innkeeper made a damning statement. "Happen it was that doctor what killed him. The rogue was having it away with the fellow's wife."

Sofia's heart lurched.

Someone wanted to ensure Mr Gentry paid the price.

What other surprises awaited them?

Mr Gentry glared at the innkeeper. "Who in God's name told you that? The man died less than an hour ago."

"Freddie told Pete the Piper. He said O'Connor had a price on his head. Pete told Mildred, the wife, and she told me in bed last night."

"Did anyone tell Mr O'Connor?" Sofia said.

The innkeeper shrugged. "I said he should watch out for a doctor named Gentry, but O'Connor thought he was a cat with nine lives. I'm surprised the killer sliced his neck and not his ball—"

Faint whispers drew their attention. A few people had gathered thirty feet away—a stable boy, a coachman and a curious traveller—staring with morbid fascination. More men came, some craning their necks and standing on tiptoes, the whispers growing to a cacophony of shocked gasps and worried speculation.

Aaron Chance stepped forward, and the throng stepped back.

"There's nothing to see here," Mr Chance said sternly, shooing the crowd away like they were stubborn sheep. "Wait inside until the magistrate arrives." He turned to the innkeeper. "No one leaves until we can establish their whereabouts tonight, including those working in the stables."

While Mr Chance managed the scene, Sofia approached the subdued Mr Gentry. She touched him gently on his broad back, the need to comfort him being her priority. "Take heart. Mr Daventry is an excellent enquiry agent and will help to clear your name. And as you know from attending the boxing bouts at Fortune's Den, everyone wants Mr Chance fighting their corner."

He looked at her, his blue eyes dull, though they were no less remarkable. "I've spent months searching for clues but always come back to the same question: Why hurt innocent women to punish me?"

"I'm sure you've done nothing wrong." What crime had *she* committed to be auctioned like meat at the market? "Mr Daventry is the best person to advise you. He knows how devious minds work. I will help any way I can."

"You have troubles of your own."

"In giving, we receive. Perhaps the Lord will look upon me graciously and rain a plague down on the Merricks."

One could live in hope.

He didn't smile. "I'm trained to deliver a dose of optimism with every diagnosis, yet something tells me to prepare for the worst."

Tension clawed the air as if something dark and inevitable was about to unfold. "Think positive thoughts." It was easier said than done. "What lifts your spirits?"

He snorted as he glanced at the eerie woodland behind. "Is this where I'm supposed to follow my own advice and walk in the verdure?"

"I merely want you to focus on what gives you pleasure."

His gaze dropped to her mouth. "If I do that, Miss Moorland, we'll find ourselves in a wealth of trouble. Best we concentrate on escaping our burdens and not the power of one simple kiss."

Simple?

Yes, kissing him came as easy as breathing.

There was nothing complicated about the touching of mouths.

Yet in that breathless moment, she'd become a slave to her desires. Excitement still thrummed in her veins, lingering like the tug of addiction.

"Our kiss was anything but simple, sir."

He seemed to drink her in, his gaze piercing through her spectacles. "All the more reason to remember I'm your employer, and it wouldn't have happened if you'd stayed at home."

The sensible comment brought a mix of sadness and relief. Soon, survival would be her only concern. Knowing they would never kiss again felt like a brick wedged in her chest.

"As you say, it's of no consequence now."

An awkward silence ensued.

The crowd dissipated as the innkeeper ushered the patrons

back to the taproom. A task made easier when Mr Chance insisted on paying for their drinks.

Mr Chance returned to the crime scene and drew his wife aside. They spoke in hushed voices. Then he captured her chin, kissed her tenderly on the lips, and assured her all would be well.

The couple looked solemn when they faced Sofia.

"You being Mr Gentry's alibi causes a slight problem," Joanna said, pursing her lips. "Constables are open to bribery. If the crime is mentioned in the broadsheets and your names appear together, the Merricks will easily find you."

Sofia felt the blood drain from her cheeks. There had been nothing to tie her to Mr Gentry. No reason for Judith to visit the doctor's practice. She had used a different apothecary and not bought dried herbs at the market.

"It won't matter," she said, determined to remain calm. "I can take the coach to Southampton and find temporary lodgings there." She had her mother's brooch and earrings and would sell them if necessary.

Mr Gentry's resigned sigh left a puff of white mist in the air. "You cannot leave London. The magistrate will demand you remain in town while he looks for evidence to prove I'm innocent."

"It could take weeks, maybe months before they exonerate Gentry," Aaron added.

"Months!" Sofia clutched her throat and heaved a breath. "I doubt I'll survive a week. You saw the list of names. At least ten men are willing to buy me at auction. Judith will put a bounty on my head." She racked her mind to think of a solution. "What's the penalty if I abscond?"

Joanna reached for Sofia's hand and clasped it tightly. "You entered the inn around the time of death. If you run, they will presume you had a part to play and may issue a warrant for your arrest."

"We're at fault," Aaron said dourly. "We encouraged you to come here, although none of us could have predicted the shocking turn of events."

Sofia hung her head, closing her eyes against a sudden tidal wave of tears. Despite every effort to find a way forward, she was trapped.

Mr Gentry spoke then, his voice tight. "There's nothing to fear, Miss Moorland. Being a gentleman, I'll do what's expected."

She raised her head, her eyes meeting his. "What's expected?"

"We'll marry. I'm sure the Earl of Berridge can persuade the bishop to process the paperwork quickly and grant us a common licence."

Chapter Six

Cavendish Square, Mayfair
Home of the 4th Viscount Hanberry

Dawn had broken an hour before Reid returned to his grandfather's home in Mayfair, tired and exhausted from the endless questioning and lack of sleep. While the world woke to a bright April morning filled with promise, he walked amid a cloud of despair.

Burns, the butler, scanned Reid's morbid black attire—a fitting ensemble for a man who'd barely escaped the noose— and received his dusty hat, explaining Lord Hanberry was in the dining room, enjoying an early breakfast.

An honest conversation with his grandfather was long overdue.

But how did Reid explain he was being framed for murder when the news would have the viscount clutching his heart and slumping over the fine china? How could he reveal his plan to marry his herbalist when the shock might send the lord to his grave?

His grandfather's bushy white brows rose when Reid entered the elegant room. From the head of the table, he captured his monocle, looked at Reid's attire and frowned. "Don't tell me there was another accident on the road last night. Coachman drunk again, I presume. There should be a law against imbibing spirits when in charge of a horse."

"Yes, it might prevent the reckless young bucks from downing brandy while racing their curricles. A young woman was maimed during a midnight charge along Park Lane last week."

"I recall no mention in the broadsheets."

Reid nodded when the footman offered to pour his coffee. "It wasn't reported in the broadsheets because the injured woman was a maid." He moved to the sideboard and lifted the lid on a silver tureen.

"Ah." His grandfather gave a nod of recognition. "I suppose such casualties are to be expected in the metropolis."

Reid filled his plate with ham and eggs, though he barely had an appetite for anything but the taste of Miss Moorland's lips. "To your earlier point, many accidents are preventable." He sat adjacent to his grandfather, as was their usual morning custom. "Is there a reason you're up with the larks?"

"I'm to visit Chesham Park for a few days. Romford negotiated the purchase of ten hectares to the south. You know these men of business are pedantic. He wants me to survey the area and read the small print."

"Send Uncle Edmund or Algernon."

The viscount balked. "I'll not put my faith in those

feather-headed fools. They haven't a brain cell between them."

"Perhaps it's time they showed an interest in land management."

Much to his chagrin, the viscount had recently turned eighty and wouldn't live forever. Cousin Algernon had studied the Classics at Cambridge and had just returned from his third Grand Tour, a sure sign the future of Chesham Park was bleak.

"They cannot manage their own purses, and waste ridiculous amounts at the tables and bordellos." The viscount eyed Reid as he sipped his coffee and was quick to broach a contentious topic. "If you managed Chesham Park, I could die a happy man."

"You know why that's impossible."

The viscount glanced at the footman. "Leave us and close the door."

Once alone, his grandfather proved he was not averse to begging. "Nothing is impossible. Give up the practice and accept the position of estate manager. Edmund will see it's a wise decision if it enables him to continue his lavish lifestyle. The neighbouring Bretton Hall will be yours. It's what your father would have wanted."

Reid relaxed back in the chair. His grandfather had grown tired of most tasks but was determined to do things his way. A trait that had caused untold misery thirty years ago.

"You know I share my father's passion for medicine."

"And look where it got him. Dead before his time." The viscount grasped Reid's arm with his gnarled fingers and a strength that belied his years. "If you're worried about Edmund, I can—"

"I'm not worried about Edmund. I'm afraid of no man." Except for a faceless killer who struck without warning.

"Good. Good. Then come with me to Chesham Park. Let Turner deal with your patients. Let the man run the practice if it pleases you. Set your sights elsewhere. You have a duty to this family."

Reid inhaled a calming breath.

The time to tell the truth was nigh.

"I can't leave. I have decided to marry."

A stunned silence ensued, then a beaming smile lit up his grandfather's wrinkled face, and he clapped his hands in glee. "Well, this is excellent news, my boy. Root through the invitations on my desk. The Earl of Ravenhope's youngest daughter is out and is said to be a beauty. Mind you, she is a bit of a dullard but comes with a dowry that would make Croesus blush."

Reid inwardly groaned and wished he had a large brandy to hand. "I have already chosen my bride."

His grandfather's eyes sparkled. "Viscount Brigham's daughter? I know you treat the lord's ailments and have dined at their home." The old devil winked. "Why, this is splendid news, truly splendid."

"I'm not marrying Brigham's daughter."

A peer's daughter did not marry a doctor.

He was marrying an intelligent woman with a wealth of common sense, though the unexpected pull of attraction stirred something far more salacious.

"Who is she?" Sensing the tension, his grandfather's happiness turned to bitter suspicion. "Tell me you're not marrying for love. Love is fickle and shifts with the tides. You understand that better than most."

The sudden weight of grief settled in Reid's chest.

He would never forget his mother's mournful wail when she received news of his father's death, killed by mortar fire while treating injured soldiers near La Haye Sainte. But what killed her was the letter hidden amongst his personal effects. A love note from his mistress.

"I'll never marry for love," he said coldly.

"Thank heavens for that."

He would marry out of duty and because he couldn't see an innocent woman hurt by circumstances he had helped to create. Besides, what more could he hope for than to marry someone who shared his interests, a passionate woman unconcerned with vanity? Someone strong who understood the importance of living separate lives?

"I'm marrying my herbalist."

The world seemed to stop and hold its breath.

The viscount stiffened. "I beg your pardon?"

"My herbalist. We plan to marry by licence." To expedite matters, Aaron Chance agreed to present Reid's case to the bishop to prevent the paperwork from being lost amid the pile.

"Your herbalist?" His grandfather's mouth twisted like he'd sucked a lemon. "What lunacy is this? We agreed you would marry someone of respectable standing. A lady of good breeding."

They had agreed no such thing.

Reid snorted. "Perhaps you've forgotten I'm your son's bastard. It's one thing to deceive strangers; it's another to deceive a daughter of the nobility. My conscience won't allow it." Indeed, it was a conversation he'd have with Miss Moorland before they exchanged vows.

"Your conscience?" the viscount scoffed. "Half the babes in the *ton* are sired by men who aren't their fathers. No, I'll hear no more talk of marrying your herbalist. And let's not mention what possessed you to hire a woman, by Gad."

"I gave her my word."

Miss Moorland had refused at first, knowing he'd been backed into a corner and not made the offer willingly.

I can't let you do this, sir. I'll not add to your burdens.

Perhaps you might save me from them, madam.

"If you think I'll permit you to marry a commoner like your father, you're mistaken." The words left the viscount's mouth in haste, though he soon realised his error. "I mean no slur on your mother's character but merely wish to state she was not of blue blood."

The resentment Reid thought he'd buried surfaced. "Life always makes us pay for our mistakes. You caused my illegitimacy when you lied to my mother. Part of me will always distrust your motives." Yet he'd wanted to believe things would be different now.

The viscount thumped the table. "I'll hear no more talk of you being baseborn. That woman ruined everything when she told you. We agreed to take the secret to the grave."

Reid was born three weeks early, a tiny babe who fooled the masses. Fate had conspired to bring his father home. And the baptism reflected a date of birth that was wholly fictitious.

"What of the midwife who attended her? The friends who helped her until my father discovered the truth? What of her *pious* father who threw her out when he noticed her swollen stomach?"

"Keep your voice down. Do you want all and sundry to hear?" The viscount dragged his hand through his mop of white hair. "It was thirty years ago. Why would anyone care now? Besides, there's no proof. Any whispers can be blamed on gossip."

The viscount slept easier at night, having erased his mistake.

"If I know the truth, others might. Can you imagine what would happen if I married into the nobility and blackmail letters arrived with the morning post?"

"I did everything in my power to make amends. Your father should have told me about his plans before he left for Edinburgh. I cannot be expected to trust the word of every waif and stray who knocks on my door."

"Waif and stray?"

"I speak in general terms. Stop looking for a reason to whip me."

An uneasy stillness settled around them.

Should Reid mention he had been falsely implicated in a murder?

No. His grandfather would attempt to ride roughshod over him. He wouldn't look for the culprit but merely find ways to make the problem disappear. He didn't care if they hanged the wrong man.

They ate their breakfast in silence, the air of disappointment growing heavier with each tick of the mantel clock. Reid felt like a fifteen-year-old boy again. He could still picture those quiet meals together as they both battled their grief. Yet he had never been made to feel like a burden. Guilt and a deep sense of loyalty ran through his grandfather's veins. Reid loved him and loathed him—a strange concept few would understand.

"I ask that you respect my decision." He knew he would have more chance of catching a star in a bottle. "We have not been intimate, in case you fear she trapped me into marriage."

He thought of Miss Moorland and their imaginary night at the Adelphi—a passionate encounter that heated his blood. As they would need to consummate their union, he hoped the reality would be just as enthralling.

"Then why, in God's name, would you marry her?"

"I placed her in a predicament." In truth, her desire to help him caused the issue. The situation may have been prevented if he'd simply been honest. "As a gentleman, I offered a solution."

The viscount mumbled under his breath. "With your bloodline, I doubt she took much persuasion."

A knock on the door brought the footman carrying a letter on a silver salver. Although the viscount straightened, the footman addressed Reid.

"For you, sir. I'm to inform the sender that you've read the missive. His footman is waiting at the door."

Reid snatched the note, broke the seal and read the message. "Confirm I'll keep the appointment." After dismissing the footman, he turned to his grandfather. "I'm to meet the Earl and Countess of Berridge at Fulham Palace this afternoon for an audience with the bishop. I trust you'll not interfere."

His grandfather gripped the table and stood slowly. "You mean to spite me, is that it? Don't tell me this is a case of history repeating itself. At least your father thought he loved your mother. Must I spend my whole life suffering imbeciles? Am I to bear witness to another tragedy?"

Reid downed his coffee. He understood his grandfather's disappointment, but he would not bear the burden of his family's legacy. "I have patients to visit." And he had to call on Mrs Ludgrove before she met a grisly end. "I wish you a safe journey to Chesham Park."

"All that promise wasted on a whim," his grandfather grumbled as he hobbled from the room without a backwards glance.

A deep empathy for his father settled in Reid's bones. The pressure to please was suffocating. The weight of expectation was a cross too heavy to bear.

Perhaps rebellion was in the blood. Much like his forebear, he refused to become his grandfather's puppet. Indeed, his father's last letter to him had carried an important message.

Be your own man.

No matter the cost.

Sofia paced the floor in the dispensary, wringing her hands and trying to come to terms with last night's events. It didn't help that she had only slept for an hour and hoped work might distract her from thoughts of Mr Gentry.

She could not marry him.

No matter how tempting the proposition.

Had he offered of his own free will, she may have accepted out of sheer desperation. But to spend their lives bound together, knowing he'd had no choice? It would bring nothing but untold misery. He deserved better. A point she would make clear when he returned after visiting his morning patients.

It was best to write a note, leave London and save him from a wretched fate. The sale of her mother's brooch should fetch twenty pounds. That would cover the cost of a packet boat to France and a year's basic lodgings. Dover was a better option, and the stage left The Golden Cross at eight the next morning.

She braced her hands on the workbench, a flurry of emotions twisting knife-like in her gut. How would she fare alone in a foreign country? How could she leave when every fibre of her being urged her to stay? The dilemma proved confounding. How could she abandon Mr Gentry in his hour of need?

Mr Hickman's breathless voice reached her ears, his panicked stutter suggesting he was dealing with a disgruntled patient. It was probably Mr Dennison's footman, come to demand a jar of leeches for the third time this week.

"Stop faffing, man, I know my way," came a masculine voice Sofia didn't recognise. "I don't need a chaperone."

She straightened as an elderly gentleman dressed in finery appeared in the doorway. "May I help you, sir?"

The fellow leant on a silver-topped walking stick. "How much do you want?" His scornful tone hit like a sharp slap. "Name your price."

"I beg your pardon? Are you referring to the leeches?"

"Leeches!" he bawled, nostrils flaring. "You're the leech, madam." His dull blue eyes fixed her to the spot while he lingered in the doorway as if to enter was beneath him. "Five hundred pounds? Might that persuade you to retract your suckers, or do you mean to drain him dry?"

Sofia stared, somewhat baffled.

"Five hundred pounds for what, sir?"

That's when he crossed the threshold, and the air turned arctic. He raised his cane, prodding it at her like it was an extension of his finger. "By Gad, you're a cunning devil. A veritable vixen. I'll agree to a thousand, no more. You can have the money within the hour."

Sofia shook her head. "You have me at a loss, sir. I fear you've confused me with someone else. Allow me to call Mr Hickman so he may—"

"Oh, I can see why he likes you." Disdain filled the gentleman's eyes as he lifted his monocle and scanned her sad dress. "You've got the same innocent look his mother had when she came begging at the door. An air of sweetness disguising a hidden passion. I imagine you beguiled him with knowledge of your witch's potions."

That's when she realised the man with the acid tongue was Mr Gentry's grandfather. "Might you come to the point, my lord?" She wasn't afraid. Nothing was as terrifying as Mr Merrick's sinister stare. And she'd learned to take criticism during lessons in confidence at The Burnished Jade. "You're attempting to bribe me to do what, exactly?"

The lord sneered. "You know damn well why I'm here. Refuse my grandson's suit, take your money and leave. Herbalists are ten a penny. He'll soon fill the vacancy."

Most people in her situation would grasp his hand and thank him. She could live comfortably for years on such a vast sum.

"I'm afraid I cannot do that." Her being arrested for absconding wasn't the issue. The magistrate had been quite clear. She was to remain in town until he had the villain in custody. No. She suspected Mr Gentry would be furious at his grandfather's interference. "Not without discussing the matter with Mr Gentry."

The lord's cheeks ballooned like a storm cloud about to burst. "Don't try my patience, girl. I don't know what hold you have over him, but you'll do the decent thing and stop this foolery."

Tears pricked her eyes, but she took a calming breath.

"I'm a woman, not a girl. Mr Gentry is a strong-minded man of thirty. An honourable man." A handsome and somewhat dangerous man, too. "I'm surprised you've not stopped to ask what prompted him to make such a grand gesture."

"Why would he?" Mr Gentry said, appearing in the doorway behind his grandfather, his face hard as stone. "My grandfather has no interest in people. He cares about land and legacy."

The lord turned swiftly, his face flushing like a thief caught escaping with the silverware. "That's not true. I care about you. This creature has bewitched you. I've seen—"

"Her name is Miss Moorland, and you will show her some respect." Mr Gentry met her gaze, letting her see the pain behind his stern facade. He stepped into the room, closing the door behind him. "There's a reason we agreed to marry."

"Yes, she's been drugging you with her potions."

Mr Gentry ignored the outburst. "There wasn't an accident on the road last night. A man was murdered. He was found gripping my calling card."

The elderly man frowned. "Was he a patient?"

"No, but I've lost four patients since the beginning of December. All women of a certain age, though their conditions were minor." Mr Gentry inhaled deeply before explaining he believed they were murdered, each victim a means of drawing him closer to the hangman's scaffold.

The lord stared, aghast. "Why didn't you mention it to me? I would have hired the best investigators and called the coroner to account. I'd have demanded the Home Secretary put his best man on the job."

Mr Gentry paused before saying, "I can handle my own affairs. The culprit covered his tracks. The only way to catch him is to predict his next move. I cannot risk the truth being buried only to resurface years from now."

"Perhaps he's a grieving husband who blames you for his wife's death or a father angry at losing a beloved child. I said this work comes with too many risks."

"Who can say?"

A shadow of suspicion passed over the lord's features. "Surely you don't think it's someone we know."

Mr Gentry shrugged. "Jealousy makes men do foolish things."

They mentioned no names but were clearly discussing the same person.

The lord cast Sofia a disparaging glance. "What bearing has this on your need to marry your herbalist?"

Sofia's pulse rose. She looked at Mr Gentry, willing him not to mention the Merricks' plan. Based on the disdain emanating from the viscount's pores, he would be the first to tell Judith where to find her.

"I wasn't entirely honest earlier."

Please don't tell him.

"By all accounts, you've not been honest for months," the viscount scoffed. "Your father kept secrets. I presumed the pain they caused would be enough to deter you from doing the same."

Mr Gentry shifted uncomfortably, and a lie fell easily from his lips. "I know your views on love, which I shared until I met Miss Moorland." He moved to stand beside her, taking her hand in his. It was warm and comforting despite being a prop in a play. "She is extremely bright. We have similar goals and aspirations. I admire her resilience and respect her desire to change opinion."

"Devil take it, I feel like I've leapt back in time and am

listening to your father's drivel." In a temper, the viscount struck the floor with the end of his walking stick. "Have some sense. If you marry her, you'll come to regret it. You've inherited your father's foolish heart. Your mother held him to ransom for years. Why do you think he accepted a commission?"

Mr Gentry released her hand and pulled back his shoulders. "Isn't it time you were on the road to Chesham Park? Don't let me keep you. As you refused to attend my parents' wedding, don't feel the need to rush back for mine."

His grandfather shuffled towards the door, muttering foul words under his breath. "Had I upped the stakes to two thousand pounds, she would have taken the bribe. Remember that when you say your vows."

The viscount left the dispensary, but Mr Gentry didn't see him out. Instead, he closed the door, breathed deeply and stared at nothing.

Sofia came to stand beside him, placing a gentle hand on his back. "I suspect you rue the day you agreed to hire me. It's not too late to call him back and explain we've changed our minds."

He faced her, brows drawn in confusion.

"This is all my fault," she said before he could speak. "I'm not your responsibility. I would have agreed if you'd wanted to marry for convenience, but you were forced to make a declaration. I cannot allow you to make such a sacrifice. I'll find another way to escape Judith's clutches."

"It's not your fault."

She expected him to bemoan their fate, not remove her spectacles and place them on the workbench. Nor tease a lock of hair from her bun and watch it slip slowly through his fingers.

"Perhaps I have selfish reasons for suggesting the match." His eyes trailed over her jaw and throat, leaving a scorching path in its wake. "Perhaps I want a night like the one we shared at the Adelphi."

Either his grandfather had stolen his sanity, or Mr Gentry desperately needed a distraction. Why else would he stare at her with strange fascination?

"Only one night," she teased. "What was it about our imagined encounter that lives in your memory?"

He dragged his teeth over his bottom lip, something he did when deep in thought, a sight that held the ladies at The Jade spellbound.

"Maybe I long to see the treasures you hide beneath that saggy dress. When we're married, I'll buy you a wardrobe of clothes that hug your figure."

"This dress used to fit me perfectly. When the Merricks left for Scotland, I cut the grocer's bill by limiting myself to one meal a day, and put the money aside for my escape."

"You've been starving yourself?" His expression tightened while his tone rang with concern and disbelief.

"I'm not starving," she reassured him.

His hand came to rest on her waist. "We'll dine out tonight. You'll have whatever pleases you. We'll order two desserts and bring one home."

Sofia swallowed. "Home?"

"I'll remain here with you until we marry. You need someone to protect you from the Merricks, and I have tenants in my house in Jermyn Street. They'll require three months' notice."

Mr Gentry painted an idyllic picture, one that would fade in time. Not on her part. Who wouldn't want to marry a handsome man who valued a woman's work? Yet she feared he

had another motive for saving her. One relating to his parents'
tumultuous past.

It came with a depressing realisation. She liked seeing the
glow of desire in Mr Gentry's striking blue eyes. She liked
hearing the sensual hum of his voice. It wouldn't be a
marriage of convenience if she fell in love with him.

It would be an unbearable tragedy.

Chapter Seven

Talk of a romantic dinner and a fantasy evening at the Adelphi reduced Reid's burning need for justice to a simmer.

Had his grandfather aired his concerns respectfully, Reid wouldn't be so damned angry. Yet the words the viscount used betrayed his disgust. Words like *waif* and *stray* and *that woman*. Words, like his disgraceful actions, that roused a deep distrust in the man who longed to mould Reid in his own image.

"There is another way to solve our problems," Miss Moorland said brightly. "We could pretend we're married. It would save me from the Merricks and prevent you from making a dreadful mistake."

"Pretend?" Did she not see the flaw in her logic?

"What harm will it do? When the truth comes to light, we could say it was part of a plan to catch a killer."

He should be overcome with relief, not feel a rising rebellion in his chest. The practicality of Miss Moorland's suggestion would not silence the gnawing need to kiss her again.

Nor would it banish the primal urge to strip her out of that unflattering dress.

"We're good at letting our imaginations run wild." A slow smile curled her lips. "My heart flutters whenever you mention the Adelphi."

The angel on his shoulder prodded him, quick to point out the problem. "If we live here under the guise of being married, we'll have to share the same bed. What if the lines between illusion and reality become blurred?"

Her gaze slid over his body like she had already lost the battle, but she shook her head and raised her chin. "Why would they? When we consider what's at stake, I'm sure we can exercise restraint."

"I'm not sure we can." It may have been possible before they ravished each other's mouths at the Hare and Hounds, but he was more than eager to repeat the experience.

Furrows appeared between her brows. "Of course we can. We're intelligent people unswayed by moments of fancy."

"You underestimate the power of a passionate kiss. Permit the rogue in me to reveal your error." He captured her chin, lowering his head until their mouths were mere inches apart.

She gasped softly.

"Your heart is racing, Miss Moorland." Excitement shone in her eyes like the moon's rays on a verdant forest. "Your lips part like they have a will of their own."

"You know how to unnerve me, sir."

"Yet you're not afraid." He touched his mouth to hers, relishing the hitch in her breath as he pulled away. "I seek the sensual woman you suppress. The one you hide because you believe she has no place in a man's world."

"Society will always restrict my options," she said, their

hot breath mating in the ether. "A lady must choose between marriage and ambition."

"What if I said you could have it all, Miss Moorland?" He brushed his lips over hers again, a delicate whisper of a kiss that barely lingered before parting. "What if I unlock the shackles and let you take what you desperately desire? It would be our secret."

Her throat worked tirelessly as she fought to regain control.

"Use me … use me for your experiment," he whispered, the ache in his abdomen tightening as blood pooled in his loins. "Take what you want without abandon. Explore the desire I know pulses in your veins. I know how badly you want to taste—"

Miss Moorland seized him, clasping his coat lapels in her dainty hands and yanking his mouth to hers.

She kissed him, a wild, passionate assault that hardened his cock in seconds. There was no time to breathe, no time to think, no time for anything but this savage need for each other.

His heart galloped.

His pulse soared.

They were kissing open-mouthed, their tongues slipping through the seam of their lips, stroking, teasing. Erotic thoughts swamped him: the need to inhale the musky scent of her arousal, to drive into her wetness and feel the tight hug of her around his swollen cock.

His fingers chased down her back, sinking into her soft buttocks. He gripped her fiercely, the need to lose himself in her evident in his grinding hips and guttural groans.

They stumbled backwards, falling against the workbench

as their hands raced over each other in a frenzy, tugging at clothes in a desperate bid to ensure neither broke contact.

He reached behind her, swiping away documents and baskets of herbs, ready to lift her onto the table and wedge himself between her parted thighs.

That's when the damn pestle rolled onto the floor and landed with a clunk, the sound bringing them hurtling back to reality.

Mother of all saints!

Miss Moorland dragged her mouth from his, heaving a breath while her eyes glimmered with a fervent hunger. "Good heavens! That was … that was …"

"Incredible?"

"Dangerous."

"Indeed. It's hot enough to send the mercury soaring." He battled for control, though lust called for him to lead the charge. "You see how easy it is to succumb to our passions." Hell, Reid trembled like a schoolboy tossing off while spying on a maid. "There's no hope of us sharing the same bed."

Miss Moorland touched her swollen lips. "No, not when you can count seduction amongst the skills you've mastered. As with most things, I'm out of my depth with you, sir."

"It's not me, madam. I may have teased a reaction, but you're responsible for the throbbing bulge in my trousers."

A flash of pride darted over her features. "I am?"

"I'd beg you to touch me, but I suspect it won't end well." If they were married, he'd hike up her skirts and have her on the workbench. "Passion can be dangerous."

"Or enlightening. I've just thought of an alternative to marriage."

"Yes?"

"The degenerates cannot bid on my virginity if I'm no

longer chaste. Indeed, there'd be no reason for them to offer marriage at all." She smiled sweetly, which made her next comment more shocking. "The solution is simple. If you're willing, you can take my virtue."

Reid had received many scandalous proposals in his time, many too vulgar to mention. Never had a woman offered herself on a silver platter with no care for her own pleasure.

He'd dismissed the suggestion, explaining that drastic measures were unnecessary. Hickman's sudden knock on the dispensary door had brought a halt to the conversation, and Miss Moorland focused on preparing a mustard poultice and filling a basket with the required tinctures.

Even now, as Reid sat opposite her in his carriage en route to visit his patient, Mrs Ludgrove, thoughts of making love to her rebounded in his mind.

Perhaps she *had* used a potion to bewitch him. The curious blend of wisdom and wildness certainly held him captive. Miss Moorland was like a complex tapestry; every thread was rich and varied, and every study offered an enchanting surprise.

How would that translate in the dark realms of his bedchamber? Would her hands be as bold as her opinion? With her passion raw and unguarded, would her touch be his undoing?

"Mr Hickman was none too pleased at me leaving the dispensary." She drew her gaze from the window. "I'd agreed to sit with him and explain the use of clay to reduce swelling."

"We have more important matters to contend with." Reid

felt a stab of jealousy. His secretary spent more time in the dispensary than at his desk. "Besides, he believed the story about introducing you to female patients."

"Yes, the idea sounded plausible." She eyed him over the rim of her spectacles. "Unlike my suggestion about you taking my virtue, which doubtless sounded like the ramblings of a madwoman."

Reid found himself smiling. "There was method in your madness. You came to a logical conclusion based on your dire circumstances."

"Well … and our kiss this morning had me thinking about the cure for hysteria."

"It did?" Lust pulled at him like an anchor in a storm. He imagined stealing her journal, scrambling madly to her notes on the condition because he'd wager she'd documented how it felt to come by her own hand.

"Wasn't that the point of the exercise?"

"Yes, it was."

"And you were right." A crimson glow touched her cheeks. "Something happens when we kiss. Excitement surges like a drug through my veins, hot and intoxicating. I forget everything but the craving for more."

His mouth went dry. The desire to have her was an ache he struggled to suppress. It was a perfect time to make a confession. "Can I trust you with a secret, Miss Moorland?"

She sat ramrod straight. "Of course."

"It's important you know the truth in case we find ourselves at the altar. It may explain my grandfather's vehemence." He held her gaze. "Give your word you'll not repeat it to another soul."

Miss Moorland crossed her heart. "You can trust me."

Reid tried not to think about his mother when he said, "I

was born a week before my parents married. It's a complicated story we can discuss another time. But my grandfather manipulated the facts to hide my illegitimacy."

Her brow quirked in surprise. "How? Did he pay people to lie?" she said without judgement.

"No, but my baptism records do not reflect the actual date of my birth. To my knowledge, it is a well-kept secret. But if I marry, I cannot deceive my bride."

"I see." She looked calm, her gaze steady, unblinking. "I appreciate your honesty and would expect nothing less from a gentleman of your good standing. It's not important, as there's no need for us to marry if you're happy to pretend."

"Would it be important if we were marrying?"

She thought for a moment. "No."

"I'm baseborn, Miss Moorland."

"You're a gentleman to me, sir."

He snorted. "The way we kiss says I'm no gentleman."

"Are you suggesting I'm not a lady?" she said, amused.

"You're a remarkable lady."

She smiled. "Then there is no argument."

As they fell into a companionable silence, he recalled what the countess had said about her a mere month ago.

Miss Moorland's father was a gentleman who fell on hard times after marrying his second wife. There was no come-out, which is just as well as she's not one for crowds.

Reid imagined her at a society ball, quiet and restrained, pressing herself to the wall so she might blend into the background. Few men would notice her subtle beauty or the fiery spark in her eyes or the passion filling her heart. Miss Moorland was a diamond hidden in plain sight.

"I believe I have a solution to our problem," he said. Surely a lady who wished to break free from the rigid confines of society craved adventure. He'd be the one to give it to her.

"Which problem exactly?"

"The scandal of us sharing a bed when we're unwed."

"Will the solution spare us both from the chains of matrimony?"

"Indeed. It will enable us to create a convincing illusion."

She arched a brow. "I must say I'm intrigued, Mr Gentry."

He grinned, ignoring the fact his friend Rothley would need persuading. "We'll stay at the Marquess of Rothley's estate, Studland Park. It's a half-hour ride from town. The Merricks can't reach you there, and there'll be no one to question the authenticity of our fake marriage."

She pursed her lips, her fingers twisting the hem of her coat sleeve. "Stay with the marquess? I have nothing suitable to wear."

"Rothley won't give a damn if you wear a coal sack. I'll speak to him this evening." He was to meet his friends at White's, an appointment he planned to cancel, but the Countess of Berridge was right. It was time he was honest with those closest to him. "Rothley's support will add credence to the deception."

Miss Moorland wasn't convinced. "I doubt he'll want house guests. He's a private man. On the rare occasions when he visits the countess at The Jade, he shows little tolerance for strangers."

There were many reasons for Rothley's insular attitude. None that Reid had the right to mention. "If you can withstand Aaron Chance's abrupt manner, you can withstand Rothley's indifference."

"I suppose."

The carriage drew to a stop outside Mrs Ludgrove's townhouse in Chandos Street, Marylebone. Reid alighted and assisted Miss Moorland to the pavement.

"How will we question Mrs Ludgrove without causing alarm?" she said, her gaze flitting to their joined hands. "She'll wonder how we know about her visit to the Hare and Hounds."

Reid considered the problem. "We'll suggest there may be an issue with the laudanum I prescribed for her sleeping disorder. I'll pretend I saw her at the coaching inn."

"Very well."

Mrs Ludgrove's butler looked relieved to see them and beckoned them into the house. "The mistress is in the drawing room, sir, nursing one of her megrims. She'll be grateful you arrived so promptly."

Puzzled by the fact they were expecting him, Reid introduced Miss Moorland as his colleague and herbalist. "Follow me, sir. I shall announce you both at once."

Stretched out on the gold damask sofa, her white cat curled beside her, Mrs Ludgrove acknowledged them by raising a limp hand from her brow.

"Thank heavens. You must have sensed the distress in my note," said the attractive woman in her early fifties. "I cannot bear the pain a moment longer."

As Reid hadn't read the note, he was careful with his reply. "Can you explain the symptoms to me again, Mrs Ludgrove? I've brought my herbalist, Miss Moorland, in the hope she might suggest a suitable remedy."

Mrs Ludgrove lifted her head as if it were filled with lead, each inch a struggle with gravity, and scanned Miss Moorland through narrowed eyes. "Is she not a bit young to offer advice?"

Miss Moorland spoke up. "I've been studying herbalism since the age of ten, Mrs Ludgrove. Nature often provides the answer to every ailment."

"Not mine," the woman protested. "Ask Mr Gentry. I've been suffering sleepless nights for months. And these terrible headaches have begun to appear at odd hours of the day."

Reid approached the sofa. "Headaches are often a symptom of sleep deprivation. We never established a reason for your restless spirit. The cure lies there."

"That's the point, Mr Gentry." With a groan, Mrs Ludgrove sat up, gathering the cat onto her lap. "I have slept soundly every night for the past week. I've taken six drops of laudanum as requested, but it's only recently started taking effect. It's most peculiar."

"May I see the tincture?" He suspected she'd been doubling the dose.

"Pinkerton!" she called before ringing the tiny hand bell on the side table. The sudden din made the cat leap to the floor and dart behind the sofa.

She sent her butler to fetch the tincture from her nightstand.

Miss Moorland mentioned the headaches while awaiting the servant's return. "Too much laudanum can cause dizziness and a throbbing head. Might these new pains coincide with your improved sleep?"

"Well, yes." Mrs Ludgrove huffed as if affronted. "I'm not an imbecile. That's what I'm saying. Might there be a problem with the tincture?"

A shiver of suspicion ran down Reid's spine. "Have there been other symptoms? Nausea? Forgetfulness?"

"I misplaced my mother's pearl earrings. I woke in a stupor and couldn't remember where I put them." She looked at the butler as he entered the drawing room. "And I've had Pinkerton hunting high and low for my ruby brooch."

"As I said, madam, you wore the brooch on your outing with your cousin in Upminster and returned home without it. There's still no reply from the missive you sent to her."

"Upminster?" Reid said, stealing an opportunity to mention the Hare and Hounds inn. "Yes, I thought I saw you at the fair and later at a coaching inn on the Barking Road. I called out, but the inn was crowded and you failed to hear me over the high-spirited revellers."

Mrs Ludgrove's face turned ghostly pale. "The Barking Road?" The question burst from her lips in a shrill squeak. "I did visit an inn on the journey home, though the name eludes me."

Pinkerton handed Reid the tincture. "It's the bottle you sent with the new delivery boy two weeks ago, sir."

Reid's heart raced. "I didn't send a tincture with a delivery boy." He examined the label on the brown bottle. "This looks like mine. It's from the same apothecary on Long Acre."

He removed the cork and sniffed the infusion. The bitter smell of opium laced with sharp spirits had him jerking his head at the unexpected potency. "And you've been taking six drops of this before bed?"

Mrs Ludgrove winced. "Perhaps a little more. The glass dropper is fiddly and quite temperamental."

Reid gave Miss Moorland the bottle, seeking her opinion.

She sniffed and came to the same conclusion. "The ratio of opium to alcohol is higher than you usually prescribe. Far higher than you would recommend for a sleeping draught."

"Indeed." He needed to question Hickman and the apothecary as a matter of urgency. "It explains the dizziness and headaches and Mrs Ludgrove's memory loss."

Miss Moorland drew him aside and lowered her voice. "We need to be honest with her. We cannot leave without warning her of the potential danger."

He agreed—touching her upper arm to reassure himself more than her—and addressed Mrs Ludgrove. "I must ask a delicate question."

The lady clutched her lace-trimmed chemisette to her throat. "Does it relate to the tincture?"

"I didn't send the tincture. It's far too strong. I suspect whoever did, wants to ensure your memory is hazy." Noting the confusion in her eyes, he added, "I must inform the magistrate at Bow Street. He will send a constable to take a statement."

Reid inwardly cursed his nemesis.

Once word got out, he would lose half of his patients.

"A constable?" Mrs Ludgrove said, a frisson of fear in her voice. "But … but … I don't understand. Why would anyone want to hurt me?"

Reid wished he knew the answer and vowed the cunning devil would pay with his life. He looked at Mrs Ludgrove, wondering how to ask if she had a lover.

Miss Moorland came to the rescue. "There is talk of a man from Barking preying on widows." She crouched before Mrs Ludgrove, the action matching the caring tone of her voice. "He may be a thief, targeting attractive, mature women. It's said he uses laudanum to subdue them because the ladies are often intelligent and astute. He's known to frequent the Hare and Hounds."

Although Mrs Ludgrove shook her head dismissively, she slapped her hand to her mouth like she might vomit.

"Have you encountered such a fellow?" Miss Moorland continued. "If you would rather not speak to us, you must mention it to the constable. And you mustn't take any more medicine until we find out who sent the bottle."

A grave silence ensued.

Mrs Ludgrove's eyes grew watery, the whites streaked with red veins.

"We'll leave you to rest." Miss Moorland stood and brushed her skirts, her compassion evident in her measured movements. "You may send for me or Mr Gentry if you have any concerns."

Reid reiterated the sentiment.

They were about to leave when Mrs Ludgrove uttered, "Wait! His name is Mr Fellows. He works at Coutts. I met him at a bookshop in the Burlington Arcade. We take supper together at Antoine's every Wednesday and have done for the past month. He invited me to the fair in Upminster, to dine at an inn and stay—"

She stopped abruptly, omitting the part where she had shared a room with him at the Hare and Hounds and he took more than her ruby brooch.

"Was he present when you misplaced your earrings and brooch?" Reid asked.

"Yes," she said, averting her gaze.

"If you could describe him, it would be a great help." Miss Moorland spoke in the soft, polite voice that put people at ease. "I wouldn't want to cast aspersions on an innocent man, but it's important to check the facts."

Mrs Ludgrove's cheeks flushed a mortified pink, her posture stiffening. "Mr Fellows claims he's thirty. He has brown hair and an athletic physique. I believe he studied mathematics at Cambridge, though it could be a lie."

I know what you're thinking.

I'm a lonely, old fool.

The unspoken words lingered in the air.

Miss Moorland gave an unaffected smile. "Thank you, Mrs Ludgrove. The information will prove invaluable. We'll leave you to rest now. A pleasant stroll around the garden and a cup of valerian tea may help you sleep tonight."

They bid the lady good day and withdrew.

"We'll visit again next week," Reid said, retrieving his hat from Pinkerton. "Send word to the practice if her condition worsens or you receive any unwanted gentleman callers."

Pinkerton frowned. "Unwanted gentleman callers, sir?"

"Mrs Ludgrove should avoid visitors for ten days." Reid prayed the devious Mr Fellows was their man and they would have him in custody soon. "I'm confident the tincture is making her ill." The excessive dose of laudanum had caused her symptoms. "But we cannot rule out an infection."

Pinkerton nodded. "We'll take every precaution."

"Forgo your half-day off this week. Someone should be here at all times, just until Mrs Ludgrove makes a full recovery."

Mrs Beckman had died when her only servant was absent.

They left Pinkerton issuing orders to the maid and returned to the carriage. Reid checked his watch and instructed his coachman, Nokes, to drive to Fulham Palace.

"Fulham Palace?" Miss Moorland settled into the seat. "We don't need a licence for a fake marriage. Why trouble the bishop?"

"The licence lasts three months. As we cannot anticipate the depth of the Merricks' depravity, we might need to marry in a hurry."

"I suppose staying vigilant is wise."

Reid had other reasons for wanting the document.

Something surprising happened when they kissed. Lust banished every decorous thought and intention. This forced proximity didn't help matters.

And perhaps he would use the licence as bait.

A way to test his grandfather's loyalty.

To determine if he could trust his own kin.

Chapter Eight

Fulham Palace, the Bishop of London's residence, exuded an old-world elegance, its ivy-covered walls and quaint leaded windows giving a sense of storied history and quiet charm.

Mr Gentry's need to have the bishop process their application quickly, reflected a deep concern for the future. Had rumours about the auction reached his ears? Had he discovered something sinister in Mr Merrick's past? Did fears of the unknown assailant drive his urgency to secure the document?

The answer became apparent when Mr Gentry's carriage pulled into the cobbled courtyard and they alighted to speak to the Earl and Countess of Berridge. The couple stood at the palace's heavy oak doors as if preparing to leave, not seek entrance.

"You've had a wasted journey," Aaron Chance said, a thread of annoyance in his tone. "We arrived as your grandfather was leaving. The bishop agreed to a fortnight's grace before considering your application."

Mr Gentry stiffened. "A fortnight? On what grounds?"

Joanna looked rather pale as she took a calming breath.

"Your grandfather seeks confirmation of Miss Moorland's age and marital status. He was quite insistent. The fact she has no dowry causes the viscount some concern."

"But I do have a dowry," Sofia informed them, "from my paternal grandmother. The document is held at Waters & Finch solicitors in Newcastle Street."

It was her only safeguard from an uncertain future.

Mr Gentry blinked in surprise. "You never mentioned it."

"I would have if we'd decided to marry. With the interest gained, it's worth a thousand pounds and is tied to a marriage contract until my twenty-eighth birthday. If I remain unwed, I can draw the funds as an allowance."

"Do the Merricks know?" Joanna said.

"I suspect so, but Judith avoided the topic." Her stepmother had taken every document from the study to store in a secret location. Whenever Sofia asked questions about money or her father's will, Mr Merrick's menacing stare rendered her mute.

"So you planned to hide abroad for the next five years," Mr Gentry stated as if the idea had merit, "and return to claim a yearly portion."

"As you know, that was my second option. A foolish idea to pursue a career in medicine led me to think I might hide in London." The prospect of working was like a beacon of hope in the darkness, one Mr Gentry had lit with his own hands. "One's passion can be a hindrance."

"Not always," he said as if referring to their last kiss.

Aaron Chance spoke up. "I doubt news of your dowry will appease the bishop. Now that questions about the marriage's legality have been raised, he will proceed with caution. Perhaps a letter from the solicitor would suffice."

Sofia nodded. "I can visit the office on Monday, though

we no longer need a licence. We've settled on a plan that suits us better."

A simple plan that didn't bind them together for life.

"Yet I'm determined to acquire one," Mr Gentry said with some vehemence. "If only to spite my grandfather." He explained they had agreed on a fake marriage until the murderer was caught, and the Merricks gave up their pursuit of her virtue. "He's visiting his country estate for a few days and cannot discount the claim."

"We will confide in the viscount when he returns from Chesham Park," Sofia added, feeling happier now she wasn't forcing Mr Gentry up the aisle with a metaphorical blade to his back. "We'll make no formal announcement but will ensure the Merricks hear the news."

Joanna gave a disapproving frown. "And when the truth comes to light, what then? Mr Gentry will remain unscathed while your reputation lies in tatters. He'll receive a congratu-latory slap on the back at White's while you will be shunned and called a harlot."

Shame, as heavy as a falling tombstone, crushed Sofia's chest.

Perhaps running was her only option. It was better than spending her life tied to a man whose desire mellowed to indifference. It was pointless pretending she could marry for convenience, not when her admiration for Mr Gentry might develop into something more profound.

"I shall do what all scandalous women do," she said, determined not to cry. "I'll leave England for the Continent."

"How very Byronesque," Joanna said, pausing to take another deep breath. "Let's pray those abroad admire your rebellious spirit." She shared a strange look with Mr Gentry, a silent message that caused him to give a curt nod.

"We'll meet at Daventry's office on Monday," Aaron Chance said. "Hopefully, his investigators will have information from those working at the Hare and Hounds. Finding the fiend who murdered O'Connor will bring us closer to the truth." He glanced at his wife as she gripped his arm to steady her balance. "Are you unwell?"

"I'm fine." Joanna's strained smile said she was not fine.

"I said there was something off about the salmon last night," the earl complained. "You looked pale when you woke this morning."

"It's not the salmon," she said, turning her attention back to Sofia. "Ask the solicitor for written proof of your age, marital status and dowry, and we will give it to Mr Daventry. He has friends in Whitehall who will speak to the bishop. Regardless of your plans, gaining a licence is a wise move, and Aaron can secure a clergyman at a moment's notice."

Mr Gentry agreed. "We must prepare for every eventuality. I'll not allow my grandfather to manipulate me as he did my parents."

Matters had become complicated, Sofia realised.

Marrying was about more than saving her from the Merricks or from ruin if they did something sinful when they kissed. The more his grandfather tried to control him, the more Mr Gentry rebelled.

"I shall visit the solicitor first thing Monday morning and have the information with Mr Daventry before noon. We can —" Sofia stopped abruptly when Joanna closed her eyes and clutched her chest.

Aaron Chance looked like his world was about to come crashing down. He captured his wife around the waist. "Let me carry you to the carriage. We'll have Gentry examine you."

"I don't need a doctor, just a chamber pot and a fan. The nausea and dizziness will pass. Besides, I saw Dr Fisher this morning when you met with your brothers at Fortune's Den."

"Dr Fisher?" The life drained from the man's face. "Why the devil didn't you mention it before?"

Joanna laid a calming hand on her husband's chest. "I planned to tell you at home tonight, but you'll probably die of apoplexy if I don't settle your fears."

"You're not sick?"

"No, Aaron. I am with child."

He stilled, though his throat worked tirelessly. "With child?"

"Don't sound so surprised. You're an intelligent man. If you consider what happens between us most days, you can make the calculation." She smiled as she smoothed her hand over her abdomen. "With God's grace, you'll be a father in early autumn."

Sofia tried to avert her gaze to allow the couple a private moment, but tears welled in Aaron Chance's eyes, the shocking spectacle holding her entranced.

He coughed to clear his throat.

He opened his mouth to speak but couldn't.

Joanna swept her arms around his neck. "Are you happy, my love? Is your heart full of joy like mine?"

Mr Chance gazed at his wife like she was the air he breathed. "It's so damn full it might burst." Warmth radiated from him, an inner glow of love he could not disguise. "You know I'll not let you out of my sight."

"I know," she said, sounding happy in her surrender.

Mr Gentry cupped Sofia's elbow and drew her away.

His touch had the restless thrum of desire coursing through her, a fickle feeling without substance. "I dare you to look at them and tell me true love does not exist," she said. "Love can transform people, whether it lasts a month, a year or a lifetime."

What must it be like to feel that level of devotion?

As a woman without means, she had no choice but to focus on earning a living. But to love someone unconditionally, was that not the greatest of life's gifts?

"I've seen what happens when love turns to despair," he said, his cynicism like a medal of honour he wore with pride. "Love is like a slow walk off the plank. Few are destined to survive."

"Have you ever been in love?"

"Of course not. I avoid it at all costs."

Was that why he'd made such a grand gesture at the Hare and Hounds? Did he believe they were in no danger of being anything more than friends and perhaps occasional lovers?

"May I ask why?" Should they be forced to marry, it was important to rid herself of any delusions. "At this stage, I feel it's vital we're honest."

Mr Gentry's sigh sounded like it came from the soul. "My mother loved my father until the day she died. My father loved her enough to sever ties with his family, but those feelings dissipated as quickly as a morning mist. Losing him broke her heart."

Sofia's parents had shared a stoic love rooted in respect and friendship, not a burning desire to kiss rampantly and live under each other's skin.

"Love is imperfect. There is still beauty in its impermanence, in a sunset that fades, in a rose that blooms in the summer sun, in an embrace that lives in the memory long after a loved one has departed."

"There is no beauty in betrayal," he snapped.

Sofia stopped to consider the point.

"No, you're right," she admitted. Judith's betrayal was a blight on every happy memory. Sofia found it hard not to blame her father, not to see him as a weak fool instead of the kind, intelligent man she loved. "I'm sorry for suggesting otherwise."

Mr Gentry's blue eyes softened. "Don't be sorry. Friends value each other's opinions, even when they disagree. Which is why we must be honest about the nature of our relationship."

It was hard to know what they meant to each other.

"In that we're friends and colleagues who've kissed?"

Kissing failed to describe what happened when their mouths met. It was more an explosion of raw emotions. A desperate need for something she could not define. When nothing mattered but the next taste or tender touch.

He smiled, and her heart skipped a beat. "You speak like there's no hope of us kissing again, Miss Moorland."

Yet she would devour him in a heartbeat.

"Had I not arrived at the Hare and Hounds when I did, I doubt we'd have ever kissed." Then she would have thought kissing a chore, the taste of a man's lips as potent as watered-down wine, not something hot and intoxicating.

"You didn't answer my question."

"You didn't ask a question."

Her heart stuttered as he stepped a little closer. "Do you think we'll kiss again, Miss Moorland?"

His husky tone caused a swirl of heat in her stomach.

"Would you like to kiss me again, Mr Gentry?"

"You know damn well I would."

Upon their return to the practice, and as a result of Mr Gentry's relentless questions, Mr Hickman confessed to knowing nothing about the tincture sent to Mrs Ludgrove.

"I—I assure you, sir, the sleeping draught was not among those sent out with the delivery boy." Mr Hickman scanned the open ledger on his desk. He found Mrs Ludgrove's name, his finger shaking as he prodded the entry. "You prescribed a sleeping remedy during your last visit in March. It came from the supply you carry in your case."

Mr Gentry strode to his office and returned with his black leather bag, popping open the brass clasps as he plonked it on the chair. He rolled out a velvet wrap, removed the small brown bottles nestled inside and placed them on Mr Hickman's desk, next to the bottle taken from Mrs Ludgrove.

"What do you notice?" He struggled to keep his anger at bay but did not let Mr Hickman speak. "While the bottles are identical, the contents are not."

"May we smell them all?" Sofia said, encouraging Mr Hickman to help her remove the cork stoppers and inhale the infusions.

"That bottle did not come from my bag." Mr Gentry pointed at the offending article. "Mrs Ludgrove might have overdosed on opium had I not made a house call today."

Mr Hickman's breath came in shallow pants. "I can't explain it. Miss Moorland makes the tinctures now, though it may have been part of an old batch and it's the apothecary's mistake."

Sofia shuddered. Was the panicked fool trying to blame

her? "The mistake is not mine. I had the scales rebalanced and ordered new measuring spoons."

"You're missing the point, Hickman," Mr Gentry countered. "Who the hell delivered the tincture to Mrs Ludgrove?"

"I'll speak to the delivery boy tomorrow. Perhaps he can shed light on the matter."

"I want answers today. Search the ledger. Make a list of all patients we've supplied with sleeping draughts and send out replacements. Write to them. They're not to accept a delivery of laudanum without an accompanying letter."

"I'll dispose of those in the dispensary and make a fresh batch," she suggested. "Mr Hickman can work with me to ensure there are no mistakes."

Mr Gentry nodded. "Make Turner aware of the problem upon his return." He glanced at Sofia, his anger dissipating slightly. "Be ready in an hour, Miss Moorland. You'll accompany me to the apothecary to ensure he's not at fault."

Mr Wiggins, the grey-haired apothecary in Long Acre, scratched his head as Mr Gentry bombarded him with questions. "My reputation is at stake. Are you telling me anyone can walk in off the street and purchase the same tincture? Is there nothing to differentiate the bottles you sold me from those you sell to the public?"

Mr Wiggins shook his head. He took two bottles from the oak shelf behind him. "See the label in red? That's fifteen per cent opium, only prescribed to those with severe pain and who agree to sign the register. The one with black writing is a ten per cent solution for those with minor ailments. There's even less in a paregoric."

Sofia removed Mrs Ludgrove's bottle from her reticule and showed it to Mr Wiggins. "Would you mind smelling this, sir, and advise what percentage is opium?"

He took one whiff and frowned. Wetting the end of his finger with the infusion, he dabbed the liquid onto his tongue, giving a sharp hiss. "That is my label, but I didn't make the tincture. It's too strong. I'd say the fool who cut the opium failed to dry it out properly, or maybe there's a problem with his scales."

Mr Gentry pinched the bridge of his nose and sighed. "So you're saying it's impossible to trace the fellow? How the devil am I meant to prevent it from happening again?"

Mr Wiggins gave an apologetic shrug.

"Might we scan the register you mentioned?" Sofia asked, though she doubted the villain had recorded his name. "You could leave it open, and I might steal a glance while you're serving a customer. You could hardly be blamed for my snooping."

The apothecary shook his head. "It would be a betrayal of trust."

"Sir, perhaps you fail to understand what's at stake here," she said, pressing her case. "The bottle can be traced to you. If a patient dies of an overdose of laudanum, you'll be the first person questioned. Can you prove you didn't make a mistake with the measurements?"

The man couldn't argue with her logic. He glanced furtively at his busy assistant and whispered, "Give me a minute, then come through to the back of the shop."

Sofia gave a discreet nod as Mr Wiggins slipped away.

She felt Mr Gentry's hand skim her waist the second they were alone, the gentle glide of his fingers making her stomach flip.

"What happened to the woman who stuttered when asking to examine my implements?" he whispered against her ear. "This newfound confidence is having an odd effect on me, Miss Moorland."

Sofia swallowed deeply. The rich timbre of his voice had an odd effect on her, too. "You're not the only one who gives lessons at The Burnished Jade. When a lady debates a topic with Aaron Chance, she learns the power of persuasion."

"You should use your talent more often. Perhaps persuade me to show you the cure for hysteria. I could give you a private lesson. One I guarantee will feel vastly superior to the experiments you conduct alone at home."

An image of them kissing shot into her mind, them panting into each other's mouths as his hand dipped between her thighs.

She turned her head a fraction and gazed into his mischievous eyes. "I find it hard to believe you'd not fumble," she lied. He knew how to heat her blood. "I know myself extremely well, whereas you hardly know me at all."

"I learn quickly, Miss Moorland, and was always top of the class at Cambridge. I know exactly where I would begin." He lowered his voice to a husky whisper. "I'd stroke you everywhere, saving that tight little bud until last."

Desire struck like a fire bolt to her core, the bud in question now hot and pulsing. "Anything more than kissing would be dangerous." And pleasurable beyond measure.

"Avoiding danger is why we kissed in the first place."

Mr Wiggins popped his head around the door, breaking the spell, and beckoned them into a tiny office crammed with boxes and bottles and reams of brown paper. "I'll wait in the shop and tell my assistant the lady felt faint. Be quick. You've a few minutes, no more."

The thick tome on the desk drew Sofia's attention. She squeezed past Mr Gentry, the mere brush against his hard body sending tingles dancing over her skin. "Thank you, Mr Wiggins."

The apothecary kept a record of those who purchased poisons and potent tinctures. His diligence was commendable. Many didn't care about the consequences when selling remedies.

"Come and examine the list," she said, flicking to the section marked 'high concentrate opium preparations'. "We'll begin in November last year, a month before the first suspicious incident."

With space tight, Mr Gentry moved to stand behind her. His presence made it hard to focus on the names written on the page. He leaned into her while looking over her shoulder.

"I know Henry Jackson of New Street." He slid his arm over her hip and pointed to the entry on the page. "His usage is recreational. He believes he's a gifted poet and spends his days seeking enlightenment."

Her pulse quickened. "Might he have a gripe against you?"

"Not that I'm aware." He shifted, the movement teasing the ache between her thighs. She could feel his gaze on her, not the register. "Nor does he fit Mr Fellows' description."

"Mr Fellows may have worn a disguise—a wig or blocks in his boots—though it's harder to fake an athletic physique."

She closed her eyes against the potent scent of his cologne as he bent his head to study the list.

"This reminds me of that night in my study, Miss Moorland. It began much like this. Me, standing behind you at the desk. The delightful press of your buttocks against my groin."

The devil liked to tease her. It was her own fault for

admitting her heart fluttered whenever he mentioned the Adelphi.

"How could I forget?"

He drew his long, elegant finger slowly down the page like he was tracing a tantalising path from her throat to her navel. "There's something desperately erotic about two people being rampant when still fully clothed. It's hard to read these names when I want to toss up your skirts and take you while you're still wearing sensible shoes and stockings."

She pursed her lips tightly so as not to whimper. An inner battle ensued. A shy woman should blush and change the subject, yet she liked this game. She liked this game far too much.

"What did you enjoy most about our amorous night in my study, Miss Moorland? Don't be shy." The warmth of his breath tickled her neck as he turned another page. "Tell me while I scour the list."

She should have ignored the challenge but couldn't.

"I liked it best when you were on your knees." She should stop there and allow his imagination to run riot, but the sudden rasp in his throat betrayed an eagerness to hear more. "And when you rose between my legs like Poseidon—your eyes as dark and mesmerising as the sea's hypnotic pull—ready to take what you wanted without abandon."

A soft groan escaped him. "What a surprising woman you are, Miss Moorland. You're a better storyteller than you are a herbalist, and you excel at making potions."

"Perhaps I'm an oracle, not a storyteller, and you should keep the lid on your ink pot. One never knows when a prediction may come true. I would hate to ruin your Aubusson rug while in the throes of passion."

"Minx," he whispered against her neck. "Do you know how hard you've made me?"

"So that's not a granite pestle in your pocket?"

"Were we anywhere else, I'd suggest you take it out and inspect it yourself. It's a rather good grinding tool."

The door creaked open, making them both jump.

Mr Wiggins peered through the gap. "Any luck searching the register?"

"Give us another minute," Mr Gentry said with his usual authority.

Mr Wiggins nodded and closed the door.

"No more games." Sofia stepped aside, motioning to the tome. "Concentrate on the list. We mustn't waste this opportunity by acting like randy rascals."

He laughed but rolled his shoulders and took on a serious expression. His finger followed the names and the reasons listed for the purchase: rotten teeth and gout being the most common ailments.

When he got to the record for February, he inhaled sharply and looked at her. "You said you lived with the Merricks on Dean Street near Soho Square."

"Yes, that's right." Every muscle hardened, bracing for an impact. "Why? Have you found something important?"

"Mr Merrick of Dean Street purchased two tinctures of high-strength opium for a tooth abscess."

Sofia's blood ran cold. "But Mr Merrick doesn't have an abscess. Sadly, he's in excellent health."

"Wiggins!" Mr Gentry called. He waited for the apothecary to enter before demanding he explain the sale of two potent tinctures on the same day. "It's enough opium to knock out a horse, let alone numb pain."

Mr Wiggins came to inspect the records. "Ah, yes. Mr

Merrick is a regular customer who's been suffering with toothache for months. He was off to Scotland and begged for an extra bottle to take with him on the road."

"Did you examine the abscess?"

"No. Is that a problem?" Mr Wiggins asked nervously. "Maybe his cheek looked swollen. I can't recall. Mr Merrick was happy to record the purchase in the register. As you know, society gents are less forthcoming."

"No, they prefer to keep their opium addiction a secret. Most refuse to send a servant, fearing the gossipmongers will find out." Mr Gentry spoke like he knew the identities of these men.

It's why Mr Wiggins jumped to an assumption.

One that proved to be the lead they needed in the case.

"I pride myself on being discreet, sir. I know your cousin puts on a brave face, but that illness he caught in Athens left him in desperate need of relief. Praise the Lord he's on the mend."

Mr Gentry's eyes flickered, a brief sign of surprise before he hid behind his polished veneer. "I hoped my cousin's need would be temporary. I'm sure you understand why I preferred not to prescribe the tincture myself."

Mr Wiggins nodded. "He said something similar when he bought one of the weaker preparations, and I pointed out that you supply the same bottles."

"What did the gentleman say?" Sofia asked, anticipation a prickling unease beneath her skin.

"He said it was time he took matters into his own hands and dealt with problems himself."

Chapter Nine

Reid felt the usual niggle of resentment when he mounted the stone steps to White's. He was not a member based on his own merits but an interloper, owing his place at the prestigious club to his grandfather's relentless efforts and his own close friendship with the Marquess of Rothley.

Reid scanned the impressive hall while the liveried footman took his hat and coat. After the farce with the bishop, he half expected a steward to appear to revoke his membership.

After all, meddling was his grandfather's favourite hobby.

He found Rothley in the library, sitting alone, reading from a small leather-bound book beneath the lamplight. Rothley looked up as if desperate for a distraction, his dark gaze narrowing on Reid.

"So, my elusive friend finally makes an appearance." Rothley slammed the book shut and tossed it onto the walnut table, then whispered through gritted teeth, "Where the hell have you been? You've not replied to any of my notes. I called at the practice this afternoon. Hickman said you're rarely there these days. I hear Monroe is handling your surgical procedures at Guy's."

Reid motioned to the footman and ordered brandy. "Since when did you read Keats?" He sat, gathering the book and flicking through the pages. "When did you begin caring about the beauty of life instead of viewing everything as a Shakespearean tragedy?"

Rothley released a weary sigh. "I don't read romantic drivel by choice. Joanna insisted we discuss an *Ode on Melancholy* when we dine next week. I suggested Southey's *The Battle of Blenheim*, but the countess is so enamoured with her husband that she's on a mission to see me wed."

"She means to lighten your heart. She knows you won't take a bride while you're still mourning the death of her brother."

Joanna feared Rothley would marry for spite, not love.

"Justin is not dead." Rothley enunciated every word, giving the table a thump for good measure. "I'd stake my life he's not buried beneath that headstone at St Michael's."

When a gamekeeper found Justin's corpse in a woodland hideout ten years ago, Rothley was adamant it was not the body of their missing friend. The coroner identified the deceased based on his hair and clothes, height and build, and the onyx signet ring, a family heirloom, tucked inside his coat pocket.

"Can we agree on one point?" Reid said. "If Justin is alive, he doesn't want to be found." Although why he would disappear for a decade remained a mystery. "Joanna is right. You cannot sacrifice your own happiness for someone who could be living abroad like a prince."

Rothley sat rigid in the chair. His forbidding presence had the power to empty a room. Indeed, all the nearby tables were unoccupied. "Injustice is a cross I'm forced to bear. I'll not rest until I know whether my friend perished or lied through his back teeth."

Reid considered mentioning Miss Bourne—the woman Rothley had hoped to marry before she disappeared into the night after accepting a bribe from his father—but it would only sour his friend's sullen mood.

He thought of Miss Moorland.

What was her price?

He would not blame her if she'd snatched the banknotes from his grandfather's gnarled hand and boarded the first boat to France. Unlike Rothley and Miss Bourne, they were not in love. That said, Miss Moorland was not a devious vixen. Loyalty came to her as naturally as breathing.

"Just like I'll not rest until I know what you're hiding," Rothley continued, eyeing Reid suspiciously. "Do you mean to put me in an early grave? If not, do me the courtesy of telling me what the hell is going on."

Reid snatched the snifter from the footman's tray and emptied it in one swift motion. "What do you know?"

"That you employed Miss Moorland as your herbalist and snuck off with her for hours today after arguing with your grandfather." Rothley spoke with his usual aplomb. "Are those not the actions of a man with a secret?"

Reid glanced behind, scouting for eavesdroppers before confiding in his friend. "I've been falsely implicated in a murder."

A shadow of unease crossed his features. "Murder?"

He told Rothley everything: the growing suspicion about

his patients, the nights spent at the Hare and Hounds looking for a killer, Miss Moorland seeking him out. "She's my alibi. The dead man had my blood-stained card in his hand. I'm grateful she arrived when she did."

Tension creased the corners of Rothley's eyes, the only sign he found the news unsettling. A man of his wealth and status could make problems disappear. Nothing fazed him except being deceived.

"Miss Moorland certainly has gumption." Rothley summoned the footman, ordering him to bring the brandy decanter. "When she first visited The Jade, she was rather a timid thing, always lost in the pages of her books."

Now Reid knew why. Her knowledge of herbs and medical procedures was exemplary. It's the reason he'd done the unthinkable and hired a woman. That, and her desperate plea for help, had touched his heart like an echo from the past.

"*Timid* is not a word I would use to describe Miss Moorland."

"What word would you use to describe her?"

Intriguing—she surprised him at every turn. *Intrepid*—she showed courage in the face of danger. *Insatiable*—kissing left them both craving more. He could not stop dreaming about her mouth.

"Miss Moorland is honest. I respect her opinion."

Was that why he'd told her his darkest secret?

Did their survival not depend on them battling the storm together?

Rothley arched a cynical brow. "Her opinion in or out of bed? There's an odd glint in your eyes whenever you mention her name."

Reid firmed his jaw. "The lady is my herbalist and merely

wishes to help prove my innocence. We're good friends, nothing more."

"That's a blatant lie. You're dying to grab me round the throat and defend her honour." A smug grin played on Rothley's lips. "So, you're besotted with your herbalist because she saved you from the noose."

"I'm not besotted with my herbalist."

Preoccupied, perhaps.

Curious, even.

Rothley hated untruths and so poked harder. "And now your grandfather knows of your fondness for your seller of simples. I can't imagine he took the news well. He disapproved of your mother's lowly status, and she was a parson's daughter. The man has an aversion to peasants."

Reid hadn't the patience for Rothley's bitter diatribe tonight. "If you've nothing useful to say, I may as well leave." He stood abruptly. "Perhaps if you focused on the living, not the dead, I wouldn't need to keep secrets."

Reid moved to step away, but Rothley caught his wrist. "Forgive me. I've been in a devil of a mood all day. Nothing matters more than our friendship. Stay. Let me help you. We'll drink and play cards."

"You always win," Reid said with a sigh.

"Because I have nothing better to do at night than wager with scoundrels and dissolute rogues."

"I thought you'd agreed to attend an evening of music and dance at The Burnished Jade." Reid returned to his seat. "I thought you had no appetite for spinsters and wallflowers."

Rothley gave a dismissive wave. "I don't. I bore myself to death and need no help in that regard. But Joanna knows how to twist me around her finger. How could I refuse her request when she said I'm the closest thing she has to a brother?"

No, Rothley did his best to fill Justin's shoes in his absence.

"But you haven't danced since that provincial ball we attended in Cambridge ten years ago. I recall you prancing around in a cornfield with your breeches wrapped around your ankles."

Rothley smiled at the amusing memory—a happy time before tragedy struck and his life became unbearable. "I wasn't prancing. I was celebrating the serving wench tossing me off. I doubt the ladies at The Burnished Jade will be as forthcoming."

If you're willing, you could take my virtue, sir.

Miss Moorland's enticing offer slipped through Reid's mind.

He wanted her—but hadn't the heart to ruin her.

"One may surprise you, though Joanna wants an excuse to watch you marching down the aisle."

Rothley winced like he'd eaten rotten guinea fowl. "I'd rather march to the gallows. I might visit a dockside tavern tonight in the hope of catching a tropical fever."

They laughed, refilling their glasses when the footman arrived with the decanter. Reid reminded Rothley he'd catch more than a fever from a sailor's doxie, then returned to serious matters.

"There's something I need from you. I wouldn't ask, but I'm desperate. And after tolerating your foul temper, I deserve some recompense."

Rothley studied him over the rim of his glass. "I would be intrigued were I not apprehensive. You pride yourself on being your own man."

"I'm only at this table because of your sway with the committee," he mocked. "You're the closest thing I have to a brother. That doesn't mean I won't punch you if you insult my herbalist."

Rothley's hard, almost wolf-like eyes softened. "You know I'll do anything you ask and would lay down my life if need be, but don't keep me in the dark again. I assume this relates to the dead stable hand."

"In a manner of speaking." He leaned closer, lowering his voice. "I offered for Miss Moorland, but she would rather pretend we're married than shackle herself to me."

Rothley blinked like he had dust in his eyes. "Why the blazes would you marry your herbalist?" He sat forward, looking confounded by the puzzle. "I mean, she's pretty in an unassuming way … and those lips … a man could sink—"

"One more word and I'll put you on your arse."

"Are you this protective over all your employees?" Keen not to aggravate matters, Rothley raised his hand in mock surrender. "The lady clearly has enough common sense for both of you, but you don't need to marry the chit to ensure she's your alibi."

"It's not that." Knowing he could trust Rothley with his life, he mentioned the Merricks' plan. "Miss Moorland has two options: marry or leave England."

Or give Reid the gift the degenerates wished to purchase.

Rothley rested his elbow on the table and rubbed his jaw. "I heard whispers of an auction but thought it drunken nonsense. There are other ways to solve the problem. We could dispose of Merrick swiftly. You could join the auction and cast the winning bid."

Although ridding the world of a man like Merrick was tempting, the marquess fell under the Crown's protection— the King would move mountains to avoid a scandal—whereas Reid would likely face the noose if caught.

"I save men's lives; I don't take them." Yet someone was desperate to prove otherwise. "I'll not risk Merrick capturing her, either."

"Then what can I do?"

"Support our fake marriage. Invite us to spend our honeymoon at Studland Park. Let us reside there until this dratted business is over."

The marquess flinched like he had swallowed a sharp bone. "Stay at Studland Park? I'd rather strangle Merrick with my cravat than suffer house guests."

"I wouldn't ask if there were another option." Reid mentioned his grandfather's meddling. "Studland Park will be a safe haven. Miss Moorland hasn't slept properly for weeks. Every slight creak of the boards has her fearing the Merricks' return."

Rothley ran his finger over his lips. "And you think she'll have an undisturbed night with you sleeping in the adjoining bedchamber?"

"Put me in the east wing."

"And have it said I'm the one tupping Miss Moorland?"

"I'm not *tupping* Miss Moorland."

"Perhaps you should. Then there'd be no one to bid on her virtue. A wild night of pleasure could save her life."

Reid snorted. "Miss Moorland suggested as much."

Rothley's elbow almost slipped off the table. "Good God! What the hell goes on behind closed doors at The Burnished Jade?"

"The ladies learn to use their voice to their advantage. Miss Moorland can be quite persuasive." She could disarm a man with one kiss. "Which is why I'll take a chamber in the east wing."

"Like hell. You'll play the satisfied groom if you want me to go along with this ridiculous charade."

Reid smiled to himself. Despite his friend's brooding countenance, he was dependable to a fault. "One more thing. Miss Moorland hasn't eaten a decent meal in weeks, and your cook is the best in Christendom. I would like her last days in London to be amongst her finest."

Rothley cursed and thrust out his left arm. "Perhaps you'd like to pierce my vein with a cannula and pump a pint of blood."

"Don't tempt me. Blundell is always seeking volunteers for his research in transfusions."

Rothley reached for his brandy. The silence stretched as he swirled the amber liquid in the glass like it held the secrets of the past, present and future. "Your grandfather's actions represent everything I despise about the aristocracy, everything I loathed about my own father. Stay at Studland Park for a month. I'll ensure Miss Moorland has a room fit for royalty. I'll have Molière prepare a feast. Hell, she can even ride my prized Arabian."

Reid sensed there was a caveat. "But?"

Rothley's eyes darkened. "You'll include me in the investigation."

A few tense seconds passed.

"I'll include you—" Reid paused, raising a hand to their friends Rutland and Dalton as the men entered the library. "If you agree not to seize control and swear to follow my command."

The marquess grumbled under his breath. "I'm happy to play the errand boy as long as I'm not kept in the dark."

"Very well. You can begin by discovering if the Merricks have returned from Scotland." Reid stood and moved his chair to make room for their friends. "And you can attend the meeting at Daventry's office at noon on Monday."

"When should I expect the newlyweds at Studland Park?" Rothley mocked. "My staff will need time to recover from the shock. They're not used to visitors."

"Miss Moorland is staying with the countess tonight." Reid had been too afraid to leave her alone while he dealt with other matters. "I cannot miss my morning appointments at Guy's, but you can expect us early evening."

"Excellent. We'll dine at eight."

"You will be on your best behaviour?"

"Having heard what happens at The Burnished Jade, I'm confident Miss Moorland can handle my sarcasm."

They fell silent as their friends neared the table.

"Drinking from the decanter already?" Rutland said, amused.

Dalton snatched Reid's glass and downed the contents, grumbling, "Devious bastards."

While Viscount Rutland was the epitome of refinement, with perfect posture and a warm smile you could trust, the elegant dimple in his chin chiselled by the finest sculptor, Dalton carried the untamed energy of a pirate. His heavy brow shielded dark, suspicious eyes, the deep cleft in his chin hinting at a life spent chasing danger.

"That cheating rogue, Wroxeter, is dicing with death." Dalton dropped into a seat and grabbed the decanter. Liquor spilled onto the table as he sloshed more brandy into his glass. "He's working with Bellingham. They've invented a series of code words so they know what damn cards to play." Dalton knocked back his drink and growled rather than hissed.

"Your troubles are a drop in the ocean," Reid said before

updating his friends on the current state of affairs, including swearing them to secrecy regarding his marital status.

Rutland's eyes widened. "And Rothley thought he had problems. Our friend contemplated jumping from Westminster Bridge to avoid that dratted soiree at The Jade."

"In the hope of catching a chill," Rothley corrected. "With these sturdy shoulders, I'm more than capable of swimming to the riverbank."

"Why the hell are we sitting here?" Dalton complained. "I know of only two men who'd want rid of the *ton*'s most celebrated doctor."

"My uncle Edmund and his spawn Algernon."

"Let's frighten them into confessing." The devilish glint in Dalton's eyes said he'd relish the prospect of putting a blade to the men's throats.

"I have no proof my uncle is involved." There was nothing to connect his family to the victims. "Algernon bought laudanum from my apothecary in Long Acre. By all accounts, he's been ill with an infection he caught in Athens."

Rutland kept his voice low, asking, "And all the patients were women of a similar age and status?"

"All widows in their fifties."

Rutland arched a brow, his interest piqued. "I'm told there's an unsavoury bet in the book downstairs. Your cousin's name is listed."

"What sort of bet?"

"The contenders must woo women twice their age. There's some sort of points system. The first to three hundred points wins everyone's thousand-pound stake. It's been going on for months. I hear Winslow is already fifty points ahead, though your cousin is closing the gap."

What the devil?

Reid frowned. "Who keeps score?"

Rutland shrugged. "Perhaps you should ask Algernon. Your cousin entered the card room a few minutes ago."

Desperate for answers, Reid was on his feet and striding along the red-carpeted landing to the card room. He found his cousin, observing two lords playing a game of Écarté.

"A moment of your time, cousin." Reid gripped Algernon's elbow, digging his fingers into the knobbly bone, a small retribution for all the cruel jibes the fop had made about Reid's mother.

Algernon lacked the strength to free himself, jerking like a fish caught on a line. Reid released him once they reached a shadowy corner of the landing.

"What on God's green earth is wrong with you?" Algernon whirled around and stared down his aquiline nose. He had a mop of brown hair like a schoolboy and the ruddy cheeks of a man twice his age. "If this is about our grandfather gifting Bretton Hall to me, take it up with him."

The comment hit like the sharp lash of a whip.

Bretton Hall would have been Reid's father's rightful home—a grand inheritance for a son of noble lineage—until he defied expectations and wed a humble pastor's daughter. Bretton Hall was the carrot his grandfather dangled to prevent Reid from making the same mistake.

"He must have visited you before he left for Chesham Park." Reid imagined the old man spreading gossip like a rat did disease. "I assume ownership comes with certain stipulations."

Algernon's smug sneer grated. "It's mine if I marry Viscount Brigham's daughter. It's no hardship. As you know, she's a sickly chit who'll likely not survive the birthing bed."

Reid was forced to quell the rising fury in his chest.

Did this weasel have no conscience?

"Does our grandfather know of your fondness for ladies in their fifties? I'm told you're part of a wager posted in the book downstairs."

Panic tightened Algernon's face. "I'm sure he knows it's just a lark. A bit of harmless tomfoolery." He ran his fingers along the collar of his shirt as if feeling the noose of obligation. "It's nothing he didn't do in his day. Besides, it's about camaraderie, not winning the prize."

Reid couldn't believe he was related to this halfwit. "How are you supposed to prove you've won?" he said, feigning interest. "Who keeps score?"

"The waiter at Antoine's keeps a written record."

"Antoine's?" Reid recalled Mrs Ludgrove had supper with Mr Fellows at Antoine's. He would find the names of those engaged in the wager in the book downstairs.

"It's a coffeehouse that serves a simple supper of an evening. We must abide by a certain criteria, a complex and tactical list." Algernon spoke like he was part of a military strategy to save the Crown. "A kiss on the hand earns five points. It's ten for the cheek and so forth."

One day, this imbecile would hold the title of Viscount Hanberry. Reid was glad his mother was a lowly pastor's daughter. It must be where he gained his common sense.

"And do your victims know you're spreading a sickness you caught in Greece? Do you take laudanum for the crippling aches or are the draughts a cure for ennui?"

The fop trembled like a trapped hare before finding the courage to argue. "It's none of your damn business. You're only here because our grandfather overlooks your working status. They'll strike your name off every guest list when my father inherits."

"What does that say about you?" Reid countered, wondering why his uncle wanted to see him shamed amongst his peers. "When our grandfather prefers a working man to the future Lord Hanberry?"

"Not anymore," Algernon said proudly. "Bretton Hall will be mine. Grandfather has a duty to keep a pure blood-line. Yours is like watered-down wine, tasteless on the palate. Had your father not married a peasant, things may—"

The punch stole the last words from Algernon's mouth.

Reid grabbed the fool round the throat, glad to see blood coating his white teeth. "Speak about my mother again and I'll rip out your tongue. My father tended troops on the front line while yours lounged in a bordello. My mother was commended for her charitable work while yours seduced her footmen, then tossed them out."

Amid Reid's mounting rage, Rothley stepped into the fray. "Release him. This isn't who you are. Call him out if necessary, but don't brawl in the corridor like a thug from the rookeries."

Algernon gathered strength from Rothley's intervention, blood bubbling at the corner of his mouth when he cried, "Take the dog to the pound where he belongs."

Rothley whirled around and rose to his full height. "Don't make the mistake of thinking I won't shoot you between the brows. Offend Gentry and you offend me. Trust me, you don't want to dice with the devil."

Dalton decided to give his two pennyworth. "Avoid walking near dark alleys for a few days. Rogues often lurk in the shadows, waiting to pounce."

Rutland ignored the quivering popinjay and draped his arm around Reid's shoulder, drawing him from the fracas.

"Your enemy wants to break you. To provoke you into reacting like a man capable of murder."

The villain's plan had worked.

Anger was like a poison in his veins, infecting his rationale.

"You must think of Miss Moorland," Rutland continued in the velvet voice that brought calm to any situation. "Fear clouds her judgement. She's living under constant threat. She has no home and no future. Every door will be closed to her when the truth of this fake marriage comes to light."

Miss Moorland was a constant presence in his mind.

He liked having her there, liked having her in his dispensary, liked their playful banter and their fervent kisses.

"Miss Moorland is an extraordinary woman who's become a prisoner of her sex and her stepmother's evil ambitions." He felt duty-bound to protect her.

"None of which is your responsibility, yet you've made it so. You must search your heart and consider why."

Reid shrugged. "She needs me."

"And it feels good to be her saviour?" Rutland stopped outside the door to the library. "Marriage is about more than love, as your grandfather persists in reminding you. You need a wife who stimulates you body and soul."

"Miss Moorland certainly does that."

Her insightful opinion aroused his mind.

Her touch set his body ablaze.

"Then why pretend? Marry her, and the problem with the Merricks disappears. She can work for you without censure, and her honour is restored."

Rutland made it all sound simple.

The lord could see a clear path on a fog-drenched night.

"There is one minor issue." Miss Moorland would rather

face ruin than force his hand. "She refuses to accept my proposal."

A slow smile curled Rutland's lips. "Good Lord, this business with the dead groom has blinded you to what is obvious to most."

"Which is?"

"Look at you. You're more than capable of seducing a woman. Make it impossible for her to say no."

Chapter Ten

Studland Park's Palladian-style facade glowed beneath the setting sun. Amber hues caressed the countryside, drawing Sofia's eye from the house—that looked as impenetrable as its master—across the sprawling landscape.

Mr Gentry shuffled closer to the window, his knees brushing against hers as he admired the grand mansion. "Studland Park has over two hundred rooms, which is ironic when Rothley lives in six of them."

Sofia met his gaze, wondering why she found his voice more soothing than birdsong, why the golden highlights in his hair were more spectacular than Studland Park's stunning vista.

"It must be so lonely here," she said, the words rousing unwanted images of her own family home: the forgotten clothes in her armoire, the abandoned dressing table, a Moorland family heirloom. "You would think the marquess would welcome visitors."

"Rothley distrusts most people."

Doubtless there were many reasons for the lord's cynicism, the uncertain death of Joanna's brother being one. Rumours suggesting the marquess had killed his friend had him mounting a search that lasted a decade. An endless battle to prove his innocence and silence the gossips for good.

Joanna's advice at dinner last night entered Sofia's mind.

The marquess can be intolerable, but he's a good man at heart. His forthright manner is his suit of armour. A protection against invaders.

"Given that Lord Rothley dislikes guests, how can I make my presence less burdensome?" Hopefully, in a mansion this size, there would be no awkward encounters in the corridor.

Mr Gentry stared at her for a few heart-stopping seconds. A smile quirked his lips. "Be yourself, Miss Moorland. Rothley respects honesty above all else. Don't be afraid to challenge him. I'm confident he'll see what I do."

And what was that?

Curiosity sparked, but she couldn't resist teasing him.

"Let's hope not. We kiss at every opportunity."

"Not every opportunity." He ran his thumb over his bottom lip, a sensual gleam lighting his eyes. "We haven't kissed since our delightful experiment yesterday."

Yet the memory had left a permanent imprint in her mind. It was like his essence still lingered on her lips, the ache to feel the heat of his mouth deepening by the hour.

She gave a coy grin. "If you're to take my virtue, we'll need to kiss again soon. Ruining me is the only way to save me."

She made her deflowering sound like a business transaction.

Yet the thought of this man settling between her thighs

had every inch of her skin tingling. Heat flooded all the forbidden places like the fast pulse of a raging river.

Mr Gentry didn't give a husky chuckle like he did when playing pretend. "Bedding you may seem like a simple solution, but I will only take your virtue if we're married."

"Oh." The news was more a disappointment than a shock. It was ludicrous to imagine he would bed her without thought or conscience. So why did she feel a sudden stab of rejection? "I thought … well … after our heated conversation in Mr Wiggins' office, it feels like we've shared more than a kiss. There's a vivid realism to our stories."

"Trust me. If we were in bed, you would know the difference."

Would she?

What could be better than the dream?

Her heart couldn't beat any faster. In her wild imagination, there wasn't an inch of skin he hadn't already kissed. She'd dreamt of treating patients and tending the poor, making love to Mr Gentry in a plush room at the Adelphi and on the dispensary floor.

Reality could never match such high expectations.

"It's not that I don't want you," Mr Gentry said, his voice a tight tremble. "By God, every kiss and erotic fantasy feeds a need I can barely control."

The same desperate desire flowed through her, too.

"I understand." She gripped the edge of the seat tightly, her fingers itching to touch him. Why was everything so complicated? "It's hard to know what's real or what we've invented as part of the plan."

The threat to their lives was real.

The passion in their hearts was real.

The pressure to stay one step ahead of the Merricks was real.

"We should stop inventing romantic tales," she added, though the vivid stories spoke to a part of her she barely knew—the awakening of the sensual woman she suppressed. "We've reached a stalemate. You won't bed me and I cannot marry you. Let's not kiss again. Let our problems be our focus."

He fell back against the squab, wincing like he'd sat on a tack. "You always offer a sensible solution, yet I look at your lips and feel the twisting ache of an addict."

He did?

"It's natural we should find comfort in each other's arms." Though the line between desire and solace had blurred quite considerably. "We're both seeking an escape from a dreadful injustice. I assume the hunger will lessen in time."

"Not when Rothley insists we play the newlyweds in front of his staff. He'll not have the *ton* thinking you're his mistress. If we're to stay at Studland Park, we must pretend we're in love."

I'm not sure I need to pretend, she said silently.

"It shouldn't pose a problem. It's not like I'll flinch if you touch me." Her breathy sigh would be a natural reaction. "Besides, how do people behave when they're in love?"

His gaze drifted, a distant search through his memories. "Love lives in the simple gestures. A lingering look. The secret caress of fingers when the world is watching. Brushing dust off a coat as an excuse to touch because love has its own gravitational pull."

"Fixing a strand of hair that's out of place." She fought the temptation to lean forward and brush the errant lock from his brow. "You sound like you speak from experience."

"My parents loved each other madly in those early years, or perhaps they were good at playing pretend, too."

A strained silence ensued.

There was no time to decide how to ease the sudden tension.

The carriage stopped outside Studland Park's sweeping stone staircase. The ornamental lamps were already lit, the soft glow an invitation to a world where opulence reigned.

"Be prepared, Miss Moorland. The mansion house is far more splendid than the Adelphi."

Why had he mentioned the Adelphi?

Had he not heard a word she'd said?

"If we're meant to be married, you must call me Sofia. And nowhere is better than the Adelphi."

"Sofia." The word left him with a soft sigh, his lids flickering like the sound soothed his soul. "An apt name for a wise woman, though it fails to describe the magical quality that makes you unique."

For her own sanity, she ignored the compliment.

"And how am I to address you, sir?" Hopefully, he wasn't one of those stuffy husbands who insisted on being called 'mister'.

"Call me Reid. I'm named after my maternal grandmother."

"Her name was Reid?" she teased.

He smiled, and the world felt right again. "Moira Reid. She died long before I was born, but I like to think I possess her tenacity."

"It's certainly a quality I admire in you."

Goodness, could she not follow her own advice?

She nodded to the liveried footman, standing on the gravel drive like a monument to formality. He opened the carriage door while his white-wigged twin let down the steps and offered a gloved hand.

Sofia alighted, feeling like a lost orphan in her plain blue cloak and sturdy boots. Mr Gentry's tailoring was impeccable. The footmen moved to retrieve their luggage. One seemed surprised her tatty valise was so light.

"Come and meet the housekeeper, Mrs Boswell." With a guiding hand on her back, Mr Gentry swept her up the stone steps, as grand as a staircase to heaven. "This place would be in turmoil without her. She will ensure all your needs are met."

"Does Mrs Boswell think we're married?" It was one thing to lie to the Merricks, another to deceive a kind-hearted soul.

"Rothley told her we're on our honeymoon."

"Our honeymoon?" Good grief. "Could we not have said we married last week? Mrs Boswell will think it odd I'm wearing this old dress." The housekeeper might wonder why a man of his status would marry a rag doll, not a porcelain one. "I don't even have a trousseau."

"I've taken care of everything."

His reply drew her up short. "You have?" He had bought her stockings and undergarments and a nightgown so sheer she may as well wear nothing?

"The countess came to my aid. I paid her a visit this morning while you were working in the dispensary. She seemed confident her gowns and slippers would fit you."

A sudden bout of nerves had Sofia grabbing his hand. "What time did we marry? Where was the ceremony? Someone is bound to ask."

He threaded his fingers through hers, as tightly as lovers' twined limbs. "Ten this morning at St Bartholomew's. Lord and Lady Berridge were our witnesses." He held her gaze and captured her chin. "All will be well, Sofia. You must trust me."

She looked up into his compelling blue eyes. "I do."

Perhaps her mind was conjuring stories again, but she felt a pulse of energy between their palms, evidence of their quiet connection. The tenderness in his eyes mirrored the gentle stroke of his thumb across her chin.

"Once we find O'Connor's killer, you'll be free to leave London, if that's your desire. Until then, the Merricks must believe we're married and I am your protector."

Fear seized her, his words conjuring a horror she had not envisioned. "What if Mr Merrick hurts you?" Victor lurked in the shadows whenever Judith lashed out, watching like a predator with a thirst for blood. "What if he seeks to make me a widow?"

Such thoughts were absurd.

But so was the idea of auctioning a lady's virtue.

Mr Gentry's mocking chuckle sounded like a dare. "I'm not afraid of the Merricks. I'm more than capable of defending myself."

Her traitorous gaze moved to his firm biceps. The fabric of his coat clung to the powerful muscles like they were carved by an expert sculptor. The urge to touch him and kiss him took hold.

He wasn't the only one fighting an addiction.

"Try to look like a happy bride." He wrapped his strong arm around her and guided her into the vast marble hall to meet the awaiting housekeeper. "Ah, Mrs Boswell. I trust you've been resting your ankle every evening as advised."

The housekeeper, a slender woman in her forties, curtsied. Her warm smile would put anyone at ease. "A little of that ointment you prescribed and half an hour propped on a stool, and it's fine for another day, sir."

"That's good to hear." He introduced Sofia, drawing her hand to his lips, the light kiss sending a delicious shiver to her toes. "My wife is somewhat nervous. The house can be as intimidating as Rothley."

The lace trimming on Mrs Boswell's white cap quivered as she chuckled. "To those unfamiliar with his ways, nothing is as intimidating as the master."

"Gossiping about me again, Mrs Boswell?" The marquess strode towards them, dressed for dinner in a crisp white shirt and tailored evening coat, though he gave the impression a wolf lived beneath the finery. "Perhaps it escaped your notice, but we're dining in an hour, and Mrs Gentry is still wearing her travelling cloak."

Mrs Boswell inclined her head. "The preparations are underway, as ordered."

Preparations? Sofia presumed they'd take a casual supper.

The marquess stepped forward and bowed. "Welcome to Studland Park, Mrs Gentry. My ancestors were tyrants and philanderers, but despite common opinion, you'll not find a harem of women lounging in the grand salon."

Months ago, she might have floundered under the weight of his obsidian stare, stuttering while trying to form a reply. But as the countess often said: Never show a man you're afraid unless you want him to kiss you.

"No, I imagine you choose your companions wisely, my lord." Sofia dropped into a deep curtsey. "A lady would need to be extraordinary to hold your interest. In such circumstances, one woman would suffice."

A flicker of amusement lit his dark eyes. "What a shame the *ton* lacks your insight, madam. Though I confess, I prefer the company of my Irish wolfhound. Perhaps one day I may be as fortunate as Gentry and find my perfect bride."

"The perfect bride does not exist, my lord. Love may creep up on you, a sliver of a feeling that takes root and grows with time." She glanced at Mr Gentry. The intimate feelings hadn't just taken root. They spread through her like a rampant vine, leaving no part untouched. "My husband found me irritating before he came to respect my opinion."

"That's not true," Mr Gentry said, his warm gaze a caress. "I found your passion for your work remarkable, your knowledge as good as any man's, but feared encouraging your ambitions."

"Let's not dwell on that now." The marquess clapped his hands as if desperate to end the conversation. "Molière will throw a tantrum if we're late for dinner. Make haste, Mrs Boswell, get our guests upstairs or I'll deduct the smashed Sèvres from your personal allowance."

Mrs Boswell found the threat amusing. "Molière knows there'll be a mutiny if he touches the china. And I wish you well finding someone who can manage a house this size, my lord."

The marquess pulled his gold watch from his pocket and checked the time. "No more dawdling, Mrs Boswell, or our guests will be bathing in the fountain." He addressed Mr Gentry. "I'll be in my private drawing room when you're ready. We can await your bride there."

Mrs Boswell led them on a long walk up the carpeted marble staircase and down a landing the length of Dean Street. "The master insisted you have the marchioness' suite, Mrs Gentry. There's no finer bedchamber in all of England."

The housekeeper threw open the double oak doors with such gusto Sofia expected to hear trumpeters heralding a fanfare. She entered the majestic room slowly, stepping tentatively on the vast Persian rug as if it were made of eggshells.

"It's spectacular." Indeed, she couldn't quite catch her breath.

The gold Rococo four-poster bed looked like it belonged to Aphrodite. A blue fresco of angels decorated the high ceiling. The crystals hanging from the chandelier looked like they had been crafted by the gods. The walls were a warm cream, the decorative stucco a sumptuous pale gold, yet the open door to the dark, masculine room adjacent stole her attention.

Mrs Boswell heard Sofia's silent concerns. "Mr Gentry will occupy the grand chamber. Lord Rothley prefers his old room in the east wing. You'll find the key to the adjoining door in the escritoire, though I doubt you'll need it tonight."

Mr Gentry captured Sofia's hand—another act in their play—drawing her farther into the chamber. "Have you ever seen a room as splendid as this?"

"No." The rug was a soft cloud beneath her feet, but she would rather the cold tiles in the dispensary, her toes warmed by the heat of Mr Gentry's feverish kisses.

"I hate to rush you." Mrs Boswell gestured to another open door. "But your bath is ready, Mrs Gentry, and we mustn't keep the master waiting. I'll find a cap for your hair. You'll not want to get it damp."

Two maids entered, each carrying a satin gown—one a sumptuous garnet red, the other a deep cerulean blue like Mr Gentry's eyes. The maids arranged them carefully on the bed, then stood with their hands clasped, awaiting instructions.

"I shall be in my chamber if you need me. I'll leave the door open." Mr Gentry smiled before disappearing into the dark-panelled domain.

She watched him go.

The last year had been a whirlwind of worry and bouts of sheer terror. When she prayed to her parents for help, they must have listened. Everything changed the day Mr Gentry hired her.

Sofia fell into a deep reverie as the maids undressed her and tucked her hair into a pink silk cap. The water in the huge copper bath warmed her cold, tired limbs. The soothing smell of jasmine oil relaxed her troubled mind.

She tried not to think about Mr Gentry stripping off his clothes, or his pleasurable groan as he slid his muscular frame into the water.

Mrs Boswell appeared in the doorway of the candlelit bathing chamber. "His lordship hopes you'll do him the honour of wearing his mother's parure tonight. There's a choice of two on the dressing table. Will it be the sapphire and diamond choker or the ruby pendant, madam?"

Sofia hesitated.

Neither, but it would be rude to refuse.

"Perhaps I could ask your husband's opinion?" Mrs Boswell gave a coy grin. "You might like him to choose your gown tonight."

Sofia didn't need a man to tell her what to wear, nor did she care about expensive jewels, but everything about the last hour had been overwhelming. Agreeing would appease the marquess and give credence to their matrimonial tale.

"Yes. Tell my husband I will wear whatever pleases him."

One maid tittered as she poured water over Sofia's soaped shoulders, while Mrs Boswell left to seek Mr Gentry's approval.

Seconds passed before Mr Gentry did the unthinkable and entered the bathing chamber like he had every right to be there. His clean shirt was open at the neck, revealing the strong column of his throat. "Leave us."

The maids leapt to attention, not as fast as Sofia's heart lurched or the speed with which she covered her breasts.

"But, sir, we only have forty minutes until the dinner gong." Mild panic laced Mrs Boswell's voice. "And Janet needs to style Mrs Gentry's hair."

Mr Gentry's mouth curved into a slow, mischievous smile. "Inform his lordship there'll be a short delay." He kept his gaze fixed on Sofia, wetting his lips as he stared at her bare shoulders. "Close the bedchamber door on your way out, Mrs Boswell. My wife will ring when she's ready."

The servants left them alone.

Their gazes locked amid the sudden stillness.

"You shouldn't be in here," came Sofia's hushed protest.

"We're married."

"No, we're not."

"As to that, I've been thinking." He moved towards her like a panther on the prowl, power in every sleek step. "Perhaps you were right."

She swallowed. "Right about what?"

Right that he was dangerous?

Right that kissing was an addiction?

"That saving you from the Merricks matters more than easing my conscience." He crouched beside the tub, his gaze moving over her body, unhurried, deliberate, the light hum in his throat a sensual song. "We agreed honesty was the best policy, yet neither of us has been truthful."

"I've never lied to you."

But he had clearly lied to her.

"You say you want me to bed you to save you from being forced to marry a degenerate. That's not entirely true, Sofia."

He stood, shocking her again by dragging his shirt over his head and casting it on the chair. "It's an excuse to have what you desperately crave."

Sofia stared at him. At his broad chest and sculpted muscles. At the soft dusting of hair and small, perfectly round, brown nipples.

The ladies at The Jade would swoon if they saw him now.

Her nipples hardened.

Her sex ached beneath the water.

"You claim you've been untruthful, too," she stated, though wanted to pant and whisper, *God, you're magnificent.*

He knelt behind her, removing the silk cap and combing his fingers through her hair. "I've lied more than once." Pressing his mouth to her temple, he whispered, "I didn't need you to take down your hair at The Burnished Jade, but I was curious to see the woman, not the scholar."

"Did the exercise sate your curiosity?"

"No." Warm fingers stroked her neck before he brushed her hair behind her ear. "It fed a need to know more. A hungry need that makes a man reckless."

She knew that feeling well: the pooling pressure between the thighs, the low, coiling ache that stole every inhibition.

"What other lies have you told?" She dared to lower her arms and lap water over her tight nipples, drawing his greedy gaze to her breasts.

He wrapped her hair around his hand, the light tug sending a wave of pleasure to her toes. "That if I'm to take your virtue, we need to marry. We need to marry because I want you more than once."

More than once?

Sofia wasn't sure if he'd repeated the statement in that deep, gravelly baritone or if it echoed in her mind. Either way, her body responded, the pulsing muscles in her core almost begging her to concede.

"Lust is no more a reason to marry than desperation is."

"You forget admiration and friendship," he uttered, brushing his mouth against the shell of her ear while trailing his fingers over her collarbone. "You need a man who'll satisfy your needs and ambitions."

This imagined union still lacked one vital ingredient.

But did love really matter?

Was it not a luxury afforded to the few?

"Perhaps we should explore what marriage means," he said, his breath hot against her neck now. "Let me touch you. Open your legs for me, Sofia … let me ease the tension throbbing in that swollen little bud."

Her pulse soared, her heart thumping drum-like in her chest. "But we'll be late for dinner." It was an excuse she prayed he'd ignore.

"You're halfway there, love. It won't take long." His fingers moved, a soft, teasing glide to the damp valley of her breasts. "It will be our experiment, something to add to those erotic notes you hide in your precious journal."

Sweet mercy!

"Say it, Sofia. Say you want *me* to make you come."

Oh, God, just do it!

"I … I do." She wanted his hands all over her body.

"I need to hear the words." He moved like an assassin in the night, rounding the tub and capturing her mouth in a swift and silent kiss. He was on his knees, leaning over her naked body, his hand lightly cupping her breast. "Say it. *Make me come, Reid.*"

She arched her back, her nipple grazing his palm, her throaty moan a white flag of surrender. "Touch me." She opened her legs wider, captured his hand and slid it down between her thighs. "Make me come, Reid."

He was panting now, a flash of triumph in his eyes. "Make no mistake," he growled, yet his fingers moved achingly slowly through her folds. "When we make love, we'll set the house ablaze."

Chapter Eleven

Reid wasn't being pleasured, yet he was about to spill in his trousers.

The sight of his *wife* writhing against his hand in the bath, her round breasts bobbing beautifully in the water, had his stiff cock weeping. He'd always known her dowdy dress hid a treasure of secrets. But by God, her skin was pale, soft and smooth as alabaster.

"I'm so hard for you, Sofia."

Candlelight caressed the delicate curve of her thigh. Mesmerised, he watched her expressions as he stroked her sex. Her pillow lips parted on a sensual moan, the sight adding to the uncomfortable bulge in his trousers.

He remembered the first time his body hardened when he looked at her, when she was oblivious to him sitting in a booth in Pickins coffeehouse and sat engrossed in her sacred journal. The first slide of the pencil across her luscious lips had been his undoing.

He experienced a similar stirring whenever she asked probing questions, and when they kissed like lovers who'd been parted forever.

But this … knowing he was responsible for her greedy little pants … was the most arousing experience of his damn life. Only a fool would name him the seducer. She brought him to his knees at every turn.

As if to prove he was a slave to her wants and desires, she reached for him, cupping his neck, drawing him to her breast.

He settled his mouth over her nipple, teasing the peak before sucking long and deep. The air about them crackled, alive with a wild energy.

"I need more of you, Reid." She grabbed his hair in her small fists. "Don't … don't stop touching me."

He was half in the water, his face and hair wet, the sweet taste of jasmine on his lips. Hell, if she wrapped her fingers around his shaft, he'd come in an instant.

"Look at me," he demanded, rubbing her bud with his thumb and sliding two fingers inside her. "I want to watch you come, Sofia."

She cupped his cheek, each breath coming faster than the last. Her whole body convulsed, her eyes fluttering closed as her muscles clenched around his fingers. "Reid."

"That's it, love. Hug me hard."

Beauty shone from her as she arched her back against the pleasurable waves. Candlelight shimmered across her wet skin, each water droplet glowing like liquid gold.

Sofia opened her eyes, drawing him into the velvety green depths. A blissful smile touched her lips. "If this is how you treat hysteria, I may require a daily appointment."

"I'll make it a morning ritual."

Her hand slipped to his shoulder. Her sweet hum of approval said she liked exploring the shape of his muscles.

"Shall I touch you, Reid? Consider it training for when you trust me with your male patients."

He might have laughed but a sharp stab of jealousy pierced his heart. "We'll save that for our next illicit encounter. Rothley will be wondering where the hell we are."

"Rothley!" She sat bolt upright. "Good Lord. He'll be furious."

Reid struggled to tear his gaze from her breasts. "Rothley may seem annoyed, but he'll relish the chance to tease us." He stood and offered his hand. "Let me help you out of the bath."

When she rose in the water, a sweet tremble of nerves on her lips, thoughts of making love dissipated. An ugly vision gripped him—her being paraded at auction before a group of depraved men.

He reached for the towel, wrapping it tightly around her shoulders and rubbing her arms dry to chase away his fears.

Mistaking his attentiveness for guilt, she rested her damp palms on his bare chest. "I wanted you to touch me. I urged you to do so and regret nothing. Everything that happens between us is beautiful."

The last statement roused something fierce inside him. A raging need to protect her, to protect this invisible bond that grew stronger by the day.

His throat tightened as he helped her step out of the bath. "I'm myself when I'm with you."

He didn't know what that meant.

He hadn't the time to consider it either because the clang of the dinner gong rang in the distance, not once but three damn times.

"We're so late," Sofia groaned, snatching his clothes off

the chair. "Quickly, put on your shirt before I call Mrs Boswell. She's going to know we've been intimate."

He reached for her hand, giving it a reassuring squeeze before dragging on his shirt. "She'll think we've done more than kiss."

If Mrs Boswell did, she gave no indication.

She shooed him from the room while issuing orders to the flustered maids. "You'll have to braid her hair. It's so damp the pins won't hold."

Amid a cacophony of hurried complaints and rustling fabric, Reid dressed and waited for Sofia on the landing.

Half an hour later, she appeared wearing an elegant red gown that skimmed every curve. Her braided hair was coiled high in an elegant bun at her crown, a few tiny red roses tucked into the plait.

"You look beautiful, Sofia." The ruby pendant drew his gaze, the red teardrop resting above the lush curve of her breasts. "Lock the adjoining door tonight," he whispered, the need to make her come again firing vivid images in his mind. "After our amorous interlude in the bathing chamber, I don't have the strength to stay away."

She leant into him, the smell of jasmine filling his head. "I left my spectacles on the dressing table. I might enter your bedchamber by mistake."

"By mistake?"

"Particularly if it's dark."

He pictured himself naked on the bed, anticipating the first touch as she groped at the coverlet. "Should you encounter something thick and hard, know I left the pestle in the dispensary."

"Good. I'm interested in examining your other tools."

They were laughing when they entered the dining room.

"Ah! The newlyweds have dragged themselves from the bedchamber," Rothley said, sounding more amused than irritated. "The soup is cold. I'm only glad the countess suggested we start without you."

Hiding his shock upon seeing other guests seated around the walnut table, Reid inclined his head and inwardly groaned. "You never mentioned hosting a dinner party."

"Did I not?" Rothley faked a frown. "A wedding is something to celebrate, and I'm hardly rousing company."

The Earl and Countess of Berridge and Mr and Mrs Daventry greeted them, offering their felicitations for the servants' benefit. The curious glint in the ladies' eyes said they knew exactly why he and Sofia were late.

Sofia stiffened beside him, her cheeks turning the same vibrant shade as her gown. "Sorry if we've spoiled your dinner. We've hardly had a moment to breathe since we arrived."

"No," Rothley said with an amused sneer. "It's surprising how exhausting dressing can be."

"Ignore him." Lady Berridge beckoned them to the empty seats flanking Rothley at the head of the table. "We were all running a little late tonight. And it must be at least a quarter of a mile to the upstairs chambers."

"Should I have sent a sedan?" Rothley mocked.

Two footmen drew out the chairs, served the soup and poured the wine. After Rothley complimented Sofia and admired his mother's ruby pendant, the conversation turned to the other reason Daventry had come.

"I have important news which cannot wait until tomorrow." Daventry cut a striking figure. His sharp mind and dangerous air made people sit up and take notice. "Assuming you're happy to discuss the investigation here."

"It will save a trip to your office tomorrow," Reid said.

"Before we continue, I have something you may need." From the seat beside Sofia, Daventry retrieved a folded document and handed it to her. "Read it, but mind what you say in company."

Sofia glanced at Reid before unfolding the missive and scanning its contents. Her eyes widened, though he couldn't tell if she was excited or afraid. She handed Reid the paper, a slight tremble in her fingers.

He suppressed a gasp. It was a special licence signed by the archbishop. It bore their names, residencies and cited the private chapel at Studland Park as the authorised location for the ceremony. "How the devil did you get this?"

A smug smile settled on Daventry's lips. "The Church refuses to allow an aristocrat to meddle in ecclesiastical affairs and agreed to abide by the law of the land."

The countess cleared her throat. "I explained the problem to Mr Daventry last night and agreed to fund the cost of the … document … if granted."

Reid could not permit her to pay for the privilege of him marrying. "I appreciate the gesture, but I'll have the funds sent to you tomorrow."

The countess looked at Sofia, a warm smile touching her eyes. "There's no need. The ladies of The Jade are important to me. The gift is for Sofia, along with a ticket for a packet ship sailing from Greenock to New York in a fortnight, should she need to escape."

"A lady must have options," Mrs Daventry added.

An uncomfortable ache settled in Reid's chest. He didn't want Sofia to leave. He didn't want to be a puppet, either, with other people pulling their strings. Everyone seemed to think they had a right to dictate the course of their lives.

"Only if those choices are her own." He looked at Sofia, dressed in clothes and jewels that didn't belong to her and wearing expensive perfume. A facade he had helped to create.

She was never more beautiful than when grinding herbs and flower petals. When she wore her old dress and home-made scent and asked intriguing questions.

But the desire to speak to his wife and elicit her opinion was overshadowed by Daventry revealing important information.

"As to other news," Daventry began, his tone grim. "The Merricks have returned from their trip to Scotland. Mr Merrick visited the solicitor this afternoon and asked about the details of your dowry."

Sofia paled. "Then time is against us." She glanced at her soup and gulped. "They'll search every back alley in London looking for me."

"Don't worry about the Merricks," Reid said, his hatred for the strangers like acid stinging his tongue. "They can't hurt you." It wasn't true. They could hurt her in ways he dared not imagine.

Her weak smile was a flimsy mask to hide her unease. She faced Daventry. "Mr Merrick is not my guardian. He has no legal right to make an enquiry. The details are confidential."

"He gave quite a persuasive argument."

"You mean he used his fists," Aaron Chance said.

"My agent found Mr Waters cradling bruised ribs and a guilty conscience. He told Merrick no claim had been filed. No one had sought evidence for a marriage contract."

"What did Judith say?" Sofia asked, looking shaken.

Daventry shrugged. "Merrick went alone."

"Alone? But she never leaves his side."

"Might we eat while we talk?" Rothley instructed the footmen to remove the soup dishes before serving himself a fricando of veal and sweet bread.

Once they had filled their plates from the ten platters on the table, Daventry returned to the topic of Judith Merrick.

"Since the incident at the Hare and Hounds, I've had someone watching the house in Dean Street." Daventry paused to sip and savour Rothley's finest claret. "The Merricks returned home yesterday morning, just after dawn. The jarvey picked them up from The White Horse in Fetter Lane."

"Yes, they took the stage from The White Horse two months ago." Sofia sat rigidly, every taut line on her face showing disdain for her step-parents.

"Within thirty minutes of the Merricks arriving in Dean Street, the cook and housekeeper scurried out the front door, their carpet bags tossed to the pavement."

Sofia clutched her hand to her chest. "Judith must have learned of my escape and blamed Mrs Pugh. Though I'm surprised she got rid of them. Judith is lazy by nature and wouldn't dream of washing her own stockings."

Daventry removed a notebook and pencil from his pocket and scribbled something on the page. "If Mrs Pugh was dismissed without notice, where would she go?"

Sofia thought for a moment. "Her sister lives and works at The Castle Inn on Wood Street, and you'll find her brother at the cooperage on Great Hermitage." With a thread of enthusiasm, she added, "I could visit both places tomorrow. See if either of them knows why the Merricks threw Mrs Pugh out."

The guests exchanged nervous glances before Rothley dabbed his mouth with a napkin and said, "This Merrick fellow needs a good thrashing. I say we beat him, hide him inside a wooden crate and put him on a ship for Calcutta."

"Men like Merrick always find their way home," Aaron Chance warned. "There's only one way to dispose of him for good. Merrick needs to feel the sharp press of steel against his throat."

Plagued by a rising annoyance, Reid growled, "I will deal with Merrick if the time comes. I'm quite capable of protecting my wife."

Killing a man was a last resort.

"If I could just talk to Mrs Pugh," Sofia began.

"I'm not sure that's wise," the countess said, worrying her lip.

"Mrs Pugh is rarely sober. She'll be no threat."

"I'll have one of my agents deal with the matter," Daventry said.

Reid waited for Sofia to argue her case, to see the fiery passion that lived beneath her calm mien, but she glanced at the salmon on her plate and sighed.

Daventry cut into his veal. "Regarding the murder at the Hare and Hounds. The witnesses claim a disgruntled husband killed O'Connor. They believe he entered and exited through the woods."

"It doesn't explain how O'Connor had my calling card." Had Reid left it in his pocket and dropped it by mistake? Was the murderer hoping to cast the blame at anyone's door, or was this a personal vendetta?

"The magistrate wanted to post a reward for information. I persuaded him against the idea. Many innocent men have hanged so a pauper can line his pockets."

"I assume you questioned the serving wench," Sofia said.

Daventry nodded. "A constable did. She never left the

inn. She said she barely has time to breathe, let alone talk to punters."

Sofia's brow rose, and a spark of curiosity lit her eyes. "When I was forced to serve drinks at Judith's rowdy parties, I kept my head bowed and hardly spoke, yet heard many vile conversations. None of which are repeatable."

"Perhaps the wench might speak to a woman," Reid suggested.

Sofia smiled. "Precisely."

"My agents know how to tease information from a witness," Daventry began, "but I'll do as you suggest and send a woman to question the serving wench."

Sofia's eyes dulled, and she looked deflated.

It was obvious she wanted to question the wench herself.

Reid stood, much to everyone's surprise. "If you'll excuse me. I would like to speak to my wife alone outside."

He rounded the table and offered Sofia his hand.

She went with him, saying nothing until they entered the library, a grand room with dark polished wood, red velvet furnishings and mullioned windows.

He closed the door, leading her through the darkness to where the glow of moonlight poured softly through the glass panes. "You must tell me what you want, Sofia."

She stared into his eyes and smiled. "Is this not a conversation for the bedchamber? Or are you referring to how we're being pushed from pillar to post like babes in a perambulator?"

There was a reason he'd not confided in anyone until now. Why he had spent months trying to gather facts and find the villain.

"Men like Daventry and Aaron Chance function best

when they control a situation. Rothley would die for me but is a damn sight more amenable."

"It does feel like we've been shoved to the wings while others take the stage." She laid her hand on his upper arm. "I'm not complaining. At the Hare and Hounds, Mr Daventry was the voice of reason, and the magistrate fears him."

"I appreciate his help, too. His men are amongst London's finest enquiry agents, but I cannot sit around here and let other people solve my problems."

"Our problems. You're here because of me."

"That's why I'm asking what you want to do. Be honest." At dinner, she had kept her opinion to herself, and he needed to know why. "Don't let anyone take your voice or choose your fate."

She hesitated. "I don't want to sound ungrateful. Everyone has been so kind and helpful, and it's hard to fight when you're alone and unarmed."

"You're not alone." He was fighting a battle, too, but refused to be relegated from Field Marshall to Private in his own damn army. "We'll support each other. Take control of our own affairs."

She nodded before smoothing her hands down the elegant gown. "I don't feel myself here. It's like I'm a stranger in my own skin. Well, except for the exquisite moment we shared upstairs."

He brushed the backs of his fingers across her cheek. "That gown fits you like a glove, but you've never looked more beautiful than when I pleasured you in the bath."

She closed her eyes briefly as if the waves of ecstasy still flowed through her. "These aren't my clothes or jewels. I don't belong here and prefer my room at the practice. I mean the marquess no disrespect, but this house has no heart."

No, the place was as grim as a mausoleum.

"Then tell me what you want to do," he reiterated.

The fire of passion sparked in her eyes. "Return to the practice and my work in the dispensary. Question the serving wench and Mrs Pugh's relatives. Lead the charge together, not wait here like preened popinjays."

"Then we'll be rebels." He captured her hand, pressing a tender kiss to her knuckles. "What about the marriage licence?" he said with some hesitancy. "If we're to face our foes and indulge our desires, you need the security marriage provides."

She looked up, her uncertain eyes meeting his. "What if I'm not enough for you, and you grow to resent me?"

"No one can predict the future, but I imagine you'd be more than enough for any man."

Water gathered in her eyes as a pensive smile touched her lips. "That's the nicest thing anyone has ever said, but there's a chance we'll tire of each other and be nothing more than friends."

"And colleagues," he reminded her. "And though you cannot train in medicine, you could open a charitable foundation and treat the poor. We could have a rich and fulfilled life without the pressure of falling in love. Love rarely lasts anyway."

Yet the thought of her saying no roused an ache in his chest and a tight knot in his gut. The air between them thinned as if signalling her quiet retreat. The need to possess her made him want to don a periwig and gown and argue his case.

"My parents were happy, and they were friends," she said.

"My parents were so in love in the beginning, it killed my mother when my father betrayed her." A lie could destroy a relationship in seconds. "As long as we're always honest, we'll have no issue."

She exhaled slowly. "So you would tell me if you wished to take your pleasure elsewhere?"

"Take my pleasure elsewhere?" His incredulous snort was loud enough to rattle the dinner gong. "I thought you knew me better than that. If we marry, I'll bed no one but you, Sofia."

"Oh." She bit her lip. "Even if you fall in love with someone else?"

"Trust me, I won't. I'm married to my work, as are you. We'll have the same expectations, expectations few people understand."

With her, he didn't need to worry about working late. He could discuss his patients, and she would listen. They would ease their troubles beneath the bed sheets, and she didn't care if he was baseborn.

"And you require the same commitment from me?"

"I'll not share you with another man," he growled. The thought had the devil's serpent writhing in his chest. "Not ever."

Long seconds passed before she nodded. "Then I accept."

She said no more, and he didn't demand a detailed explanation, though the rush of elation was euphoric.

"Shall we put Aaron Chance to the test and see if he can summon a clergyman here?"

She blinked rapidly. "You mean marry tonight?"

"Why wait? If we're to tackle the villains, there's no better time." They were neck-deep in the mire and would keep each other from drowning.

"Very well. I expect the countess will be pleased."

"Rothley will be ecstatic."

"The marquess wants us to marry?"

"If it means we'll leave him in peace and return to town."

Everyone's eyes were upon them when they entered the dining room. The guests put down their cutlery and gazed with eager curiosity.

Once seated, Reid nodded for Sofia to speak as agreed.

She took a fortifying sip of her wine and faced Rothley. "My lord, we thank you for your hospitality but plan to return to town in the morning."

Rothley's mouth quirked. "Is it not in your best interest to remain here? Few people dare to approach the gates, let alone mount the steps."

"We're extremely grateful for everyone's help but have decided to take charge of our own affairs." She glanced at those seated around the table and smiled sincerely. "If you still want to assist us, we have a list of tasks."

They had made a brief list before leaving the library.

Everyone offered their unwavering support.

"Daventry, we would be grateful if your agent could continue watching the Merricks," Reid said, wanting to know when the devils ate and slept and breathed. "And check if Coutts has an employee named Mr Fellows."

"Of course."

"We'd like to review the witness statements from the patrons of the Hare and Hounds," Sofia said.

Daventry arched a brow. "That won't be possible. The details are confidential. The magistrate may grant me access to the files. I can relay pertinent facts but nothing more."

Reid thanked him before turning to Aaron Chance and mentioning the wager in the book at White's. "I need to know the names of the women these reprobates targeted. Many of those taking part frequent your gaming hell and will undoubtedly be in your debt. I'm sure they'll be eager to co-operate."

Aaron Chance's arrogant grin said he'd enjoy throttling a rogue or two. "Your cousin is on the list. Am I permitted to ruffle his feathers?"

"Pluck them out for all I care."

Rothley leaned back in his seat, sipping claret. "I pray my task is a damn sight more interesting."

"I'm trusting you with a matter closer to home. When my grandfather returns from Chesham Park, I need to know where he goes and who he visits."

Guilt surfaced. During the fifteen years he had lived with his grandfather, Reid had questioned his mother's account of her tragic tale. But the viscount's words to Sofia in the dispensary exposed a cruel side to his character.

Was it all just bravado?

Would his grandfather mellow once he learned they had wed?

Rothley's indifferent mask slipped, his dark eyes shining with a fierce determination to protect those who mattered most. "You distrust him?"

Family should be about more than blood.

Family should be the shelter one sought in a storm.

With a heavy heart, he sighed. "Something tells me I should trust my grandfather as much as I do Victor Merrick. But I hope he proves me wrong."

Rothley raised his glass. "I shall leave no stone unturned."

"One more thing," Sofia began, "perhaps *we* could make a wager."

"A wager?" Aaron Chance sounded intrigued.

"Yes, on how quickly you can summon a clergyman. We want to marry here tonight."

Chapter Twelve

Had they made the wager, the Marquess of Rothley would have won.

Mr Collard, vicar of the parish of Islington—and under the marquess' patronage—was summoned to Studland Park from his home a mile away.

Within the hour, Mr Collard stood inside the private chapel tucked amid the mansion's grand halls, dressed in his black cassock and starched collar and gripping his worn bible.

While Mrs Boswell had gone to make a small posy from the vases of flowers distributed around the house, the marquess drew Sofia and Reid aside in the panelled corridor near the chapel.

"You're free to refuse the offer," the lord began in a strangely soft tone as he retrieved a small box from his coat pocket, "but I've had this for almost a decade. While I have no desire to taint your union, you don't have a ring."

Sofia took the proffered box, her breath catching in her throat upon seeing the emerald and chrysolite ring inside.

"Good heavens. It's beautiful." She wanted to ask who it belonged to and why the marquess had it in his possession but daren't.

"It might not fit. You can have it resized at Woodcroft's in Bond Street and send me the bill. Consider it my gift to you both."

She glanced at Reid and smiled. "There's no reason to own something sentimental. Ours is not a love match."

Reid disagreed. "It's a generous gift, Rothley, but I can't let my wife wear another man's ring."

The marquess looked ready to drop to his knees and beg them to take the dratted thing. "Let it be a temporary solution until you purchase a replacement. After which, Mrs Gentry may wear it to the theatre or a soiree at The Burnished Jade."

Fearing the marquess wouldn't rest until they agreed, she said, "I'd be happy to accept the gift in the manner it's intended." If only to ease the man's tense expression.

The lord exhaled like he'd been holding his breath for ten years. "Love is a fool's dream. Marriage was meant for practical purposes. I respect the wisdom of your decision to wed."

Sofia noted the shadows of sadness behind his dark eyes and the palpable sorrow shrouding the house. "There is something you might do for me in return, my lord."

"Yes?" came his wary reply.

"Would you give me away?"

He gulped. "Give you away?"

"Mr Gentry regards you as family." And the lord looked lost at present and needed a purpose. "I hope to feel the same in time."

He bowed. "It would be an honour."

The countess appeared from the chapel, wondering what was holding up the proceedings. "Are you ready, Sofia? Mr

Collard can barely keep his eyes open and is likely to fall asleep where he stands."

"Yes, I'm just waiting for Mrs Boswell. She's keen to ensure I have a posy to match my gown." She had changed into the blue gown, red being a scandalous colour for a bride. "We'll be along in a moment."

The countess returned to the chapel seconds before Mrs Boswell came hurrying down the corridor, carrying a posy of white violets and blue forget-me-nots. She had crafted a wreath of myrtle for Sofia's hair.

"I'm sure you know myrtle is a symbol of love," the housekeeper said, positioning the wreath on Sofia's head so it sat low like a crown.

"I'm sorry we weren't honest earlier," Sofia whispered.

"You had your reasons, I don't doubt." Mrs Boswell noticed the velvet ring box Sofia clutched in her hand, recognising it instantly. With a blink of shock, she met the marquess' gaze.

"It's time to close a door to the past, Mrs Boswell," his lordship said, sounding world-weary. "Even if the *opportunity* presents itself again, which I doubt it will, I'm an unforgiving devil."

Mrs Boswell's rheumy eyes betrayed a deep sadness, too. "There's a reason we get a crick in our necks when we keep looking back. Focus on the present, or you'll miss the path ahead."

"A small step is better than none," he agreed.

"Happen there's a lot to celebrate tonight, my lord."

The marquess grimaced. "That's enough sentiment for one day, Mrs Boswell. Light the fire in the ballroom and have Jacob grab his fiddle. We'll take drinks there after the ceremony."

Despite being in company, Reid took the ring box from her hand and kissed her tenderly on the forehead. "I shall see you at the altar, Sofia."

She watched him enter the chapel, his confident strides chasing the faint flickers of apprehension away. Hopefully their desire for each other would last longer than a season.

The marquess offered his arm. "Ready, Miss Moorland?"

"Yes, my lord."

She had pictured her wedding day many times during the last month. The nightmare involved being spirited from the house in the dead of night by a depraved monster. Being drugged and tied to the marital bed, hours of slow torture before the salivating Mr Harrop finally had his wicked way.

The reality was a dream in comparison.

Mrs Boswell thrust the posy into Sofia's hand, snapping her from her reverie. "In the absence of family, I'll gather the staff so they might give a warm cheer once you've exchanged vows."

"Thank you, Mrs Boswell."

A hollow emptiness accompanied the sudden sting of loss.

Sofia fought to hold back tears at the sight of the empty pew where her mother would have sat, focusing instead on walking in step with the marquess—not her father, sadly.

"This is no way to start married life," she whispered, "but I will do everything possible to ensure Mr Gentry doesn't regret his decision."

Indeed, I don't know where I would be without him.

Lord Rothley looked ahead. "Gentry is his own man. He wouldn't marry you if he didn't want to. Besides, I've seen the way he looks at you."

Her heart skipped. "How does he look at me?"

"I'm sure you know, Miss Moorland."

Was it the same way she looked at Reid as she moved slowly towards him and the sleepy-eyed vicar? Like she was counting the seconds until they kissed again? Like the desperate need to feel the heat of his skin had her pulse pounding in her throat and her breath coming too quickly?

The witnesses had gathered near the altar, though Sofia barely acknowledged them until the countess stepped forward to take the posy.

"Have faith," Joanna whispered, kissing her cheek.

Faith was all she had. And a strange mix of lust and longing for the man soon to be her husband.

Reid took her hand, stroking his thumb softly over her knuckles in the same hypnotic way he'd teased her sex. "Do you need your spectacles? I want you to be sure you're marrying the right man."

A calmness settled in her chest. "I am marrying the right man." She didn't need her spectacles to know that. She felt the truth of it deep in her bones.

Desperate to begin, the vicar glanced at his open bible, suppressed a yawn and straightened his spine. "Dearly beloved—"

Judith would have found a clergyman who took bribes to ignore the bride's wails and the rope binding her feet. Mr Collard spoke like a true servant of God and his lofty tones could be heard in the heavens.

But the ceremony had hardly begun before he glared at them beneath bushy red brows and delivered a stark warning. "Marriage is not to be taken lightly, or wantonly; but reverently…"

She could attest to the latter—there wasn't a man she

respected more than Reid Gentry—but the strong desire to slake a physical need was a compelling factor, too.

Mr Collard continued extolling the importance of love and commitment, a sermon that should have forced her to stall the ceremony and beg for the Lord's forgiveness.

Yet throughout the devout speech, Reid held her hand in his sturdy grip and did not let go despite the vicar's frown. Life pulsed between their palms. It chased up her arm, filling her heart with hope.

"Who giveth this woman to be married to this man?"

Rothley stepped forward with tight shoulders and a tense jaw. One might think he had an aversion to pious men. "I do."

He didn't have to place her hand gently on Reid's because her betrothed had already claimed her.

The vicar addressed Reid. "Wilt thou love her, comfort her, honour and keep her in sickness and in health?"

"I will," Reid said without hesitation.

She lied, too, when asked if she would obey her husband. A spirited woman could not temper her passion once she'd found her voice.

And then came their personal vows, promises they must keep for a lifetime, not merely until a killer was caught. They pledged their troth and bowed their heads in prayer. Before she caught her breath, they were pronounced man and wife.

"Those whom God hath joined together, let no man put asunder."

Men would try to tear them apart, starting with Victor Merrick.

But Sofia didn't tremble in dread.

Her heart swelled with pride upon being declared Mr Gentry's wife. She admired his work and his courage when facing the enemy. He would always be a strong figure of support, and he valued her opinion. And heat curled low in her belly at the thought of sleeping beside him tonight.

Strangers swamped the candlelit chapel: maids and liveried footmen acting as well-wishers, clapping and cheering and showering them in flower petals.

Someone in the crowd called for Reid to kiss her. A motion endorsed by Mrs Boswell. The Daventrys were quick to join the appeal.

"Every union should be sealed with a kiss," Mrs Daventry said, locking gazes with her husband to demonstrate the power of love.

"It would be rude not to," Reid said, his boyish grin turning tender when he swept his arm around her waist and hauled her close. "Perhaps we should kiss like we do in private," he said for her ears only. "Put Rothley's mind at ease."

The warmth of his body seeped through her clothes. She looked at his mouth. "Maybe not exactly like we do in private, but we must appease our well-wishers."

Whenever Reid Gentry kissed her, the world ceased to exist.

It was no different now. Every nerve in her body sparked to life. She was drunk in seconds, giddiness forcing her to cling to his coat lapels. One slow stroke of his tongue over hers was a promise of the riches awaiting her tonight.

He tore his lips away on a groan. "Forget what I said about locking the adjoining door. If you're willing, you'll sleep with me tonight."

"We're married," she uttered, laying her hand over his heart, praying in time it would beat for no one but her. "But when I visit your bed, it won't be as your wife." Their union wouldn't be based on fake promises but on a deep-rooted need that neither could deny. "I'll come as your lover."

"Would it be rude to leave now?" he whispered.

Aware twenty people watched them, she patted his chest. "Let's appease the guests for half an hour. Besides, a little frivolity will settle my nerves."

Mr Daventry approached, giving Reid a congratulatory slap on the back. "Glad to see my efforts in obtaining a licence weren't wasted."

Lord Rothley spoke up, inviting everyone to the ballroom to continue the celebrations. "I'll need a bottle of brandy to make the next hour bearable. It's nights like this I wish I had an opium addiction."

Joanna gripped the lord's arm. "Come. My husband won't mind if you claim the first dance. I hear your footman plays an excellent tune on the fiddle."

"Dance with your husband, Joanna. He'll do anything to please you. A chorus of angels wouldn't rouse me to the floor."

Mr Chance did dance with his wife. A skilled pugilist should be fluid in his movements, yet the couple's waltz was akin to a tight embrace, his hands dipping lower than they should.

Amid the marble columns and Greek statues watching from the alcoves, the Daventrys danced with finesse. Yet it was a lesson in the power of laughter and how one look could convey a soul-deep bond.

While the marquess lounged in a padded gilt chair, drowning his sorrows and getting drunker by the second, Reid clinked his champagne flute with Sofia's and made a secret toast.

"To my wife, whose courage matches her grace." He

sipped his champagne. "I look forward to experiencing the joys of married life together." The glint in his eyes said he was not referring to a cosy night spent reading beneath the candlelight.

"To my husband"—the words brought a lump to her throat. The night would be perfect if they were in love— "whose kindness, compassion and modern thinking sets him apart from other men."

He watched her down the champagne, then set their glasses on the footman's tray and captured her hand. "Are you sure you want to leave Studland Park tomorrow? It means sleeping in the room above the practice and not a chamber fit for royalty."

"I'm sure. You've been neglecting your patients. And we should tackle our problems, not run from them."

He brought her fingers to his lips. "Tackling our enemies will be dangerous. Rothley would urge us to proceed with caution, though I believe a frontal assault is the best strategy. I'm tired of hiding in the shadows, Sofia."

"Agreed. Tomorrow, we'll visit the Merricks." A chill chased down her spine. Thankfully, she would not have to face them alone. Still, the thought would keep her awake tonight. "We have an early start. Perhaps we should retire. Your touch can help me forget my fears."

She needed a better reason to lie in bed, sweat-soaked and panting.

His lopsided smile had her stomach flipping. "Let's leave now and take the celebration upstairs." His thumb skimmed her ring as he held her hand. "I'll have the vicar bless a new ring once our nightmares are over and we've dealt with our foes."

What lived in their hearts was more important than what

she wore on her finger, but she nodded and threaded her arm through his. "Perhaps we should help the marquess to bed before we retire."

Lord Rothley sat with his arms resting on his knees, his head bent low, a picture of weariness and introspection.

"I'd have better luck wrestling a black bear. I know when to leave Rothley to deal with his demons and when to offer advice. Mrs Boswell will see to him. She always does."

Mrs Boswell saw to everything. That fact became abundantly clear when Sofia entered her bedchamber. Amber flames danced in the grate, casting the room in a sensual glow. The arousing scent of jasmine oil filled the air. The maid had turned down the bed and placed a white silk nightgown on the pillow.

Reid came to stand behind her, sliding his warm arms around her waist. "I see another bottle of Rothley's expensive champagne. Would you like me to pour you a glass, Sofia?"

Nerves and the potent thrum of desire had her turning in his arms. They were so close her breasts were pressed against his chest, deepening the ache that started before they'd mounted the stairs.

"I shall abide by my vows and obey your instruction." She'd do anything he asked when that ravenous gleam transformed his features. "Do I need a glass before making love to my husband?"

With light fingers, he cupped her throat. "Why defer to me? I've never made love to my wife. I've never made love to any woman. This feels entirely different from anything I've experienced before."

"How so?"

"I could hold you like this all night and still feel sated."

A light laugh escaped her. "The moment our mouths meet,

this will become a lesson in scandal, not one of restraint." She smoothed her palms over his waistcoat, fisting the material, a primal hunger in her grasp. "And we both know how skilled you are at settling my nerves."

His gaze dipped to her lips, and her insides clenched. "I don't want you to feel afraid. I forget who I am when I'm with you and get swept along in the quest for pleasure."

"What better way to begin married life," she stated, kicking off her slippers. "I want you to seduce me. I want to be your lover. Yes, it will be wild. We've always known that."

"And perhaps too vigorous," he said with a sinful smile.

"I'll tell you if it's a problem."

Raw, masculine heat glowed in his eyes. "Good," came his languid drawl. "Tell me. Is this a problem?" He settled his mouth on her neck, kissing and sucking her sensitive skin, slipping slowly down to nip her shoulder with his teeth while he worked on unhooking the back of her gown.

A hushed whimper escaped her. "No. It's divine."

He smelled unbelievably good, dark and mysterious, like exotic musk and forbidden forests. And his hands, so large and powerful, undressed her with masterful skill.

"Is this a problem?" He tugged the short sleeves down her arms, drawing the gown off her shoulders, exposing more of her chest.

Arousal coiled through her body.

Each touch hypnotised her mind.

He was everywhere, pushing the gown over the curve of her hips, unthreading her stays and kissing the swell of her breast, his tongue dipping into the deep valley.

"I could devour every inch of you," he growled.

She was in danger of losing her mind.

Her petticoat pooled at her feet.

He exposed her breasts.

"Reid." Sweet Lord. He squeezed her buttocks, sinking his fingers into her flesh as his mouth settled over her tight nipple. Every flick of his tongue on the sensitive peak had her panting. "I need to touch you."

She didn't wait for a response and dared to slide her hand between them, shaping it around the solid length in his trousers. His manhood was thick and long and hard against her palm.

His guttural groan rent the air. "God, Sofia. Release me. Undo the buttons. Touch me. Touch me now."

Logical thought scattered like leaves in the wind when she wrapped her hand around his hot flesh. He rocked his hips, pushing his solid member through her fingers, groaning like it was the most exquisite feeling in the world.

"Glide your thumb gently over the crown," he commanded.

She obeyed, swirling the bead of moisture over the tip.

"Tighten your grip, love … yes … yes … like that."

She had read enough books to know how lovemaking worked. None mentioned that his manhood would pulse and swell and slide like silken steel between her fingers. Or that his growled obscenity would make her feel like a goddess. None mentioned the almost savage need to ravish every inch of him. Or that these things combined would cause a sudden bout of mania.

The last of her inhibitions vanished.

Shocking words left her lips without censure.

"I need you inside me, Reid." She stroked his manhood, the musky scent of him feeding this irresistible attraction. Desire licked her body like flames. She couldn't guard her heart or hide her feelings. "I need you to undress and do all the wicked things you promised."

"You'll get everything," he panted, sliding his tongue into her mouth, kissing her while shrugging out of his coat. "But we need to slow down."

"I—I can't." Lust burned like liquid fire in her veins. Now she knew why half the ladies in the *ton* were hysterical. "Hurry."

She tore at his clothes, tugging like a wildcat.

A button skittered across the floor as he pulled off his waistcoat. She fiddled with his cravat, though even the simple knot was too tricky for her trembling fingers. Gasping, they both fought to strip him naked.

Then he dragged his shirt over his head, and her breath left her lungs.

He was magnificent.

The memory of her climax in the bath came crashing back. She'd wanted to run her hands over his flawless skin, caress his broad shoulders and corded muscles—drag him on top of her in the jasmine-scented water.

Now, she followed the teasing trail of hair from his navel to his trouser waistband. His rigid manhood jerked as her gaze dipped lower, begging to be touched.

He said nothing as he removed his shoes and trousers.

When he rose he regarded her intently, his eyes dark like a midnight ocean, his slow smile making her insides clench. "Remove your chemise while I watch." He glanced at her breasts, his tongue skimming his bottom lip.

Nerves mingled with excitement as she gathered the hem.

"Do it slowly," he whispered.

She obeyed, teasing him as she raised the garment inch by inch.

He hissed a breath when she exposed her sex. "If I were a selfish man, I would have you twice tonight."

She gave a coy smile. "I want you to be selfish."

"Then prepare yourself. This night will beat our one at the Adelphi."

She stepped into his embrace when beckoned.

He held her close, the heat of his skin intoxicating. The kiss they shared wasn't desperate or savage, but a soft, slow melding of mouths that reached inside her, touching her soul.

Reid swept her into his arms and carried her to Aphrodite's bed, brushing the silk nightgown aside and laying her down. He glanced at the complicated braid secured with pins and tiny roses. "When we make love tomorrow, I want you on top of me, your hair cascading over your shoulders."

She smiled, hope springing to life in her heart.

We need to marry because I want you more than once.

He'd meant it.

Whatever existed between them would live beyond their wedding night.

Time seemed to falter when he knelt between her thighs, his eyes roaming over her with fervent hunger. "I mean to worship every inch of you. You'll tell me what you like and dislike. There must be nothing but honesty between us, Sofia."

She nodded. "I hide nothing from you."

This blossoming love she felt growing inside her didn't count.

She doubted he'd want to hear a declaration.

"God, you're so beautiful," he breathed, the compliment bolstering her confidence. "But this openness we share, it's refreshing and arousing in equal measure." He moistened his lips, his grin turning sinful. "I'm going to pleasure you, love, until I've wrung every last whimper from you. Bend your legs. Open them for me, Sofia."

The urgent fever came over them again.

Reid lowered his head, murmuring how wet she was before he circled her bud with his tongue.

Pleasure shot through her.

Every wicked kiss and suck had her arching her back, begging for more. Tension coiled deep inside her. "*Reid!*"

He must have heard something in her greedy plea. He met her gaze, his eyes a hot smoulder as he pushed two fingers inside her, pumping slowly before easing out and claiming her again.

She cried out as her climax burst through her in wave after rippling wave. Her muscles clamped around his fingers, claiming a small part of him, though she wanted it all.

Reid didn't give her a chance to catch her breath. He rose above her, positioning himself at her entrance. "Do you still want me, Sofia?"

Want him? She had never wanted anything more.

"I'm yours." Now and forever, her heart echoed. "Take me."

He stared into her eyes as he breached her, the slow, inch-by-inch intrusion stretching her wide. He kissed her, a hot assault on her senses before one final thrust saw him buried to the hilt.

They both gasped.

He stilled. "Did I hurt you?"

"No." She doubted he ever could.

"It will feel better when I move."

What could feel better than holding him this close?

Indeed, when he withdrew slowly, she felt bereft. But

then he rolled his hips and filled her so full she could not recall feeling anything so divine.

Arousal grew between them, reaching a fever pitch.

He rocked into her, each angled slide drawing her closer to her release.

She came, crying his name and holding him deep.

His thrusts came harder, his need urgent, the tempo desperate.

Unable to stop touching him, she raked her fingers over his back and buttocks.

Reid had never looked more handsome than when he spilled himself over her abdomen. His impressive chest heaved as he chased his breath. His eyes shone the brightest blue, no longer marred by shadows of mistrust. The satisfied smile on his lips held her captivated.

"That was ... that was spectacular," he purred, like his problems were a distant memory.

"Yes, it was," she said, eager to feel that close to him again.

Chapter Thirteen

Reid sat quietly, observing his wife as the carriage passed through the Islington tollgate and headed into London. While he struggled to shake the memory of their lovemaking from his mind and temper the newfound need for her, she watched from the window as fields and hedgerows gave way to the bustle of the city.

Her shoulders rose and sagged every few seconds, her weary sighs failing to lift her solemn spirit. She clutched her hands in her lap, but he saw the tremble she tried to disguise.

She was afraid—afraid of the Merricks.

The urge to settle her fears had him referring to the new hat pin the countess had given her at Studland Park. "The countess has a unique taste in gifts."

Sofia blinked, touching the decorative pearl-topped pin visible in her poke bonnet. "Pins can be lethal if one knows where to stab a man. This one is a little wider, the tip sharp as a blade."

"The countess knows how much you fear the Merricks."

Sofia averted her gaze. "Judith's erratic moods were bearable, but now Victor pulls her strings. He's a law unto himself."

Men like Merrick used fear as a weapon.

"Did Merrick ever touch you?"

Sofia shivered. "No, he enjoys being a silent participant."

Rage roiled in his chest, but he fought to suppress it. "He watched as your stepmother hurt you?"

She pursed her lips, struggling against whatever visions filled her mind. "Judith has always been cruel with her words. She found a different outlet for her wickedness when she met Victor."

"What is her gripe with you?" he asked calmly, hoping to put his pugilistic skills to the test when he finally faced Merrick.

Sofia gave a half-shrug but then explained how Judith had bled her father dry. "It makes no sense. I watched a logical man turn into a blithering idiot. He seemed blind to her manipulation."

"Perhaps your mother was the sensible one and her death highlighted his weakness." Reid's father had proven his mind was feeble during his temporary commission in Brussels.

"It makes me wonder if you ever really know someone."

It was a cue to reveal something from his past. He thought about changing the subject, but they'd vowed to make honesty the foundation of their marriage.

"That's what killed my mother in the end." His chest constricted. The tight hands of grief squeezed his lungs. He mentioned the letter found amongst his father's personal effects. "Her heart gave out when she discovered my father had a mistress."

He could still hear his mother's mournful cry when she

discovered the woman was staying in Brussels, in a village close to his father's camp.

Sofia swallowed deeply. She reached across the carriage and clasped his hand. "I know how important she was to you. I'm sure your father's selfish actions made her question every intimate moment they'd shared."

Reid recalled speaking about this once before.

His grandfather's response had been vastly different.

Can you blame him? A man needs a woman who worships him. Not one who dedicates her life to helping strangers.

"The light in my mother's eyes died when she read that letter. Hours later, I found her cold in her bed." In his grief, he'd resented her leaving, a feeling his grandfather nurtured.

She didn't care about your father, and she didn't care about you. I blame it on her upbringing and that religious zealot who threw her out.

"How old were you?" Sofia said softly.

"Fifteen."

Her breath caught. "I was fifteen when my mother died."

Losing a parent at a young age was not uncommon, especially if one lived in the rookeries. Yet the coincidence was like another string strengthening their bond.

While he had dealt with a bitter old man, she had coped with a violent step-parent. And now, two separate events had somehow brought them together.

"We have more in common than we realised," he said.

They shared an interest in medicine, social reform, and a wild passion between the bedsheets. It should have roused hope in his chest, but the road to happiness was an uphill trek they might not survive.

"Much more in common." Her coy smile evoked a picture of this morning's lesson in curing hysteria. A lesson in scandal because he'd made her climax with his mouth as she stood naked before the looking glass.

"You don't need to be afraid of the Merricks," he said, returning to the reason for her sad sighs. "While I don't make threats lightly, I'll die to protect you, Sofia."

She inhaled sharply, then threw herself into his lap.

He wanted to say any honourable husband would do the same, but his wife's mouth came crashing down on his, and he forgot everything but the arousing taste of her.

"I fear my nerves are rather frayed," she teased.

The prompt to slip his hand up her skirts encountered a setback.

The carriage stopped on Wood Street, outside the shabby Castle Inn. With a list of calls as endless as a madman's rant, there was no time to waste.

"We'll discuss the treatment for your nerves tonight," he said, smiling. "When we consider the topic of my growing ailment, too."

They alighted. The Castle Inn was closed on Sundays, so Reid thumped the door repeatedly until the landlord answered.

"We ain't open. Not unless you've hired a room." The pigeon-faced fellow peered through the narrow gap in the door, scanning their attire. "I've got a spare one going. It's yours for three shillings, including a hot supper."

Reid reached into his waistcoat pocket for a coin. "I'll give you a crown if you let us discuss the matter inside."

The fellow snatched the coin and beckoned them into the dingy taproom. Three older men sat huddled around a corner table, downing ale and putting the world to rights.

"Don't mind them," the innkeeper said, rubbing his hands

together. "They're kin, and there ain't no laws about serving family on the Lord's Day."

Reid scoffed. "I'm not here with a warrant."

The fellow looked at Sofia and gave a toothy grin. "I reckon I know why you're here. I can have June put on the best sheets and fix the room up nice for the lady." He nudged Reid and winked. "I'll even put a flower on the pillow for a price."

"Would it be possible to speak to June?" Sofia said. "I know her sister, Mrs Pugh. I heard she lost her position and could help her find another."

The innkeeper screwed up his face like he smelled something foul. "I'll give *you* a shilling if you take that drunken harpy off my hands. I found her slumped on the stairs this morning, piddle soaking her stockings."

"Are you speaking about June or Mrs Pugh?"

"June's only vice is that Congle tea from China."

"Congou," Reid corrected.

"That's it. She sings every Friday so she can buy a pound. I told her she'll have to sing every day of the week if I'm to suffer her sister."

Reid tried to stem his impatience. "Fetch Mrs Pugh and I'll give you a sovereign for your trouble."

The innkeeper's eyes widened. "Will I still get the money if she's spouting gibberish? I reckon she's still half-cut. You'll want a peg for your nose."

"Bring her here, and you'll get your sovereign."

"Can I see the blunt?"

"Fetch her!"

The innkeeper scurried away through a door behind the counter. Raised voices upstairs accompanied thuds and bangs.

A woman screamed to be left alone. She shrieked. Something smashed.

Long moments passed before the innkeeper yanked open the door and shoved a scrawny woman into the taproom. "Unless you want to sleep huddled next to a brazier tonight, you'll speak to these good people."

The innkeeper gripped the swaying woman's wrist, dragging her forward along with a stench too putrid to name. A red scratch marred his cheek. He held out his hand to Reid, keen to be paid for his trouble.

Reid crossed his palm with gold. "Leave us. Best dab some brandy on that welt before it becomes infected."

"She's a wild one this morning," the keeper warned.

Mrs Pugh cursed the fellow to Hades, her spittle pelting his face like plump raindrops. Then she turned, wobbled, and stared at Sofia. "You? Why, you little devil. I should tan your hide. That's what I should do."

Reid made to speak, but Sofia's temper flared. "Lay a hand on me, and I'll have you carted to the nearest gaol. I don't need to tiptoe around you anymore. Say what you like to Judith."

Mrs Pugh's glassy eyes rolled in their sockets and she slurred, "I'm out on my ear because of you, s-sneaking off when you shouldn't." She burped, the fumes noxious. "Merrick never gave me a chance to explain. He's already out looking for you."

Sofia pressed her palm to her chest and breathed deeply. "Then he's wasting his time. I'm married now."

"Married!" Mrs Pugh looked at Reid, her head lolling back and forth. "You don't need to lie to me no more. You left home less than a week ago."

Reid cleared his throat. "I assure you. Sofia is my wife. If you see Merrick, tell him I'll gut him like a fish if he comes near her."

Mrs Pugh chuckled, the sound fuelled by drink. "Happen you've never set eyes on the devil. One look from him will have you scarpering."

"I don't scare easily, Mrs Pugh."

A determined man was a fierce opponent.

"Merrick always gets his way. Happen he'll take pleasure in stealing Sofia back." Her cackle became a hacking cough. She pressed her mouth to her elbow, the fabric catching the phlegm. "I bet Judith is glad you're gone. She never liked the way Merrick looked at you. Your virtue was the only thing stopping him from giving you one himself."

Reid cursed under his breath.

"What did Judith say when she came home to find me missing?" There was a thread of satisfaction in Sofia's tone. "She must have been livid."

Mrs Pugh shrugged. "If she'd been there, she might have let me stay, but that devil acts like it's his house."

Sofia glanced at Reid and frowned. "But Judith was there when Mr Merrick threw you out. I was told they arrived home together in a hackney and you left shortly afterwards."

Mrs Pugh shook her head, the action causing her to grip a nearby table for support. "Judith went to the solicitors. Merrick's sister is visiting from Edinburgh for a month. The brute set her to work straight away and had her cleaning up the mess."

"Did Merrick mention anything about the auction?" Reid said, desperate to gain insight into the fiend's plan. "Do you know when the event will take place?"

"What auction?"

"Victor planned to sell me to the highest bidder."

The woman stared through bloodshot eyes. "I know he likes you serving the old gents in the new card room, but he ain't mentioned nothing about an auction."

"Think, Mrs Pugh," Sofia urged, gripping the sleeve of the sot's crumpled dress. "Did Judith discuss a party with you? A wedding celebration, perhaps?"

"She talked about having a gathering at home."

Despite pressing Mrs Pugh for answers, it was obvious she knew nothing. Maybe the liquor had rotted her brain cells. She begged Sofia for money and offered to talk to Judith Merrick, but Reid knew Mrs Pugh would hit the bottle the minute they left.

Outside the inn, he drew Sofia aside.

"We have two choices." The way she worried her lip had him sliding his arm around her waist, drawing her closer. "We pray Mrs Pugh will tell Judith you're married and they decide to leave you alone."

"Or?" She closed her eyes, anticipating the other option.

"We visit the Merricks now and inform them ourselves."

She paled, her frown betraying an inner turmoil. "We agreed to face our enemies. And it's important you know what sort of man Victor is."

"I know what sort of man he is." A tyrant and bully. A beast without morals. He smiled to chase the haunted look from her eyes. "We're married. The Merricks need to know you fall under my protection now. I'll not let them hurt you. No one will ever hurt you again."

Strange how his own words caused an ache in his chest, a twisting tug of longing that made it hard to breathe. His attachment to her deepened by the day. Nothing but the touch of her lips brought him peace.

He prayed the feeling didn't fade.

"I don't care about myself," she confessed.

Unspoken words hung in the air between them.

He stroked her cheek to settle her fears. "The key to tackling men like Merrick is to show you're not intimidated. I may play the considerate doctor, but make no mistake. I can be savage when the need arises."

Sofia clenched her fist and hammered on the front door, wishing it were Judith's smug face. Nausea roiled in her stomach. The Merricks were unpredictable. Nothing would go as planned. An argument was the least of her concerns. The meeting would likely end in a fistfight.

No one answered.

Reid stepped back, surveying the upper windows before banging on the door with his fist, too. "Daventry's man said the Merricks are home, though they didn't return until the early hours."

Were they combing the streets looking for her or trying to explain to Mr Harrop that his bride had fled? Perhaps they didn't give two hoots and were glad to see the back of her.

"Judith often spends the day in bed." Judith found rising a chore and lacked the strength to pull back the coverlet. Maybe the creaking bed had finally snapped, and the couple had suffocated beneath a mangle of sheets.

But Sofia wasn't so lucky.

Gruff shouts echoed from within the house.

A high-pitched shriek reached her ears.

The Merricks argued as much as they bounced on the mattress. After her experience with Reid last night, she knew the difference between a three-minute marathon of grunts and groans and two hours spent making love.

Seconds passed before they heard the patter of footsteps in the tiled hallway. A woman answered the door, her hair a tangle of red curls, her eyes bloodshot and her breath as stale as the dregs of yesterday's ale.

"What has ye raising the roof at this godforsaken hour?" the woman said in an irate Scottish burr. "'Tis it not a crime to knock so early on the Lord's Day?"

This woman must be Mr Merrick's younger sister. While Sofia knew he had relatives in Scotland, the man spoke with a mild London accent.

Sofia gathered herself. "We're here to see the Merricks. Judith was married to my father before she married your brother."

The woman paled. She put a shaky hand to her throat. "Then ye must be Miss Moorland. My brother has nae slept and has been mindless with worry."

Victor had never been of sound mind.

The woman beckoned them over the threshold. "Come in out of the cold. I'll fetch Victor and make a pot of tea." It wasn't cold, but perhaps it was a standard greeting in Scotland.

"I would prefer to speak to Judith."

"As I said, best come inside and talk in private."

The stranger welcomed them into the drawing room, then hurried upstairs to rouse the household.

Sofia glanced at the blue brocade sofa, a lump forming in her throat because it was the last purchase her mother made before she died. The ornate brass fire screen had belonged to her grandmother, and for a moment she forgot about the hatred and arguments and remembered what it felt like to be with people she loved.

As tears filled her eyes, Reid drew her close, the heat of his body soothing her spirit. "I know how hard it is to leave your home and start anew. There are tenants in my parents' old house, though I sometimes park outside and let the memories consume me."

Sofia leant into him. "After today, I'll never come here again. The Merricks have left their stain on everything I once held dear."

"Is there anything you want from your room before we leave?"

She met his gaze, his question filling her with glowing gratitude. "My grandmother's dressing table, though I doubt Judith will agree."

Reid dashed a tear from her lashes. "I'll offer her a sum she cannot refuse. People like the Merricks value nothing but ready coin."

The pain in her heart eased, but the thud of footsteps on the stairs had the organ pumping wildly.

Victor entered the room—vanquishing all breathable air.

Doubtless Reid was expecting a monstrous fellow with evil eyes and a toothless grin, but a master of deception had carved Victor's handsome mask.

"Sofia," he said, slapping his hand to his wicked heart like his prayers had been answered. He combed his fingers through his greying black hair. "I trawled the streets looking for you. Mrs Pugh sent me to The Burnished Jade, but I found the place in darkness."

Sofia raised her chin. She did not need to appease Victor Merrick anymore. "I left because I found a letter from Mr

Harrop confirming he wished to purchase me at auction. I believe you've invited other men to bid on my virtue."

Victor frowned, his mouth curling downwards, his thick black brows slanting though they failed to hide the sudden flare of anger in his eyes. "Harrop is a doddery old fool. Even if it were true, whatever secret arrangement he had with Judith no longer applies."

His response raised a few questions, but she needed to leave this house and refused to linger a second longer than necessary.

"Where is Judith? Scrubbing the laundry in Mrs Pugh's absence?"

A muscle in Victor's cheek twitched. He glanced at Reid for the first time but continued to ignore him. "So, you've found your voice during your little trip about town."

"I wasn't allowed a voice when I lived here."

"Lived?" Again, he looked at Reid but glared this time. "Introduce me to this gentleman, Sofia, so I might thank him for seeing you safely home."

"I'd prefer to wait for Judith."

"Judith isn't here," he snapped.

That's not what Mr Daventry's man said, though perhaps he had mistaken the Scotswoman for Judith. Both had red hair.

"When do you expect her to return?"

"Never."

A heavy silence descended, the inevitability of the word hitting like the plunge of the guillotine.

"Never?" What did that mean? "Did Judith remain in Scotland?"

"No. She complained about the cold wind and dreary skies." Crinkles appeared at the corners of Victor's eyes, though his tone held no emotion when he said, "Judith is dead. She'd taken something to help her sleep and went missing from the coaching inn near St Albans."

Sofia listened, shocked that Judith needed a sleeping tincture because she usually snored the minute her head hit the pillow. Fear crept into her heart and spread like a night frost.

Had Judith riled Victor's temper?

"A coachman found her body in the grounds of the abbey." The devil did not shudder or shed a tear. "The coroner summoned a jury of locals to examine her. They delivered a verdict of accidental death."

"When was this?" Reid said.

Victor whipped his head around. "I'll not answer your questions until I know who the hell you are."

Reid straightened to his full height, a few inches taller than Victor. "Then I'll tell you who the hell I am. I'm Sofia's husband."

Victor froze. Darkness passed over his features. "This is no time for childish games. Did you not hear me say her stepmother is dead? The house is in mourning. Have some respect."

Respect? Victor was a walking monument to insolence.

"It's true. I'm his wife." She edged closer to Reid. "I've known Mr Gentry for months. We were married in the chapel at Studland Park." And she carried no pity in her heart for Judith.

Victor stared and stared. Time stood still. A glint in his eyes said he'd found a flaw in the tale. "Yet you haven't claimed her dowry."

"I don't need her dowry. We married for love, not money." Reid didn't slip a protective arm around her waist but stepped forward, squaring his shoulders. "We're here because my wife wants her dressing table. We're not leaving without it."

A sly grin played on Victor's lips. "It's not her dressing table. I own the house and everything in it, per the details of Judith's will."

Sofia couldn't help but wonder if this was Victor's plan all along. Her beloved family home would belong to this brute. "You don't own the house until the probate court determines you do."

"To apply for probate, the executor needs the death certificate," Reid added. "The coroner won't issue a certificate for an accidental death until there's been an inquest."

Victor firmed his jaw. "The coroner gave his verdict."

"A verdict on probable cause. The inquest findings usually reach the executor in two weeks. It will be another two weeks before the case goes through probate. Anything can happen in a month."

"That sounds like a threat," Victor countered.

"Take it however you please. Luckily, the accident happened in St Albans, a mere twenty miles away. Close enough for me to attend the inquest and ask pertinent questions."

Victor raised a menacing finger. "Stay out of my business, boy, or I'll make you regret coming here with your feeble warnings."

The tension reached fever pitch.

The air crackled with the promise of violence.

Sofia knew they had evidence that might make Victor think twice about throwing a punch. "The coroner may change his verdict when he learns you purchased two bottles of potent laudanum from the apothecary in Covent Garden.

You may say they were for Judith, but it will cast doubt on your tale."

The fiend paled.

She saw a flicker of uncertainty in his eyes.

Silence stretched like a bowstring about to snap.

Victor stepped back and raised his hands in surrender, yet he would have appeared less terrifying if he'd drawn a blade. "Take the table."

Sofia gripped Reid's arm, keen to leave the house.

Reid summoned Nokes, telling him to place the table in the carriage, and they would hail a hackney.

Victor stood in the hall, his beady eyes fixed on her, not Reid and Nokes lugging the furniture. When his sister arrived with the tea tray, he dismissed her with a threatening jab of his finger.

Victor Merrick made sure he had the last word as Sofia left. The whispered statement prickled the hairs on her nape, filling her with ice-cold dread.

"Some men value virtue over experience between the bed sheets. Lucky for you, I'm not one of them."

Chapter Fourteen

They returned to the practice, arriving in a hackney to find Reid's coachman and Turner hauling Sofia's dressing table up the narrow staircase.

Turner saw them, paused and sighed in relief. "Where the devil have you been? I sent word to Cavendish Square but received no reply."

Bewildered, Reid said, "It's Sunday. You're on call this week."

"We needed to speak to you urgently. I arrived to find the house empty and feared something dreadful had occurred. I would have visited your friends but have been swamped with work all morning."

Guilt flared.

Turner had enough pressure without Reid adding to his burden. "Take the dressing table upstairs and meet me in the study. I'll explain all then."

"We have important news, too, though poor Hickman still hasn't recovered." Turner lowered his voice. "The man was a wreck this morning. I've given him a drop of laudanum to calm his nerves."

Reid inwardly cursed. He'd neglected his work these past few weeks, and his loyal employees had paid the price. He made a mental note to treat them to supper and an evening relaxing in a mineral bath at Porretta's.

Hickman shot out of his chair when Reid entered the man's office. His red-rimmed eyes said he'd barely slept. "I swear I locked the doors last night. I did the usual checks upon leaving. Some devil broke into the dispensary and stole our supplies."

Reid froze.

Cold dread crept over him.

Sofia should have been sleeping upstairs last night. Whoever broke into the premises would have encountered her.

Had hurting her been the plan?

He stormed out of the room and headed for the dispensary, coming to a crashing halt in the doorway. The shelves were empty, and the drawers overturned. Shards of glass littered the workbench.

Sofia was already there, crouched on the floor, brushing scattered herbs into a scuttle. "Why would someone do this?" Her voice quivered under the weight of emotion. "All those hours of hard work wasted."

"Leave the herbs. There may be glass on the floor." He cupped her elbow and brought her to her feet. "I'll hire someone to clean up this wretched mess."

She sagged against his chest, her distress evident in every shuddering breath. "Just when it feels like we're making progress, something dreadful happens to set us back."

He held her in a tight embrace. "Someone means to break

our spirit, but we won't let them. Everything here can be replaced. No one is hurt. That's all that matters."

The obvious culprits sprang to mind.

Did Algernon want revenge for the punch he'd received at White's? Had his grandfather hired someone to destroy the dispensary? Perhaps he meant to scare Sofia and persuade Reid to take a position at Chesham Park. Would the lord agree to accept Sofia if Reid gave up the practice and managed the estate?

Turner entered the room. He glanced at them enveloped in each other's arms and presumed their herbalist had crossed boundaries in her distress.

"I'll take Miss Moorland to your study. A nip of something strong will do her the world of good." Turner stepped closer as if to rescue Reid from an awkward encounter. "Come, Miss Moorland. I can make tea if you prefer."

Turner reached for her arm, an innocent action, though Reid felt a possessive pang in his chest, a stab of jealousy unlike anything he'd ever known.

Perhaps that's why he said, "Miss Moorland is my wife. We were married at Studland Park last night. I would have told you, but it's a complicated situation, and we invited no one but the witnesses."

Turner stared, his shock palpable in the gnawing silence.

"You're married?" he said, gulping.

Turner liked Sofia and was always attentive. He'd lent her precious books and encouraged her quest to study medicine. They'd spent hours together in the dispensary. In marrying in haste, had Reid deprived his friend and his herbalist of an opportunity to fall in love?

The thought shook him to his core.

Not because he felt remorse for putting paid to Turner's

romantic notions, but because he had a sudden desire to prove himself worthy. To ensure his bride wanted *him* and no other man.

Good Lord. Did he want his wife to fall in love with him?

Sofia must have felt the crushing weight of Turner's disappointment. She pushed out of Reid's embrace. "I'm sorry for not confiding in you, Mr Turner. Mr Gentry offered me work so I could escape my stepmother's clutches. In marrying me, he has saved me from a fate worse than death."

Turner's cold eyes warmed as he looked at her. "If you needed the safety marriage provides, you should have spoken to me."

Sofia did not ask him why. "I had planned to leave England, but matters took an unexpected turn, and Mr Gentry agreed we should act quickly."

"There was no time to consider other options," Reid said, knowing it wouldn't ease Turner's dismay. It was also a lie. Time was against them, but he'd married Sofia because he wanted her. And this strange intimacy they shared mattered more than it should.

Was he beginning to feel a deep affection for his wife?

"Well, there's nothing to be done," Turner said with a sad sigh. "Might you have the marriage annulled? Once your problems are over, that is?"

It was already too late.

Reid recalled their night of exquisite lovemaking, the strange feeling that flooded his chest when he entered her, her plea for him to push deeper. Yet he couldn't explain that to Turner.

Thankfully, Sofia was tactful in her reply. "I made a vow I cannot break. I promised to be a good wife and intend to keep my word."

Turner inclined his head respectfully. "I would expect no less from a woman of your good character, Miss … Mrs Gentry. I wish you both well."

An uncomfortable silence ensued.

Would this be the moment Sofia never forgot?

The day she learned there had been a better option?

Reid prayed Hickman hadn't marriage in mind, too.

"I had to move some appointments," Turner said, swiftly changing the subject, though his tone was noticeably cooler. "Lord Brigham refuses to see anyone but you. Other patients are of the same mind. The rest I've managed to squeeze into my tight schedule."

Reid took the veiled reprimand on the chin. "I'll be living above the practice for the foreseeable future. It means I'll be available around the clock. It will give me time to catch up on missed appointments."

He made it sound like work was his priority.

A desire to protect his wife was the only motive.

"Is that wise? Living upstairs, I mean?" Turner glanced at the mess on the floor. "The person who broke into the dispensary picked the lock. There's no sign of forced entry, and we've accounted for all the keys."

"Did Hickman not bolt the dispensary door?" Reid said before realisation dawned and he answered his own question. "He didn't bolt the door because he expected Mrs Gentry to return home."

Turner nodded. "We presumed she might be staying with Lady Berridge but couldn't be sure." He shifted, his expression tightening. "There's another problem. Your grandfather came here this morning, demanding to know where you were. He told me to 'fetch the herbalist' but I explained Miss Moorland wasn't here either."

Damnation!

His grandfather was supposed to be at Chesham Park.

An internal war with his conscience ensued. Who married without inviting their grandfather? The man had kept a roof over Reid's head for fifteen years. Yes, Reid had inherited his father's home and personal wealth, but his grandfather cared for him until he came of age.

A faint whisper of suspicion breezed through him.

One he'd dismissed many times before.

Did his grandfather care, or were his actions self-serving?

"If he comes here, don't tell him we're married." A deep sense of trepidation sent Reid's pulse skipping. "If he has questions, you'll refer him to me. Is that understood?"

He knew the viscount could be persuasive. It's why Reid lived with him in Cavendish Square, not in a house he personally owned.

Be your own man.

No matter the cost.

In his father's last letter from Brussels, he had underlined both statements. Reid always thought it meant he should follow his own ambitions. It's why he'd been so determined to train in medicine. But perhaps his father referred to the pressure to please one's kin.

Turner grimaced. "You know how Hickman panics. It doesn't help that your grandfather knows his uncle, Sir Phillip. The need to appease the privileged is in Hickman's blood."

Reid felt a frisson of alarm. "What did Hickman tell him?"

"That Miss Moorland's family lives in Dean Street and he might find her there. Hickman stuttered so badly the viscount had him repeat it. Then he blurted that her stepmother's surname is Merrick."

Sofia failed to see the problem. "It doesn't matter anymore. Mr Merrick has no use for me. He'll probably take one look at your grandfather and slam the door in his face."

But his grandfather was persistent and desperate to learn everything he could about Sofia. "My grandfather will pay Merrick for information. Victor will be more than accommodating then."

She shrugged. "What can Victor tell him, other than we're married? Your grandfather will discover the truth soon enough."

Perhaps they should visit his grandfather together, just as they had with the Merricks. "We'll tell him ourselves. I'll arrange a meeting."

He asked for an update on their patients, praying no one else had died under suspicious circumstances.

"I can spare an hour now if you want to discuss medical cases," Turner said, his tone more formal than friendly. "And you need to let Hickman know whether to call a constable. In light of your sudden *absences*, we weren't sure what to do."

Remorse hit him squarely in the chest. "Have Hickman join us in my study once he's summoned a constable. We'll discuss business matters, then spend the afternoon tidying the dispensary."

It was seven that evening by the time they cleared the debris, made fresh tinctures and bid Turner good night. Hickman had left an hour earlier, eager to return home to feed his cat.

Reid's thoughts turned to the only pleasure in his life. He stood watching Sofia add the last of the ground herbs to the new bottles. She had barely eaten today. A problem he was keen to rectify.

"Fetch your bonnet and pelisse." He closed the gap between them and prised the bottle and funnel from her hands. "I'm taking you out to supper."

She looked at him, a soft curl caressing her cheek and he remembered why he'd insisted she tie back her hair. "I need to wash and change. Perhaps we could visit Antoine's and make it a working supper."

He did want to question the waiter. Algernon claimed the man was paid to keep score for the wager at White's. Perhaps he knew the elusive Mr Fellows.

"We'll take a hackney rather than walk to the livery stables and disturb Nokes. Can you be ready in half an hour?"

When she smiled, he considered altering the plans and spending a cosy evening at home. Home? He rarely felt content anywhere. Yet here, in the simple dispensary, he felt a sudden wave of peace.

"I can be ready in ten minutes." Sofia laid her palm on his chest, reached up and kissed his cheek.

He drew her close, claiming her mouth in the same desperate way he wanted to claim her body. A need like he'd never known sparked a fire in his blood. Every silken stroke of her tongue chased away his demons. The sweet taste of her lips stirred—

She broke contact on a ragged breath. "Reid, we'll be stripping off each other's clothes if we don't stop now. If you want to miss supper, we can retire early.

Let's go to bed, he imagined saying.

But her stomach growled in protest.

"You need to eat." He pressed a tender kiss on her forehead. "We'll be each other's dessert when we return home later."

The need to feed their addiction had them holding hands in the hackney cab. He must have drawn her fingers to his lips three times or more. He wondered if this was a male form of hysteria. Bedding his wife seemed like the only thing capable of calming his rampant spirit.

Antoine's inviting atmosphere did little to temper his need.

Candlelight cast a soft glow over the wooden walls and tables. The gentle murmur of couples in conversation added to the sense of intimacy. Heat from the fire warmed him, and the rich aroma of coffee and a hearty stew teased his growing appetite.

A waiter came to greet them—a slim man, light on his feet, who introduced himself as Francois. The faint beads of sweat on his brow belied his calm composure.

"Might we have a booth?" Reid gestured to a darkened corner of the room, where no one would notice a couple kissing across the table.

"But of course, monsieur."

"We mustn't forget to ask about Mrs Ludgrove," Sofia whispered as they followed the fellow to their table.

"Let's wait until we've ordered. The man might be more amenable then." He guided his wife into the booth and sat opposite. Upon noting they served a decent enough burgundy, he asked for a bottle and two glasses.

Sofia met his gaze and smiled. "Thank you for suggesting this. I've already had a lovely time, and we've not eaten yet."

The strange feeling rose inside him again, a tidal wave of emotion that left him somewhat giddy. "I enjoy your company. And after the stress today, it makes a change to sit and relax."

He wished they had no agenda. That he wasn't scanning the room, searching for men taking part in a stupid wager. That he could ease his suspicious mind and enjoy this simple pleasure.

They ordered from the basic bill of fare: onion soup and bread, beef stew and dumplings. Sofia spoke about her grandmother as they sipped their wine, absorbed in the intimate atmosphere.

"Having her dressing table means the world." Her smile revealed more than gratitude. The warmth in her eyes and voice had him reaching across the table, his fingers engulfing hers as he clasped her hand. "My grandmother always said people would judge me for my lack of experience. That I must strive to prove I'm capable."

He smiled. "It sounds like you inherited her indomitable spirit. Both my grandmothers died before I was born. Perhaps life would have been different had they survived."

Sofia looked at him like he was a prince amongst men. "My grandmother would have sung your praises. You hired a woman to work in your practice. You gave me a chance to prove I'm capable."

"You're more than capable. People are creatures of habit. You'll be a visible presence in the practice, and they'll soon come to trust your word."

Something deep and unnameable lingered in her gaze.

Something that warmed him for reasons he didn't quite understand.

He hoped she never stopped looking at him like that.

Their soup arrived, and he found himself absorbed by her: the way she laughed, the way the candlelight danced over her flawless skin, the way she popped a piece of bread into her mouth like it was a sin, and she hoped no one would notice.

Somehow, the conversation turned to Judith and betrayal.

"Is it wrong I'm glad Judith is dead?" she asked. "She made my life miserable, and I cannot rouse an ounce of sorrow."

The comment touched on his own dilemma. "It's natural under the circumstances. She ruined the illusion that your father was perfect. And it's normal to feel relieved, not sad when someone's hurt you."

Being intuitive, she focused on the remark that revealed more about him than her parent. "Learning about your father's mistress must have caused similar feelings for you."

He swallowed past the lump in his throat. "One letter shattered the illusion of a happy family. Like you, I have questions no one can answer."

They fell silent and ate.

"Did you ever find your father's mistress?" she said, and he almost choked on a slither of onion. "Perhaps she might shed light on his thoughts."

He felt heavy, like his blood had turned to lead. "I know nothing more than her Christian name. It would mean speaking to those who served with my father, and I cannot tarnish my mother's memory that way."

She nodded like she understood.

Strangely, it took nothing more than the brush of her leg against his beneath the table to chase the uncomfortable thoughts away.

Francois came to clear their dishes.

Reid stole the opportunity to discuss the wager. "I expected to see a handful of young aristocrats wooing older women to win a bet."

"It must be hard keeping track of the points," Sofia added.

The Frenchman shook his head. "They fill the tables on quiet nights. Profits have never been better."

"How do you know who's taking part in the bet?" Reid inquired.

"They hand me a token. A brass jeton with a clover design."

Sofia clutched her chest. "My heart goes out to those ladies looking for love and are oblivious to their machinations." She sighed. "A friend comes here to dine with a much younger gentleman every Wednesday. Now she's heard about the bet she doubts his motives."

"You might remember her." Reid described Mrs Ludgrove and what he knew of the insidious Mr Fellows. "Did he show you a token? Knowing the truth would help to ease her fears."

Francois didn't need to think. "*Oui*, monsieur. They ask for this table because it is away from prying eyes." He glanced behind before whispering, "The gentleman showed me his jeton, and I marked his card before he left. That was over a week ago. And the last time he came here."

Reid kept an impassive expression.

Inside, his blood boiled.

So, the villain was a man listed in the betting book at White's. It had to be Algernon. The motive was greed and jealousy. Algernon wanted Bretton Hall. And the only way to win their grandfather's favour was to discredit Reid.

Relief flooded through him.

He'd deal with Algernon tomorrow. There'd be no more deaths. No more sleepless nights spent imagining himself cramped in a cell at Newgate. And yet he couldn't imagine his foppish cousin slicing O'Connor's throat.

Sofia was quick to satisfy a query. "You said you marked

his card. I know they've been coming every Wednesday for a month. Did he dine with other older ladies?"

Francois chuckled. "A few. But this is just one place where they have their card marked. There are others. I know an attendant at the British Museum gives ten points if the player can steal a kiss near the bust of Rameses II."

"Then the men carry their cards with them?" she said.

"*Oui*, though the cards, they are numbered. The men involved in the wager, they remain anonymous." The sudden tinkle of the overhead bell caught the waiter's attention. He glanced at the door and gave another chuckle. "Here is one now. But the poor fellow, he lags behind the pack."

Curiosity piqued, Reid peered discreetly around the waiter before shooting back into the booth in shock. While Francois went to greet his customers, he could barely catch his breath.

"Don't look, but we know the man who's just entered." His heart pummelled his ribcage, anger rising again because he had been a bloody fool.

Sofia's eyes widened. "Who is it?"

He slid deeper into the shadows. "Hickman. He's here with one of our patients, Mrs Morris. It won't surprise you to learn she's fifty and takes a sleeping draught for her nerves."

Chapter Fifteen

Sofia wanted to look behind but daren't.

She had considered whether one of Reid's colleagues was responsible for the deaths of his patients. While returning a book to Mr Turner's room, she had rummaged in his desk drawers. She questioned the delivery boy and asked Mr Hickman to help measure the ingredients. Checking to see if his nervous disposition had caused the mistakes.

"Has Mr Hickman seen you?" She reached across the table and touched Reid's forearm, knowing nothing would ease his disappointment.

Betrayal didn't always deliver a sharp blow to the gut.

Sometimes it left an empty void where trust once lived.

"No." His handsome face crumpled into a snarl. "He's just slipped Francois his scorecard while Mrs Morris is shrugging out of her pelisse."

"Did you know he was taking part in the bet at White's?" It was a foolish question. Reid told her everything and would have mentioned it sooner. "Have you had suspicions before tonight?"

"No. None." Hurt dulled his blue eyes. "Hickman struggles to pour tea from the pot without shaking. Why would I suspect him of participating in a wager for libertines?"

The tightness in her chest had her scrambling to think of a way to ease his pain. But that would mean lying—something she could never do, not to him.

"Mr Hickman could have sent the tinctures. He has access to the dispensary and arranges other deliveries." She paused, recalling his remorse when he almost shut a patient's finger in the door. "Perhaps I'm naive, but he doesn't strike me as a man who would deliberately hurt anyone."

There was no hint of the cold, calculating look she'd seen in Victor's eyes. Although some wicked men pretended to be charming, and the victims discovered the truth too late.

"I should know better than to trust those close to me," he snapped.

Distrust was a vortex that sucked the happiness out of every experience.

"We should focus on finding proof Mr Hickman sent the tinctures. His red hair says he is not Mr Fellows. Though I'm beginning to wonder if Mr Fellows is only guilty of being a cad."

Reid leant forward. "Do you know what I think? Hickman stole the bottles and destroyed the dispensary to make it look like a crime scene. He wants things to return to how they were before you arrived. When he could hide in his office and I didn't force him to examine patients."

"Maybe you're right." A constable would draw the same conclusion. "And with fewer patients, you're unlikely to need his help."

"Precisely."

Doubt formed a knot in her gut. The uncomfortable

feeling forced her to address another issue. "What do you keep in the restricted room upstairs? Might Mr Hickman have picked the lock and discovered your secret?"

He dropped his voice to a whisper. "The room is like a shrine to the deceased. I've made a profile of every victim. I've put pins into a map of the metropolis, pointing to all patients who fit the criteria."

Her breath caught. "You must show me. If the magistrate decides to search your premises, it might look like a criminal's sanctum, not a logical way of hunting for clues."

Reid scrubbed his face with his hand and groaned. "You're right. God, this is a damn mess."

"No, it's not. Every day we learn something new."

"And yet we're still clueless." He grabbed his wine glass and knocked back the contents. "Look at him." He nodded in Mr Hickman's direction. "The man's hand is steadier than a ship's anchor. He hasn't trembled once while speaking to Mrs Morris."

"Perhaps he doesn't find her as terrifying."

"Now you're defending him."

"I'm not. I'm trying to help you discover the truth. And we're not clueless. Mr Daventry said these little insights are like breadcrumbs leading us to the culprit."

Surely they were reaching the end of the trail.

He sighed. "I suppose we know Fellows is taking part in the wager. Francois will give a statement to that effect. And Fellows is using an alias. The men who frequent White's don't work at Coutts."

"Exactly," she said in a positive tone. "He met Mrs Ludgrove here numerous times. It's possible he sent the laudanum to make her more amenable. When he realised the tincture was too potent, he decided to blame you."

"Then I'm just a convenient scapegoat."

"Indeed." She raised her glass, chinking it gently against his. "From what you told me about your grandfather's original plan for Bretton Hall, your cousin has a motive to discredit you. He purchased tinctures and is taking part in the bet."

"And he fits Mrs Ludgrove's description of Fellows."

"Which means Mr Hickman destroyed the dispensary for the reason you claimed. He's afraid and didn't know what else to do."

A watery smile touched his lips. "What do we do now?"

Sofia thought for a moment. "We say good evening to Mr Hickman and his companion. You take me home and show me what you keep in the restricted room. We make a plan for tomorrow. And you make love to me in the French bed you purchased from Ingrams."

He downed his drink and grinned. "We're not leaving until you've eaten your stew. If last night is any indication, we need our strength."

They remained hidden in the booth for another half an hour, eating and drinking wine. Reid watched his secretary, giving a running commentary every time Mr Hickman touched his companion's hand.

Reid paid Francois, leaving a little extra for the valuable information. As they made to leave, her husband couldn't wait to surprise Mr Hickman.

He wore an arrogant grin as he stopped beside their table. "Hickman? You never said you were dining at Antoine's tonight."

Mr Hickman jumped in the seat, sending his cutlery crashing to the floor. "Mr Gentry. I—I don't recall you saying you were dining out, either." With a sudden shaky hand, he gestured to the attractive older woman sitting opposite. "You k-know Mrs Morris, of course."

The lady smiled. She wasn't embarrassed about dining with a man twenty years her junior. "Mr Gentry. John tells me you're married. Please accept my felicitations."

John? The couple were on more than friendly terms.

Reid made the introductions.

Sofia's stomach flipped when he called her his wife.

"What wonderful news." Mrs Morris beamed. "There's always a vibrant energy in the air when one meets a couple so desperately in love."

Sofia couldn't argue. She felt like she was floating on a wave of euphoria whenever she was in Reid's company.

"Indeed," he said, his hot hand coming to rest on her back. "Well, we'll leave you in peace. Good night. Enjoy your supper."

They left Antoine's intent on hailing a hackney but had barely walked ten yards when Mr Hickman burst onto the street, panicked.

"Sir, I want you to know that I met Mrs Morris in a book-shop quite by chance. I assure you, I did not abuse my position or deliberately seek her out."

"Ballocks," Reid said, shocking the man. "I watched you give Francois your jeton and scorecard. Does Mrs Morris know you're using her to win a wager? And don't start trembling now. You've sat as rigid as an oak the last half an hour."

Mr Hickman struggled to form a reply. "I admit I was thinking of the wager when I invited her for coffee. But things are different now."

"Then why have the waiter mark your card?" Reid countered.

"I was afraid Francois would mention the wager and

knew if I gave him the card, he would know to keep the secret." Mr Hickman turned to Sofia, a pleading look in his green eyes. "I feel some affection for Mrs Morris. She'll never understand if she knows I've dined with other older ladies."

Sofia decided to hit him with the truth. "The men involved in the wager are betraying the ladies' trust. Honestly, I thought better of you. Mrs Morris will think you're a scoundrel when I suspect the opposite is true."

"Did you bring Mrs Ludgrove here?" Reid demanded to know.

"Good grief, no!"

"What about Mrs Beckman or Mrs Nelson? Did you send those women stronger tinctures hoping to subdue them?" He gave a mocking snort. "Admit, it would be a damn sight easier to kiss a woman if she were delirious."

"No!" Mr Hickman could barely catch his breath. He glanced back at Antoine's door. "I know nothing about the tinctures but I did bring Mrs Aspall here. I was desperate and needed more points on my card."

Reid turned on his heel, throwing his arms in the air and cursing Hickman. "You deceitful devil! I should haul you to the nearest police office."

"Perhaps you should explain why you joined the wager," Sofia said, trying to bring an element of calm to the situation. "Why would you think you had a hope of winning when pitched against libertines?"

"More importantly, where the hell did you get the thousand-pound stake? You've grumbled about the purchase of new boots for weeks."

Mr Hickman cupped his face in distress, hoping the problem would disappear. He shook his head, but Reid tapped his toe, determined to stand there until he received an answer.

Francois exited Antoine's and waved at them. "The lady says your food is getting cold, monsieur."

Mr Hickman raised his head. "I'll be there in a moment."

Appeased, the waiter disappeared to relay the message.

With a weary sigh, Mr Hickman said, "You'll probably dismiss me when I tell you. But you were pressing me to accept a few patients and I can't bear the thought of …" He screwed his eyes shut.

"What have you done, Mr Hickman?" she said.

He struggled to look at Reid as he confessed. "Mr Algernon Gentry paid my stake in exchange for a list of patients who met the betting criteria. Mrs Beckman, Mrs Ludgrove and many other patients of a similar age were on the list I gave to your cousin."

A fire of hatred lit Reid's eyes. He looked like Lucifer poised to unleash his wrath and banish Mr Hickman to the pits of hell. "You gave Algernon confidential details?" he raged. "Names? Addresses? You betrayed my trust after I've done everything possible to accommodate you?"

Mr Hickman bowed his head in shame.

Oh, her heart was breaking.

For her husband, not Mr Hickman.

She supposed nothing hurt as much as his father's betrayal. But it must feel like the world was against him. If only Lord Rothley were here. He would know exactly what to say to lessen the blow.

"Why?" Reid pressed. "And don't tell me you hoped to win. You knew damn well you didn't stand a chance against the likes of Winslow. Tell me. I'll not stomach another one of your lies."

The man's cheeks flushed red. "It will sound foolish, but I wanted my uncle, Sir Phillip, to see my name in the book. If he thinks I keep company with favourable men, there's more chance of him funding a personal project."

"Favourable men?" Reid scoffed.

"How bizarre," she said, shaking her head at the snivelling secretary. "You work for a respectable man yet allied yourself with wastrels. I've a mind to inform your uncle you lack basic common sense."

Reid narrowed his gaze. "You're not a member of White's. Your application was black-balled."

Mr Hickman squirmed. "Lord Meyers owed your cousin a debt. I was permitted to take part."

Reid laughed. "No one owes Algernon a debt. Besides, I studied the betting book and your name is not listed."

"It must be." A shadow of mistrust clouded the man's eyes. "I received a card and a token. They were accepted at every named venue."

"Those keeping score don't know who's taking part. It seems I'm not the only one who's been betrayed."

Realisation dawned, and Mr Hickman started trembling.

Reid watched his employee, unaffected when the man began pleading for mercy. "I can tolerate mistakes but never disloyalty. Your actions could cost me my neck, let alone the practice. Turner will clear out your desk and return your belongings. I don't want to set eyes on you again."

Reid captured Sofia's hand, taking her with him as he strode down the street. He summoned a hackney, his loud whistle as abrupt as his curt directions.

Inside the cab, tension clawed at the enclosed space like a caged animal. She could try to soothe his pain, comb her fingers through his hair and convince him he would never have cause to doubt *her*.

And yet he would doubt her if he knew the truth.

She had misled him, too.

This marriage of convenience was not so convenient after all. This marriage was not based on friendship or ambition or necessity. This marriage was based on love.

Reid felt sick to the pit of his stomach.

When he wasn't battling nausea he felt like punching the roof of the cab until his knuckles bled. Downing a bottle of brandy might temper the fury in his veins. Making love to his wife might help him forget Hickman's treachery.

Yet he didn't want to use Sofia like that.

Resentment had no place in their relationship.

Every kiss was sublime. Every touch sacred. Something special happened when they focused on nothing but each other. He'd be damned if he'd let his devious secretary ruin something precious.

It took the fifteen-minute journey back to Leadenhall Street to calm his raging temper. Sofia was right. They had made progress tonight. But he had to tread carefully. Accusing Algernon of drugging the patients would start a family war. If it came to a battle, he suspected his grandfather would side with his son and heir, not the baseborn relative who'd disobeyed him.

Sofia sat quietly.

Perhaps she was just as stunned by Hickman's confession.

Perhaps she knew their troubles were far from over.

Indeed, fate decided to test Reid's mettle again tonight.

He recognised the elegant equipage parked opposite the practice, and knew the white-haired occupant peering through his monocle.

Reid helped his wife from the hackney and paid the jarvey. "Go inside, Sofia, while I speak to my grandfather. Wait in the hall with the door open where I can see you."

A memory surfaced, unbidden. He was just six years old when his grandfather arrived one bitter winter's night. Though his mother had hurried him into the drawing room, Reid had caught the sharp edge in his father's voice as he spoke.

You'll accept us as a family or not at all.

It seemed history might repeat itself.

Reid crossed the road and stood waiting for his grandfather to lower the carriage window. Those few strained seconds felt like forever.

"You've not been home," the lord said coldly, opening the door and beckoning Reid inside the vehicle. "And you weren't at the practice last night."

Reid remained on the street. "I stayed at Studland Park."

His grandfather's gaze flitted to Sofia. "With your herbalist?"

"With my wife."

The man paled, then uttered, "That's impossible."

"Why? Because you threatened the bishop?"

His grandfather dropped his monocle, leaving the eye glass dangling on its red string. "Can you blame me? You hardly know her and admitted to acting out of obligation. I was merely buying you time to consider other options." He grumbled to himself. "Your father was just as impetuous."

Tired of hearing his lies, Reid spoke openly. "You mention options, yet always consider your own ambitions first. You want me to marry into a noble family and are willing to force my hand."

How was that love?

His grandfather did not deny the accusations. "You're determined to set your sights low yet deserve better. If you chose a sensible lady from an upstanding family, I wouldn't need to interfere. I could rest peacefully in the grave."

"Because you hope guilt won't follow you to the afterlife?"

The lord puffed his chest. "I have no reason to feel guilty. I fixed your father's mistake. I suppose I should be grateful you wanted to marry this chit before impregnating her."

Bile rose to his throat. Had his grandfather made similar derogatory remarks about Reid's mother? "My wife's name is Sofia. And this discussion is over."

Reid turned on his heel but his grandfather cried, "Wait! I came to make peace not fuel the fire. Is Bretton Hall not an ideal place to raise a family?"

Reid whirled around. "Algernon said Bretton Hall is his now."

The old man mumbled. "You will always have first refusal. Take the position of estate manager and I shall ensure your son inherits the house. Your wife stands a better chance of being accepted if you reside in the country. You know how intolerant people are here."

He wondered if his grandfather could hear his own hypocrisy.

"It occurs to me you're the only one who finds me lacking." A mocking laugh escaped him. "You're not inviting me to reside at Bretton Hall as a gentleman and your grandson, but as your lackey. To you, I'll always be the baseborn son of a harlot."

"That's utter poppycock."

"Have you had this conversation with Algernon? He's a reprobate and a wastrel yet can do as he pleases."

Had Reid's father been a loyal man he might have had some admiration for him. He'd defied society and the patriarchy, and trampled over their expectations.

"Algernon will inherit a viscountcy," came the lord's excuse.

Yes, the rules were different for titled men.

"And that makes him deserving? No wonder my mother worked to help the downtrodden. The future depends upon educating good men, not useless toffs."

Reid marched away, knowing he'd taken the right path and had no plans to deviate.

"Just tell me you lied about marrying her," his grandfather cried.

Reid ignored him.

"Tell me my efforts weren't in vain," came his irate plea.

Reid met Sofia's gaze. She looked scared. Nervous.

He entered the practice, slammed the door shut behind him and captured his wife around the waist. "I doubt he'll bother us again."

Tears clung to her lashes, shimmering faintly in the darkness. "He sounded angry and so dreadfully disappointed."

"He's been bitter and resentful his entire life."

She eased out of his embrace. "I don't want you to choose between me and your family. I hoped your grandfather would mellow in time, but I doubt he will. Our marriage will always be a problem."

He felt a wave of alarm and sensed more than her physical retreat. "It may be a problem for him. It will never be a problem for me."

"You say that now but may come to regret your decision."

"I don't regret marrying you, Sofia."

"Relationships fail. Family bonds last a lifetime." A tear rolled down her cheek. "I don't have to stay in London. The countess still has a ticket for the packet ship to New York."

Her last comment chilled him to the bone.

"You're my family now." He cupped her cheeks and kissed her, a long, drugging kiss that made his world seem right again. "It was never a choice between you and him. He just refuses to accept he can't bend me to his will."

Her weak smile failed to reach her emerald eyes. "Don't make any rash decisions. When your problems are over, you may see things differently."

"You'll still be my wife." A fierce possession rose in his chest. She was his—for now and forever. He'd not break his vow.

"This love affair may lose its bloom. I would hate for you to sacrifice everything because you chose to help me."

He couldn't help but laugh. "Have you been paying attention to what happens when we're together? You're all I think about. You're all I want. I could spend the rest of my life between your soft thighs and die happy."

"What happens when lust loses its lustre?"

"It won't."

"Or you meet someone else you desire."

"I won't."

She dashed another tear away. "No one knows what the future holds."

Unsettled by her sudden vulnerability, he reached for her hand, driven by a need to prove her wrong. "I'll do everything I can to make our marriage work. You agreed to do the same." He threaded his fingers tightly with hers, forming an unbreakable bond. "It's been an exhausting day. Let's go to bed. We'll discuss this in the morning after a good night's rest."

She nodded.

In light of the recent robbery, he mentioned checking the downstairs rooms before retiring. "Come with me. I'm afraid to let you out of my sight."

They checked the dispensary and found everything in order. Turner's office was a mess, and Reid merely peered around the door. He checked his study, leading her inside to ensure his desk drawers were locked.

It was dark, so quiet, yet his heart raced when he caught the scent of her exotic perfume. The smell of iris and musk curled around his insides, stirring something raw and primal. A sensual hum escaped him.

Her earlier distress died on a chuckle. "Do you find something arousing about straightening papers and checking drawers, Mr Gentry?"

"The only arousing thing in here is you."

She held his gaze, desire a fire in her eyes as it roamed over his body. "Perhaps you were thinking about that night in your study when our desperate need for each other had us making love in our clothes."

"Or how badly I wanted to hike up your skirts in the apothecary's office."

"I'm not sure I remember," she said coyly, rounding the desk.

"You were reading the register," he purred, opening a ledger and beckoning her forward. "And I was studying the entries over your shoulder."

She squeezed between him and the desk and pretended to

read the ledger, his cock hardening when she hummed and said, "I remember there wasn't much room."

"Yes, it was tight." He leaned over her, pressing his erection against her buttocks. "And we had a devil of a time concentrating."

"We'd have had an extra inch if you'd removed my pelisse."

He reached around her, caressing her breasts while releasing the buttons. "Is that better?" He tossed the garment aside, cupped her throat and nuzzled her neck. God, he couldn't get enough of her.

A soft whimper escaped her. "Much better."

Lust formed a tightening knot deep in the pit of his stomach. "Can you feel how hard I am?" he drawled, grinding against her to ease the ache.

"Not as much as I would like. Skirts can be a dreadful inconvenience."

He took the bait, freeing himself before gathering her skirts to her waist, the fabric cascading like a waterfall over his arms. The first touch of his weeping crown to her bare buttocks tore a husky growl from his throat.

"Hell, everything about you is so damn divine. Part your legs for me, Sofia." He pushed through the gap between her thighs, his cock gliding through her slick folds. He didn't enter her, just teased her sex and drove them both mad with desire.

"Reid," she panted for the third time, her hands braced on his desk.

"I need to touch you. I need to taste you. I need to be inside you." He held her skirts, fisting the material in his hands. "But I want to look at you when I do. I love watching you come."

"I want to watch you, too, but I need you quickly first."

Eager to ease the tortuous agony, he entered her, pushing deep into her wet channel, loving how she stretched for him. Only him. Always him. "Hell, yes!"

Her mewl rang with satisfaction. "Oh."

"You were made for me, love." He slid in and out of her, his eyes rolling back in their sockets as she took every solid inch. "I'll never sit at this desk again without remembering how good you feel."

He thrust harder.

The pen fell off the inkstand.

A few papers flew onto the floor.

He had to touch her but struggled to hold her skirts aloft.

"I'm removing some of your clothes." In a frantic effort to undress her, he released her skirts to unfasten the hooks and eyes on her dress.

He withdrew so quickly she gave a disappointed moan.

"I'll be back where I belong in a moment," he promised her.

The sentiment was not lost on him.

There was nowhere else he would rather be.

He knew without question she was his home now.

With some urgency, he removed her dress and petticoat. "The rest can stay," he drawled, pushing her shift to her waist and lifting her to sit on his desk.

Her gaze lingered on his jutting manhood protruding through the fall of his trousers. "What a startling contradiction," she purred. "Such elegant tailoring paired with such raw masculinity."

He dropped his trousers and palmed his cock. "They're the clothes of an upstanding gentleman."

"In more ways than one."

"Lean back on your elbows. Let me see you."

She did as he asked, parting her legs. Her sultry smile said she knew her sex glistened, and that he wouldn't be able to resist sucking the swollen bud.

He was on her in a heartbeat.

Eating her. Licking. Drinking.

Tasting the sweetness that drove him wild.

Sofia came hard, her pants fast and shallow, her body shuddering violently against his mouth. "I—I need you."

Not as much as he needed her.

The compulsion to own every inch of her had him pushing inside her until he could push no more. "You're mine, Sofia." The words were a possessive growl. "Mine!"

Her warm body hugged him as he drove in and out of her.

They both moaned when he gripped her wrists and pumped so fast the desk shook. The hourglass rolled onto the rug. The papers beneath her bottom were crumpled, but he didn't give a damn.

One thought remained clear as he withdrew and his guttural groan rent the air as he spilled over Sofia's thigh.

He'd been so focused on earning a living, so fearful of making his parents' mistake, he'd neglected to make a life. He stared at his wife in awe. His future lay breathless on his desk, looking brighter and fuller than he'd ever dared to imagine.

Chapter Sixteen

"So, all evidence points to your cousin being responsible for drugging your patients." Mr Daventry rested his elbows on the desk, his hands clasped as he contemplated the information. "Doubtless he fed the ladies laudanum to make them amenable to his charms."

"We'll never get a confession," Reid said from the seat opposite. "Not when it means admitting to murder. The magistrate won't prosecute a viscount's grandson unless there's irrefutable proof of guilt."

"And your grandfather will find some other poor fellow to blame."

Doubt churned in Sofia's stomach. She had never met Algernon, but men who made wagers for a lark did not enter the stables of a coaching inn and murder a groom in cold blood.

"I'm convinced the assailant dragged Mrs Beckman downstairs," she said, recalling the bruising the coroner had dismissed. "They found the other ladies in their beds as if sleeping."

She learnt that much when Reid showed her his secret room this morning. A map of London covered one wall. There were piles of notes on the deceased: their daily habits, family members' names and addresses. They had studied the information before burning it in the grate.

"What makes Mrs Beckman's case different?" Mr Daventry mused.

"If Algernon is Mr Fellows, he was having intimate relations with at least one of the women, potentially while they were subdued." The scene in her mind bore an uncanny resemblance to her nightmares of Mr Harrop. "Mrs Beckman may have kept her wits and tried to fight him off."

"Then we cannot let these crimes go unpunished," Mr Daventry said fiercely, slapping his hand on the desk. "We need proof of guilt. I don't care if the culprit is a prince of Persia. He will pay for his sins."

Reid shifted in the seat beside her. "I suspect my grandfather would sooner lay the blame at my door than risk losing a future heir."

Sofia's heart crumpled.

Had her husband ever felt loved?

Did he think love came with strict conditions?

She wanted to jump into his lap and confess to caring, but he'd insisted they would never have to worry about fickle feelings. Life with him was beautiful. A dream come true.

She could not risk losing him. Yet she feared if she made the declaration, he would think their relationship was doomed, too.

"What about Hickman?" Mr Daventry said.

Reid sighed. "He's merely guilty of being a fool."

Was Mr Hickman a fool or a master manipulator? Did he have two faces? The lonely man plagued by nerves, and the confident man caught dining with a woman and taking part in a wicked wager?

Something Mr Turner said entered her mind.

Sometimes I wonder whether Hickman wants us to think he has an illness to hide his incompetence.

"Or Mr Hickman is extremely clever and knows how to deceive those closest to him." She had found him alone in the dispensary on numerous occasions. "It's possible he staged the robbery at the practice to throw us off the scent."

"I'll have a man watch Hickman for a few days." Mr Daventry made a note in his leather-bound book. "What's the situation with the Merricks?"

Sofia explained everything. "I wouldn't be surprised if Victor killed Judith just to claim the house. It might have been his plan all along."

Mr Daventry was not shocked to hear of her stepmother's death. "Did Judith have a will?"

"Victor says she did." She mentioned Judith had removed all the documents from the study while her father was bedbound. "My father never spoke about his money worries. Judith blamed his gambling, but Mr Chance could find no record of the debts."

Mr Daventry frowned. "But Judith did own the house?"

"I believe so, but she refused to name the solicitor dealing with the probate application or show me a copy of the will." They'd argued, and Judith had slapped her, accusing her of being rude and ungrateful. "All the solicitors I visited said they couldn't disclose confidential information."

Reid sat forward. "Why didn't you mention this sooner?"

"Because you had more serious matters to contend with."

"Have you checked the probate registry?"

"No." She felt foolish for ignoring the issue for so long. "The Merricks had me living in fear. Escaping was my priority."

"I'll have my probate lawyer conduct an investigation. He has friends in the Prerogative Court, which will save time." Mr Daventry beckoned her to the desk and offered her his steel-nib pen. "Record your father's details: full name, known address, occupation, place of birth and death." He turned his attention to Reid. "Are you happy if I send a man to St Albans to meet with the coroner?"

Reid hesitated. "I should be the one dealing with my wife's affairs. You've done enough, and I'm not even paying you."

Mr Daventry chuckled. "I expect free medical care for life. Besides, you're both needed elsewhere. The workers at the Hare and Hounds claim they know nothing and saw nothing. They distrust the local justice of the peace, yet you might persuade them to trust you."

"Did your man speak to Doyle?"

"No one has seen Doyle since the murder. He didn't return to his lodging house. I sent an agent to his mother's home in Reigate. Finding him would be a blessing."

"His disappearance is more than suspicious," Reid said.

"Yes. Either Doyle killed O'Connor, or he knows who did."

The Hare and Hounds
Barking Road, London

They waited until eight o'clock that evening before visiting the coaching inn. They spent the short journey devising a plan and kissing until they could barely breathe.

Now they'd arrived, Reid was preoccupied with her safety. "Remain in the carriage while I question the ostlers. Nokes will ensure you come to no harm."

"What about you?" Panic rose like bile in her throat. Whoever murdered O'Connor would kill again to avoid detection. "These men believe you're one of them. What if they've discovered your real identity and feel betrayed?"

"I can protect myself. The men know I have an alibi. They understand injustice, and I suspect they will be a damn sight more helpful than my grandfather."

She shuffled to the edge of the seat and gripped the door handle. "I'm coming with you. It's safer for both of us if we remain together."

He sighed, accepting defeat, and alighted.

"Stay close," he said, handing her down.

She stumbled, and he caught her, wrapping his arms around her waist and holding her tight to his hard body.

Their gazes locked.

Their breath mingled in the cool night air.

Unspoken words passed between them.

I love you danced in her heart and mind.

Nearly tumbled from her lips.

They kissed, a slow carnal mating, their tongues sliding

together like sweat-soaked limbs. Lust tugged low and deep. The yearning in her heart and soul was just as profound.

He pressed himself into her. She couldn't feel the solid ridge of his arousal through her skirts, but his grinding hips were a silent confession.

Let it always be like this, she thought.

She wished she knew the secret formula for a life filled with love. This man made her drunk, and she hoped she never spent a day sober.

"Minx," he uttered, breaking contact.

"You kissed me first."

"Because you did that thing with your mouth, and I couldn't help myself." He released her and adjusted himself in his trousers.

"Thing?"

"That coy quirk that says you want to do more than kiss."

She hit him with the coy quirk now. "Should I stop?"

He captured her chin. "Never stop."

Heavens! The potent force swirled around them again.

The undeniable energy that defied words.

Did he feel it, too?

She laid her hand on his chest. "Reid, if we don't move from here, we'll spend the night frolicking in the carriage. We need to find Mr Doyle."

"I'll be glad when this wicked business is over."

"So will I," she said, though feared what would happen when he no longer needed to play her protector—when she wasn't helping him find clues and chase villains.

They gathered their wits and strode to the stables. The woods behind had an eerie presence, like the dark verdure hid a wealth of evil secrets.

Reid entered a stall where an ostler, an older man with

lank white hair, was brushing down a chestnut mare. "I'm looking for Jack. He usually works in this row of stalls."

The fellow barely glanced Reid's way, though his manner suggested a wariness of strangers. "He's working at The Wild Pigeon in Upminster. Do you have a horse what needs tending?"

"No. What about George Trainer?"

"At the Pigeon, too." The ostler straightened, rubbing his aching back. "No one wants to work here, what with the recent murder. Davey stayed. He's nipped into the inn for a bite of supper."

Reid thanked the man.

"Everyone's afraid the mad doctor might return." The ostler brushed the horse again, smoothing its sleek fur. "They're scared he's lingering in the woods, waiting to take a knife to their throats. One mistake and they might lynch the wrong man."

The comments were a warning to tread carefully. Indeed, Sofia felt a tightening of trepidation as they approached the inn.

All eyes were upon them when they entered the taproom. Conversation died. People froze, tankards half-raised, and stared. The silence stretched until it was painful.

Reid nodded to people he knew.

No one returned the friendly gesture.

The innkeeper rounded the oak counter and approached them, keeping his voice low as he said, "Best make yourself scarce. We heard you're the doctor whose wife was friends with O'Connor." He glanced at Sofia like she was the scarlet woman. "They think you've done away with Doyle, too, and those fancy friends of yours have helped you get away with murder."

"None of that is true," Sofia whispered.

Reid looked the innkeeper in the eye. "I'm innocent of all charges, but if you spare me five minutes, I'll explain everything."

The innkeeper scoffed. "If you don't go now, this lot will beat you senseless and leave your body to rot in the woods."

Amid the tense atmosphere, Sofia noticed half the tables were empty. "Surely you want to help us find the real culprit. You'll be driven out of business when people discover the villain stayed here."

"A witness claims she shared a room with him last week," Reid added. "He tried to kill her with an overdose of laudanum."

"If he drugged the witness upstairs," she began, slightly manipulating the facts, "what's to say he won't poison your punters and blame you?"

Long seconds passed.

The innkeeper scratched his head. He looked at his customers' nervous faces and mumbled, "You'd better not be lying. Don't make me regret trusting you." Then he put his arm around Reid's shoulder and called to the serving wench, Annie, to bring tankards of ale to the table.

They were ushered to the shadowy part of the taproom, where she and Reid had shared their first kiss. So much had happened since then.

They had married.

She had fallen in love.

"You'd better begin by explaining why a man with your connections keeps company with thieves and poachers."

Reid told him everything. "I spent weeks watching the people in the taproom, hoping to catch him. He's elusive but made the mistake of targeting my patients. It's how I knew he'd brought Mrs Ludgrove here."

"Then why kill O'Connor?"

"He must have seen something incriminating."

With a quick check over his shoulder, the innkeeper said, "I never mentioned this to the constable, but O'Connor seemed mighty pleased with himself. He bragged about winning some money at a bare-knuckle brawl in Romford. Yet he couldn't remember the fighters' names or the winning odds."

Reid straightened. "Perhaps he was blackmailing the killer?"

"Something was amiss. The braggart acted like he'd stumbled on a casket of pirate gold and could do as he pleased."

The wench came with their ale.

Her hand shook as she placed their drinks on the table.

"We need you to make a statement, sir." Sofia noticed Annie watching them while pretending to clean the counter. "We heard Mr Doyle and Mr O'Connor argued over Annie."

The innkeeper laughed. "They argued about a lot of women, but Doyle has a special place in his heart for Annie. He didn't want O'Connor hurting her."

"We need to find Doyle," Reid said urgently.

"Most people reckon you killed him."

"But you know that's a lie."

He leaned forward, dropping his voice to a whisper. "Wherever Doyle is, I'd say he's afraid the magistrate will string him up for a crime he didn't commit."

"Or a crime he may have committed," Sofia dared to say. "We won't know for sure until we find him. Let's pray it's before the authorities do."

The innkeeper's shoulders drooped as he exhaled. "Listen, I want this mess cleared up, too. I can't say for sure, but Annie feels responsible for what happened. It ain't her fault. Still, I've heard her sneaking from her attic room at night."

Sofia shifted closer. "You think she's visiting Mr Doyle?"

"A loaf of bread and a chunk of cheese disappeared yesterday. Maybe if you hang around here long enough, she might lead you to him." The innkeeper suddenly grabbed Reid's forearm and narrowed his beady eyes. "They'd better not find Doyle dead. If they do, I'll tell them about this conversation."

"We want the truth, nothing more."

While they had the innkeeper's attention, Sofia asked another pertinent question. "You must have seen the gentleman who stayed in Mrs Ludgrove's room last week. They visited the fair in Upminster and dined here."

"I ain't got eyes in the back of my head. The taproom was teaming with revellers. People come from as far afield as Colchester to visit the fair. They were crammed in here like sheep in a pen."

"Think," Reid pressed. "Mrs Ludgrove's companion was young enough to be her son. It must have drawn attention if they were sharing a room."

The innkeeper tilted his head and stared at a point on the beamed ceiling. "I glimpsed him on the stairs. Brown hair. A fit-looking fellow. He was confident and wore fancy Hessians. I ain't never seen a pair with two gold tassels per boot."

While Sofia was grateful for the snippet of information, Reid sat bolt upright. "Two tassels? You're certain?"

"As certain as I can be."

She didn't have a chance to ask why it was relevant until they'd finished their ale and returned to the carriage.

"I know only one man vain enough to add an extra tassel to his boots," Reid said, muttering a curse. "Algernon insists his bootmaker adds two to every pair made."

Her breath caught. "So Algernon is Mr Fellows."

Reid nodded. "We need a witness to identify him but yes. In choosing his victims wisely, he's been able to frame me for murder and be in the running to win the damn wager. Not to mention, fulfil his desire to own Bretton Hall."

"Why does he dislike you?"

"I'm not sure he does. He's always craved approval. To do that, he has to discredit me in our grandfather's eyes."

Mr Daventry said they needed solid proof. Accusing a man based on his fancy boots and the desire to win a wager wasn't enough to secure an arrest.

"I prayed Algernon wasn't the killer." She knew there was no hope of him facing a trial. "Your grandfather will ensure he escapes justice."

"Another crook will pay for my cousin's crimes," Reid agreed, his voice laced with resentment.

"I hoped you could put your troubles behind you, not live in fear of the culprit striking again."

He sagged back in the leather seat, dragging his hands through his hair. "I'm so tired of this cat-and-mouse game. A man can only take so much. Perhaps we should both board a boat to Madras and leave this sorry business behind us."

"Madras?" How would this marriage of convenience work if they were far from home, far from their friends and the people who cared? "What would we do there?"

"The same as we do here?"

"You'd work as a doctor and surgeon, and I'd assist you?"

He shrugged. "Why not? At night, we'd lie naked in bed, a tangle of limbs beneath a single white sheet, the smell of blossom carried on the breeze, the silk curtains dancing languidly at the open window."

"You paint an idyllic picture." More so because he envisioned them together, not sleeping in separate rooms. "But what about those you care about? I fear the Marquess of Rothley would never recover if you abandoned him, too."

Sofia imagined the marquess ambling alone through his regal gardens at night, lost in his sad memories. Would he stop to touch the rosebuds, confused how such beauty thrived in an ugly world? Beneath the moon perched high in the heavens, would he stare at the sky and beg the Lord to end his misery?

"Lord Rothley's strength is a shield," she said. "It can only take so many hits before it splits in two. You have a life here. One you need to reclaim."

He released a long breath. "You're right. Though the idea of spiriting you away on an exotic adventure has some appeal."

Why? she wanted to say but suddenly noticed a cloaked figure skulking through the yard, creeping closer to the carriage.

"Reid. Someone's coming."

His eyes darted to hers, following her gaze into the darkness, before narrowing on the shadowy figure. He crossed the carriage to shield her, whipping a blade from his boot.

Concealed within the hooded depths of her cloak, Annie cupped her hands around her face, pressing close to the windowpane. She peered inside and mouthed for Reid to open the door.

"I ain't got long." Annie glanced behind as if the trees

had ears. "But Doyle made me promise to give you a message if you returned to the inn."

Reid slipped the blade back into his boot and sat forward. "Doyle? Do you know where he's hiding? Take us there. We mean him no harm. We seek nothing but the truth."

"He left for the coast this morning," Annie said, a tremble in her voice. "His cousin owns a fishing trawler near Margate. It's safer on the high seas than it is hiding out here. I'm to send word to a local inn once the cove who killed O'Connor is behind bars."

"Only guilty men run," Reid growled in frustration.

"That ain't true. He don't trust no one." She glanced around the dark yard again. "Doyle was the last person to see O'Connor alive. The local justice is looking for an excuse to stretch his neck." She reached into the pocket of her apron. "I was told to give you this."

With a shaky hand, she gave Reid a card the size of a bible.

He scanned the card, his brows rising. "This scorecard is for the bet at White's. How did you get it?"

He studied it and then handed it to Sofia.

The scorecard was a simple grid: rows marked by dates and columns with initials. Each box contained a tally, a neat recording of the person's progress.

"ANT must be short for Antoine's," she said, noting the number twenty printed in the top left corner. "B.M. the British Museum."

"I suspect H.H. is the Hare and Hounds."

"For a shilling, I mark the gentlemen's cards and copy the score into the book I was given to make sure there's no cheating," Annie confirmed. "They've been bringing ladies here for months, wooing them to get points. A kiss on the hand is worth five points. A room together for the night is worth twenty."

"Who does the card belong to?" Sofia said.

Whoever it was had too many points to count.

Annie shook her head. "I'm glad I don't know his name. He's down in the guest register as Mr Jones, but that's a lie. He was pretending to be her husband."

Yes, Mrs Ludgrove had used the alias Mrs Jones.

"O'Connor was snooping through the dining room window—he's always looking for female company—and saw the devil adding something to his wife's wine."

"Laudanum," Reid stated.

"Must be. He had her up in the room half an hour later. O'Connor held the fellow to ransom. He wanted ten pounds, or he'd tell the woman she'd been drugged. He told Doyle the next day."

Reid gave an exasperated huff. "Why the devil didn't Doyle tell me? When I asked if he'd seen anything, he said no."

"O'Connor made him swear to keep the secret. They argued because the man paid with a ruby brooch and pearl earrings. O'Connor asked Doyle to sell them, but he refused, worried someone would trace them back here."

So the men weren't arguing over bedding Annie.

Annie started fidgeting, her breath growing short and shallow. "I must get back before I'm missed. I'm happy to speak to a constable once that beast is in gaol."

It was clear Mr Doyle ran because he feared he would be the next victim, but they needed a way to identify the felon.

"Where did you get the scorecard?" Sofia asked.

"Doyle found it near the body." Annie shuffled back. "He

saw the cove thrust the doctor's card in O'Connor's hand and race off into the woods."

Sensing Annie's retreat, Reid said, "Is that all Doyle remembered? Did he confirm it was this Mr Jones who killed O'Connor?"

Annie nodded. "He said to tell you the killer is a wealthy London gent, about thirty. He wore all black except for the extra gold tassels on his shiny boots."

Chapter Seventeen

Reid usually woke at dawn with a long list of the day's appointments running through his head. He usually whipped back the bedsheets, the chill air getting his blood pumping, jolting him into action.

His blood was pumping fast this morning, but he was nestled between his wife's silken thighs, holding her hands above her head as he filled her to the hilt.

"Reid," she gasped, his name a throaty moan on her lips.

God, he loved hearing her needy pants.

He loved the way an innocent kiss set them both ablaze. That she desired him with a passion that defied logic, too. He loved that her hair was a tangled mess on the pillow. That she was happy in her own skin and nothing mattered more than sharing these intimate moments.

He loved the arousing mix of fire and tenderness in her eyes. He loved … He loved her.

He stilled mid-stroke, questioning the thought, though the feeling lived in his heart, not his head. It ran through his veins, challenging his rigid beliefs.

She held his gaze. "What's wrong? Did you remember something important about the case?"

He laughed, his cock jerking inside her. "The case? You're all I think about when we're alone like this."

His days began and ended with her.

He'd seen this level of devotion before: a kiss that lingered, the rush to dress after spending too long in bed. That grand love affair had ended tragically. He couldn't bear the thought that might be their future, too.

He bent his head and kissed her madly, lust a drug that had him hot and hard and throbbing, eager to climax after making her come twice already.

Lust failed to suppress the sudden wave of emotion every time he drove into her. It didn't stop fear creeping into his heart when he considered what he could lose. Or how the hell he would tell his wife he'd fallen in love with her when he'd promised her a life without complications.

He released her hands, knowing she couldn't resist the urge to touch him, and every caress would distract his mind. The minx rocked with him, her fingers digging into his back, then his buttocks, her tight pink nipples grazing his chest.

He withdrew quickly, spilling himself over her abdomen as they'd agreed, neither wanting to raise a child in a convenient marriage.

"I'll fetch a cloth." The power of her gaze burned him as he strode naked to the washstand. He didn't want to fool himself into thinking he'd seen something tender in her intelligent green eyes. "Prepare yourself. The water is cold."

A giggle followed her shocked gasp as he wiped the evidence of their lovemaking. He considered crawling into bed beside her and shutting the world out but had patients to see this morning. And Turner would want to know why Hickman had missed work two days in a row.

They were dressed, had eaten boiled eggs and toast, and were in the dispensary when Turner arrived. As expected, he noted Hickman's absence and came looking for answers.

Sofia smiled. "Good morning, Mr Turner. There's coffee in the pot and toast in the rack if you'd like some."

Turner thanked her. "I can help myself."

She made an excuse about looking out for the delivery boy and left them alone.

The rising ache of betrayal returned when Reid mentioned his secretary's name. "I need you to clear Hickman's desk and have his things sent to him in Stanhope Street. We have a vacancy for a secretary. You may know someone who's interested in the position. I welcome any suggestions."

Stunned and confused, Turner said, "Why? Is he struggling to cope?"

With a heavy heart, Reid explained the encounter outside Antoine's. "Your father always said Hickman was a liability. I'm sure he said the same to you."

"No. Father spent more time testing my knowledge than discussing personal matters." Turner's sigh seemed to carry the weight of the world. "Even though I dine alone now, I still find myself reciting the method for tying a tourniquet without risking gangrene."

Reid felt the sour sting of regret. He had neglected Turner while trying to ease his own suffering.

"Like your father, you've always been hardworking and dependable. I've left you to cope here while busy with personal affairs." He gripped Turner's shoulder in a gesture of brotherly affection. "I'm sorry for taking you for granted."

Turner nodded and smiled like all was forgiven.

"I just wish you'd confided in me about Miss Moorland's predicament. I would have been happy to help." Turner glanced at the dispensary door before dropping his voice. "Your view of romantic relationships is hardly a secret. I just hope you don't live to regret your decision. Especially in light of your grandfather's disapproval."

The comment roused Reid's ire.

He didn't want or need Turner's opinion on his marriage.

But he wasn't cruel or unfeeling and so said, "Sofia is my priority now. I'll do everything in my power to honour my vows."

"Of course. You always rise to a challenge."

They moved to the topic of Hickman's replacement. Turner suggested employing someone young, preferably a doctor who had trained at Guy's. "They're eager to learn and modern in their thinking, and we need someone who can do more than shuffle papers."

"Agreed." Reid had been too lenient with Hickman and felt like a damn fool. He was grateful he had one dependable employee. "Perhaps we could discuss it over supper tonight and a long soak in a mineral bath at Porretta's."

Every muscle in his body ached. And once he'd visited Algernon this afternoon, he would need to ease his mind and calm his temper.

Turner's first thought was Sofia. "Leaving Mrs Gentry here alone would be unwise. What if the robber returns?"

Cursed saints!

Reid wasn't an imbecile.

Sofia would always be his first thought, too.

"We were invited to a recital at The Burnished Jade tonight. Mrs Gentry will spend an evening with friends, and we'll put the world to rights at Porretta's." It was Sofia's idea.

Turner nodded. "It will be good to get back to normality. We could dine at the Adelphi."

"I prefer the Clarendon. It's closer to the bathhouse." At the Clarendon, Reid wouldn't spend the entire evening imagining making love to Sofia upstairs.

It was four o'clock that afternoon when Reid dropped Sofia at The Burnished Jade, kissed her and promised to return for her at ten that evening—once he'd smoothed things over with Turner.

First, he had to tackle his cousin Algernon.

Indeed, he sat outside his Uncle Edmund's house in Portman Street, glancing at the elegant facade, wishing he could tie a noose around his cousin's neck and hang him from the wrought-iron balcony. Instead, he would present the facts and inform Algernon he'd been seen murdering a man at the Hare and Hounds on the Barking Road.

"The evidence against Algernon is mounting," Daventry had said when they visited him earlier that day. "Show him the scorecard. Tell him there's more than one eyewitness. Let's see what he does next."

Doyle, Francois and Mrs Ludgrove could identify him. The French waiter agreed to meet with an artist to sketch the villain's likeness.

Reid alighted and knocked on the door.

A tense blend of anger and unease churned inside him. Knowing he might face his uncle only magnified his discomfort.

"Mr Gentry?" The ageing butler stumbled in shock as their gazes met. "Good day, sir. This is a welcome surprise."

"Hello, Redfern. Am I permitted to cross the threshold?"

As a young man, Reid had spent countless hours at his uncle's house. That changed when he came of age. Their relationship had been in a slow yet steady decline ever since.

"Of course, sir." Redfern stepped back and welcomed him into the grand hall. "Might I take your hat, sir?"

Reid removed his beaver and straightened his hair. "Keep it close. I doubt I'll be longer than five minutes. That's assuming my cousin agrees to see me."

Redfern inclined his head. "I shall enquire on your behalf, sir."

The butler entered Uncle Edmund's study, hushed whispers preceding his return. "Your uncle is home and asks that you join him for coffee or brandy, sir."

Despite a gnawing reluctance, Reid agreed. "If I'm to tolerate my uncle, I'll have brandy."

Edmund Gentry did not rise from the chair behind his imposing desk. He stared at Reid over steepled fingers and echoed the butler's sentiment. "Well, this is a surprise."

The sting of grief stole Reid's breath. With a swathe of brown hair and piercing blue eyes, Edmund bore such a striking resemblance to Reid's father it was like looking at a ghost.

"I'm not here to bring glad tidings."

"No, I don't expect you are."

Redfern entered, carrying two glasses of brandy on a salver.

Edmund motioned for him to set their refreshments on the desk, adding a curt instruction to close the door behind him. "Your father and I used to steal brandy from the decanter as boys and replace it with cold tea."

Reid sat in the chair opposite his uncle, grateful for the

solid mahogany barrier between them. "I imagine it wasn't long before Grandfather found out."

"He knew before we'd taken the first sip but enjoyed playing us off against each other. Keen to test which one of us had the looser tongue."

"Who did?"

Edmund laughed. "Me, of course. Your father had nerves of steel."

Anger flared at the compliment. "My father's loyalty was brittle where his courage was strong."

Edmund found his response amusing. "Yet the opposite might be said of you. One wonders why you live with an old man and not in the house your father bequeathed you."

Reid snatched the crystal glass and knocked back the brandy. "I've seen the damage disloyalty can do." In living with his grandfather, he'd hoped to prove he was not as faithless as his father. "But you're mistaken. I'm currently living above the practice with my wife."

Absorbing the news, Edmund sat bolt upright, intrigue alight in his sharp eyes. "In that pokey room? How interesting."

"I'm yet to give the tenants in Jermyn Street notice."

"When the devil did you marry?"

"Three days ago, in the chapel at Studland Park."

Edmund covered his mouth with his hand and laughed. "No wonder you're here. The pieces are falling into place. If your wife is happy to live above the practice, she's not a peer's daughter."

"Sofia is my herbalist."

Edmund threw himself back in the chair and raised his hands in mock surrender. "Then accept my humble apology. You have your father's gumption after all."

"What is that supposed to mean?"

"It means you've finally opened your eyes and defied your gaoler. I suspect the viscount"—disdain dripped from the last word—"is baffled. He thought he had you chained securely in your cell."

Edmund is bitter because I favour you over Algernon.

His grandfather's remark sprang to mind.

Your uncle was jealous of your father and he's jealous of you.

"Grandfather is not my gaoler." Yet he heard an echo of doubt in his own protest. "I studied medicine when he demanded I study land management. We battled for months when I left Cambridge."

"That's how conditional love works. You think you won the war, but it's all part of a master plan to control you."

Edmund is so resentful he makes up stories in his head.

"Perhaps you're delusional. We've barely spoken these last five years, and now you're lecturing me on naivety."

Yet what if his life was an illusion?

One created by a master of deception.

Edmund must have read his mind. "That's the mark of a skilled captor. The victims are clueless until they try to escape. I imagine he said vile things and made you believe I despise you."

"He said you were jealous of my father."

Edmund tossed back his brandy and grinned. "Damn right. He chose his bride and lived his own life while I was bound by the ropes of primogeniture." Edmund opened his desk drawer with the key tucked inside his waistcoat pocket. He withdrew a small stack of letters bound with black ribbon and tossed them to Reid. "But I always loved and admired my brother. We were in constant contact until the day he died."

Reid stared at the letters, confused. "But you made it clear I wasn't welcome here."

"Yes, to save all our necks. I needed *him* to think I believed the vile things he'd said about you."

Bile bubbled in Reid's stomach. "Vile things?"

"That you're as conniving as your father. You don't really care about medicine because your goal is to claim the viscountcy when he's dead. He told me to send Algernon away. Why do you think he's been on his third Grand Tour? I was told you could kill a man with a potion, and no one would know it was you."

Reid shrank in the chair in disbelief.

Deep down he knew it was true.

He'd never earned his grandfather's approval.

"That's why he persuaded you to care for him at the house. So he could keep a watchful eye on you." Edmund pushed the letters closer to Reid. "Keep them. I've been waiting for you to see the light. But we must tread carefully and ensure every move is tactical."

Reid shifted in the leather seat. His vision blurred. The solid world he'd embraced after losing his parents was a lie. He'd been living in a quagmire. Every step potentially treacherous.

"I suppose he's angry you didn't take a bride of his choosing," Edmund said.

"I followed in my father's footsteps and married a commoner. They're my grandfather's words, not mine."

"There was nothing common about your mother," Edmund snapped. "Few people possess a heart so pure. It's why your father loved her. He loved her until his dying day."

The remark took the wind out of Reid's sails.

"Of course, that was inconvenient," Edmund continued.

"Inconvenient?"

"It's all in the letters. Whatever you do, don't let *him* know you've read them. Now you've married beneath you—my father's words, not mine—you no longer serve a purpose."

Reid sat in stupefied silence.

He wished Sofia were here.

The mere touch of her hand, the light brush of her lips over his, made everything right.

"Redfern said you came to see Algernon. Are you the cause of his cut lip?"

"He said something vile about my mother."

Edmund paled. He sat straight, concern marring his countenance. "The viscount is using Bretton Hall to get Algernon to do his bidding. You must see beyond what seems obvious."

Uncertainty gripped him.

He didn't know who or what to believe anymore.

He reached for the stack of letters, sliding the top one from the pile. It was dated a month before his father died. The tone was friendly, yet fearful for the future. His father signed the letter by asking Edmund to watch over his family.

"Thank you for these." Reid tucked them away in his pocket. "My mother burnt all my father's letters when she learnt he had a mistress."

Edmund arched a brow. "Did he have a mistress? Or was it part of an evil man's plan to gain control of a young boy?" He didn't give Reid time to absorb the veiled accusation. "Whatever your gripe with Algernon, it's based on lies."

Reid shook himself and tried to focus on the real reason he'd come. "I need to see Algernon's scorecard for the wager he's taking part in at White's. Someone is attempting to frame me for murder. All evidence points to my cousin."

Edmund's calm demeanour vanished as he shot out of the chair. "The boy is a hare-brained fool, but he's not a murderer. Good God! Surely you know that. The viscount has gone too far this time." He yelled for Redfern but remained frozen in outrage as he awaited the butler. "Have Algernon join us in the study. Tell him to bring his scorecard for that stupid wager at White's."

Redfern left.

A clawing silence ensued.

"What other evidence is there?" Edmund barked.

"Witnesses described him and his double-tasselled boots. He bought laudanum from the same apothecary used to drug and kill my patients. All widows in their fifties being used by selfish men trying to win a bet. He killed the man who saw him drug one patient and left my calling card at the scene."

Edmund stumbled and fell into the chair. "He wants you to inherit the viscountcy. He wants you running Chatham Park. Is your wife with child?"

His uncle was rambling.

"No." Panic tightened Reid's throat. A few months ago, he might have accused his uncle of being dramatic. Now he knew better.

Algernon entered, his brown hair unkempt, his trousers creased like he'd been sleeping in a chair. He looked at Reid and staggered back. "What the devil do you want?"

"Where's your scorecard?" Edmund cried.

"Upstairs."

"Fetch it!"

Algernon returned with the tatty card in his hand.

"Give it to Reid."

"But—"

"Give it to him!"

Algernon gave Reid his dog-eared card. The number twenty was printed in the corner, and the boxes were filled with tally marks.

"Well?" Edmund said, impatient for answers.

Reid produced the card Doyle had found. "The murderer dropped this at the scene."

"Murderer?" Algernon winced as he glanced at the card. "That isn't a genuine scorecard. Mine is number twenty. If you lose your card, you forfeit your place."

Reid huffed in annoyance. "Are you saying it's a coincidence?"

"I'm saying someone made that to frame me for murder."

"I'm the one being framed," he countered. "You bribed my secretary to give you the names of patients in their fifties. You conned him into thinking he was taking part in the bet."

Algernon glanced at his father, his cheeks flaming. "I wanted to win the wager but was short of ladies to charm."

"You lackwit," his father grumbled.

"Four of the women you wooed died of a laudanum overdose. Laudanum purchased from Wiggins in Long Acre. The apothecary said you bought the tinctures. Apparently, for a disease you caught in Athens."

"You caught a disease in Athens?" Edmund snapped.

"No." Algernon gulped. "I purchased the tinctures to help me sleep."

"Or to subdue women so you could earn more points for the *bloody* wager," Reid cried. "You were seen pouring laudanum into Mrs Ludgrove's wine at the Hare and Hounds. You conned the woman and told her your name was Mr Fellows and you work at Coutts."

Beads of sweat formed on Algernon's brow. "What? No! That wasn't me. Mrs Ludgrove refused my offer of dinner."

Reid pressed harder, knowing it wouldn't take much to make the fop crack. "You stole Mrs Ludgrove's ruby brooch and pearl earrings."

Again, Algernon looked at his father and whimpered. "It wasn't me. Can't you see what he's doing? He wants Bretton Hall and will see me hanged to achieve his goal."

The devil's own fury rose in Reid's chest. "The groom was found murdered. Witnesses described the killer as young with an athletic build and wearing double-tasselled Hessians."

Edmund swore in disbelief.

That's when Algernon crumpled to his knees and sobbed like a babe, repeating over and over, "It wasn't me. I swear I didn't kill anyone. It wasn't me."

Chapter Eighteen

The Burnished Jade
Aldgate Street, London

"Must we suffer these pleasantries much longer?" Lord Rothley whispered to his friend Mr Dalton, seated to his right in The Jade's splendid music room. "I'd rather scour the ten-year accounts looking for a missing penny."

Occupying the chair to his left, Sofia gently nudged the marquess. "Miss Crane has spent a week gathering the courage to sing tonight. Be respectful. Pay her the courtesy of listening."

He inclined his head. "Forgive me. Sentiment brings out the worst in me."

Miss Crane clasped her shaking hands together and sang *Home, Sweet Home* as the Countess of Berridge watched with pride. She received an encouraging round of applause and left the floor, grinning from ear to ear.

The song's lyrics echoed in Sofia's mind.

Home! Home! Sweet, sweet home!

She didn't care where she lived. Her home was with Reid. Be it a cramped room above the practice or a grand town-house in Jermyn Street.

She turned to the marquess, keen to know how long she must suffer her husband's absence. "Do you have the time, my lord?"

He held her gaze like he sensed her disquiet. "That's the second time you've asked in as many minutes. Gentry *is* dining with Turner tonight?" Suspicion and a frisson of fear rang in every syllable. "Tell me he's not on a wild crusade to find the nefarious Mr Fellows."

"Be assured. He is meeting Mr Turner for supper at seven."

"I sense a but, madam."

She hesitated. "Reid wanted to visit his cousin first. Mr Daventry said he should ask to see the scorecard and mention the witnesses. Despite my protests, Reid insisted on going alone. Men rarely talk freely in a woman's presence, and he wants Algernon to admit he drugged Mrs Ludgrove."

The marquess relaxed his tight expression. "Algernon breaks ladies' hearts for sport. He's a wastrel with a brain the size of a pea, but he's not a murderer."

Sofia quickly told him about their encounter with Annie at the Hare and Hounds. The marquess had to keep his opinion to himself for a few minutes while Miss Becker played Handel's *Largo* on the pianoforte.

"Many men favour the double tassel," he said as soon as the applause died. He pulled his watch from his pocket and checked the time. "Good Lord. Is it only six o'clock? I feel like I've spent an eternity in this chair."

Ten minutes later, during a short interval where the ladies were encouraged to speak to the gentlemen present, Reid entered the drawing room.

Sofia's heart skipped a beat.

He looked breathtaking in his fashionable dark blue coat and trousers, but she noticed the subtle tension in his eyes.

He was at her side in seconds, his hand sliding over hers, his cologne swamping her senses. "I don't have much time if I'm to make the Clarendon for seven, but I wanted to see you."

I needed to see you.

She brushed an imagined speck of dust from his sleeve. "I'm so glad you came." Despite his earlier reassurances, she'd spent the last two hours fraught with worry. "What did Algernon say about the scorecard?"

Before Reid could reply, Lord Rothley joined them. "For pity's sake, save me from talk of cute pugs and hothouse flowers. Find me someone willing to discuss grave robbing or the ethics of cannibalism when shipwrecked on a desert island."

Though Reid laughed, a deep sadness lingered in his eyes —a sorrow probably caused by his cousin. "I'm sure Sofia can find a lady who's interested in the macabre."

The lord gazed at the women sitting demurely on the blue damask settee. "I suspect these ladies would find a wilting rose disturbing. Surely it's time to leave. I cannot suffer another mawkish song or ode."

"The ladies are encouraged to sing to help build their confidence. When we're here alone, we discuss all manner of morbid topics." She gestured discreetly to Olivia. "Miss Woolf is fond of the graveyard poets and enjoys discussions on life's fragility."

"Miss Woolf?" He observed the woman with hair like flames of fire. "How fitting. I despise sheep. Let's pray this one bares her teeth."

"I could introduce you."

The marquess gave a snort of indifference. "Don't trouble yourself. The night will be over soon. I'll have a case of the ague the next time the countess invites me to an event."

Knowing her husband had to leave soon, Sofia squeezed Reid's hand. "Did you see your cousin and examine his scorecard?"

He drew closer and bent his head. "Algernon confessed to giving the ladies he wooed a small dose of laudanum. But he swears he didn't kill them. He claims he never dined with Mrs Ludgrove or took her to the Hare and Hounds. He didn't kill the groom, either."

"Then who did?"

Reid looked deflated. "I fear my grandfather might be involved."

Sofia's heart sank to her stomach. "Surely not."

Please, no, she silently begged.

Fate wouldn't be so cruel.

The only family member Reid cared for wouldn't betray him, too.

Reid managed a watery smile. "I'll explain everything when I return to collect you at ten. I can't let Turner down again. The man has been running the practice these last few weeks."

"Ten?" the marquess groaned. "I'll die of boredom long before then."

"Sofia will find someone to keep you entertained." Reid gripped his friend's shoulder. "I trust you to take care of my wife until I return. Don't let her out of your sight."

Lord Rothley bowed his head. "I'm nothing if not dependable."

Reid drew Sofia into the hall. He glanced about to ensure they were alone before crushing his mouth to hers and kissing her until they could hardly breathe.

"I'm thinking of asking Turner to become my partner," he said, holding her close and kissing her again. "He might refuse. Lord knows I've given him every reason to seek a new position."

"That's a splendid idea."

"We'll talk later tonight." His gaze swept over her face as if committing every detail to memory. "I should go, or I'll be late."

She ran her hands over his shoulders and the sculpted muscles filling his coat. Love for him flooded every fibre of her being. "Our troubles will be over soon. Chaos always precedes a time of change. We'll be better people for knowing the truth."

"There's only one truth in this godforsaken mess, and that's how I feel about you," he blurted.

She failed to suppress a gasp.

Her pulse raced frantically.

How do you feel? she wanted to say, but the guests burst into the hall, heading for the music room to retake their seats for the recital.

Reid's friend, Mr Dalton, grinned as he passed. "For a couple who married for convenience, you seem surprisingly smitten. Come, Mrs Gentry, let me show you to your seat before you drown in waves of sentiment."

"I'll be back in four hours, maybe three," Reid said, kissing her hand as Mr Dalton led her away.

She held her husband's gaze until she entered the music

room. A maelstrom of feelings overwhelmed her. Amid the burgeoning bloom of love lived a sudden fear she might lose everything.

"A drink, Mrs Gentry?" The marquess offered her a silver flask engraved with a dragon crest. "It's brandy. At times like these, one needs something stronger than lemonade."

She took a sip to stem the confusing rise of panic.

"You loved someone once," she dared to say.

A muscle in the lord's cheek twitched. He paused for a few strained seconds. "You make it sound like love is a choice. It's not. It's a dratted inconvenience."

"You speak of unrequited love. I imagine that's akin to the hopeless torment one might experience in hell."

Would that be her fate?

Was she doomed to love a man who only lusted after her?

"It's a struggle one must suffer for an eternity," he agreed.

"Was my wedding ring meant for her?" Sofia looked at the sparkling gems and thread of gold string she used to secure the ring in place until she found the time to visit Woodcroft's.

"If it was, it would sit on her finger. Fate decreed otherwise."

Miss Woolf came to stand before the audience and informed them she was to recite a passage from a lyric poem.

"Not another one." The marquess shifted his attention to the petite lady with the vibrant red hair. "Give me something other than green meadows and blasted rainbows," came his muttered plea.

Miss Woolf took a calming breath. "*Elegy Written in a Country Churchyard* by Thomas Gray." She glanced around the audience, though her gaze came to rest on the marquess.

"It explores the adage: 'Though our journeys in life may differ, our destination is always the same.'"

Lord Rothley straightened. "Sounds promising."

"*Full many a flower is born to blush unseen*," Miss Woolf began in a reverent tone, "*and waste its sweetness on the desert air.*"

The words reflected a missed opportunity, suggesting time spent anywhere but in the present moment was a waste.

Miss Woolf's gaze moved to the other men in the audience as she continued reciting from the elegy. "*The boast of heraldry, the pomp of power*," she said before meeting the marquess' gaze again. "*And all that beauty, all that wealth e'er gave, awaits alike the inevitable hour …*"

"*The paths of glory lead but to the grave*," the marquess whispered.

Miss Woolf recited two more quatrains from memory and received an applause from everyone in the audience, including the awakened Lord Rothley.

The lord took a sip of his brandy. "Who did you say that was?"

"Miss Woolf. She's been a member here for two months."

"Why is she here?"

"To find friendship amongst like-minded people."

"She gallivants about town alone, I presume."

"No. Her maid is taking tea with the other servants downstairs."

"Her choice of poetry is refreshing."

"The countess encourages freedom of thought and speech."

"Indeed." He offered Sofia the flask. "Have you told Gentry you're in love with him?" When she didn't reply directly, he said, "There's a notable change in the air when you're together."

"He's a remarkable man."

"Which makes me wonder why anyone would want to hurt him."

Sofia struggled to understand how Reid found himself in this position, too. "Algernon seeks their grandfather's approval and wants Bretton Hall. Though he professes innocence, all the evidence leads to his door. We just need Mrs Ludgrove to identify him as the elusive Mr Fellows."

They fell silent as another lady took centre stage to recite Portia's speech from *The Merchant of Venice*. It was a plea for mercy and compassion, though Sofia would never forgive the man who wished to hurt Reid.

"What if Algernon is telling the truth and he didn't murder O'Connor?" the marquess said, like he'd been waiting to play the devil's advocate for the last five minutes.

Sofia scoured her mind. "I don't see who else it could be."

"Not Doyle or that poacher fellow," he agreed. "Whoever killed O'Connor killed the patients and planned to implicate Gentry."

"Or Algernon accidentally killed the patients and needed to blame someone."

The marquess sighed. "Yes, it's possible."

Mr Dalton leant towards them, his heavy brow shielding dark, intense eyes. "The motive is always greed or jealousy. Algernon is the obvious villain. What if the real culprit used Algernon as the scapegoat?"

She thought for a moment. "I suppose the question should be: Who knows the identity of Reid's patients? That would be

Mr Hickman, Mr Turner and Algernon. He bribed Mr Hickman for a list of ladies in their fifties."

Lord Rothley nodded. "Gentry's grandfather is a resourceful man."

She pushed that suggestion aside. "Mr Hickman hasn't the stomach for murder. And it's not Mr Turner." The men were close and had been for years. "Mrs Ludgrove knows him. He's treated her on at least three occasions. I checked the records to allay any doubts. And he invited me to supper on the night of Mr O'Connor's murder. Why would he do that if he had business elsewhere?"

The marquess checked his watch. "It's still early. What say we take my carriage, visit Mrs Ludgrove and ask a few pertinent questions?"

The lord was desperate to escape The Jade.

"Yes, if you promise to dance with Miss Woolf upon our return." They would have a wasted journey. Mrs Ludgrove had described Mr Fellows as having an athletic physique. Mr Turner was of average height and build.

With a quick glance Miss Woolf's way, the marquess agreed.

After hearing Mrs Reagan's dramatic parable on the value of being forthright, they left and journeyed to Mrs Ludgrove's home in Chandos Street. With each passing mile, fear formed a cold knot in her chest.

When Pinkerton finally answered the door, he was determined not to grant them entrance. "I'll let no one but Mr Gentry cross the threshold. Not until the ten days of quarantine have passed."

"You do remember me?" Sofia said. "I'm Mr Gentry's herbalist. And this is the Marquess of Rothley and Mr

Dalton." The marquess offered his calling card. "We must speak to Mrs Ludgrove urgently."

"I gave Mr Gentry my word. He trusts—"

"Step aside!" Mr Dalton pushed past Pinkerton and marched into the hall. "My patience is a coiled spring ready to snap."

Despite the butler's protests, they followed him inside.

Mrs Ludgrove was lounging on the sofa, her hair hidden in a purple turban, the cat curled in her lap. "What's the meaning of this? Who the devil are you?"

The cat hissed.

Sofia introduced herself. "Do you remember me? I'm Mr Gentry's herbalist."

Mrs Ludgrove looked terrified. "Did *he* send you?" She clutched her robe in her fist. "I've told him I don't want his rotten medicine. The game is up. There's no point keeping secrets anymore."

A little mystified, Sofia said, "You've spoken to Mr Gentry?"

"No, Mr Fellows. He's persistent. I'll give him that."

Pinkerton stepped forward. "The gentleman has been bombarding my mistress with notes. I told the penny boy he'll get a thick ear if he tries to deliver one here again."

A cold prickle made her shudder. "May I ask what Mr Fellows wants?" Did he hope to kill all the witnesses like he had Mr O'Connor? Would he lure Mrs Ludgrove to a secluded wood out of town and do away with her, too?

"To meet privately, to return my brooch and earrings. He claims I asked him to take the jewels for safekeeping. What poppycock. He could have robbed me while I was half-dazed. No. I'll let him stew a little longer."

"I trust you told the constable what happened," Sofia said.

Mrs Ludgrove's pinched expression said not. "And have my business bandied about in the broadsheets? Pinkerton told the constable I had an infection and to call next week."

"But it's imperative we find Mr Fellows." Sofia paused, unsure how hard to press the widow. Lives were at stake. "He could hurt someone else."

Mrs Ludgrove dismissed the plea. "I've told you all I know."

The widow shooed them away and fell back on the bolster cushion like a weary Cleopatra.

Sofia turned to her companions. "Wait in the hall. I wish to speak to Mrs Ludgrove alone." She refused to leave the house without clearing her colleagues' names. Indeed, Mrs Ludgrove held the key to solving the entire case.

Lord Rothley and Mr Dalton obliged.

Sofia moved closer to the sofa.

It was pointless being kind, and so she chose a different tactic. "I find your failure to take this seriously quite disgraceful. Who are you trying to protect? Surely not Mr Fellows. The man put laudanum in your wine."

Mrs Ludgrove's head jerked in Sofia's direction. "What? Who told you that? It's simply not true."

"A witness at the Hare and Hounds. Mr Fellows killed a groom to hide his secret. He won't rest until he's ruined Mr Gentry's reputation."

"Mr Fellows is a gentleman."

"No, I fear you have been duped."

The widow screwed her eyes shut and shook her head. "I just want it all to go away. I wish I'd never had that conversation in the bookshop. I wish I'd never accepted his offer to dine at Antoine's."

"You did, and the truth will prevail. The question is: What

would you like written about you in the broadsheets? Do you want to be the person who helped catch a killer or the one who aided his crimes?"

The woman paled. "Mr Fellows is not a killer. It's all a dreadful misunderstanding. Yes, I'm angry he took my brooch and earrings. If he'd needed money, I would have given it to him. It's the lies and deception. That's what I cannot abide. The sneaking about and making up stories."

Sofia feared she'd had a wasted journey and made one final attempt to get answers. "You're not the only lady he's courting. I saw Mr Hickman dining with an older woman at Antoine's."

"Who?" Her reply and bland expression confirmed their secretary was not Mr Fellows. "What has that got to do with me? Are you even listening, gal?"

A sick feeling swirled in Sofia's gut.

Her head whirled as pieces of the puzzle started slotting into place.

The note Mrs Ludgrove sent to the practice asking for Mr Gentry never arrived. They had called by chance that day. The penny boy had not lost the letter. Someone at the practice had destroyed the note.

"Why do you persist in keeping Mr Fellow's identity a secret? What are you hiding? I can only assume you think Mr Gentry knows him."

Please, no!

Could the villain be Mr Turner?

Surely not.

"It's no one's business." Mrs Ludgrove sounded quite angry now. "I gave you a false name because he said no one would understand. And he was right."

Sofia firmed her stance. She would get a confession even

if she had to strangle Mrs Ludgrove with her garish turban. "I know it's not Mr Turner," she lied, "because he's betrothed and will soon marry."

The tale had the desired effect.

Mrs Ludgrove's chin hit her lap. Her eyes bulged in their sockets. She began shaking. "Betrothed? But he can't be."

Merciful Lord!

Mr Turner was the insidious Mr Fellows!

The blood in Sofia's veins froze. Reid was with the deceitful devil now.

There was no time to press for answers.

No time to wonder about a motive.

Sofia ignored Mrs Ludgrove's sudden tears and darted from the room.

Saving her husband was all that mattered.

Chapter Nineteen

The hum of quiet conversation drifted through the Clarendon's refined dining room. While others sipped wine, laughed and spoke about a play or an aunt's upcoming birthday, Reid and Turner discussed death and morbidity.

During three courses, neither mentioned Sofia.

Reid sensed his friend's hostility and didn't want to make matters worse. It was impossible not to smile when talking about his wife. Love flowed through him in warm waves at the mere thought of her. And guilt ate away at him every time he met Turner's gaze across the table.

Tension stretched between them.

So tight it was liable to snap.

He'd planned to ask Turner to become his partner, yet something stopped him from making the offer.

Perhaps Turner still grieved the loss of his father.

Perhaps jealousy ate away at him, along with festering resentment.

"What's your view of Hickman?" Reid said, keen to

discover if losing their secretary was the cause of Turner's disquiet.

"We've been carrying him for too long." The coldness in Turner's voice embodied the noticeable change in him. A change that had grown more profound this passing week. "I'll source a replacement."

It seemed Turner had forgotten who owned the practice. "Pick four candidates, and I'll conduct the interviews."

Turner caught himself and nodded. "Of course."

The awkward air returned.

Reid considered calling it a night and venturing to The Burnished Jade rather than Porretta's Bathhouse. Hopefully, Turner's mood would mellow once things returned to normal.

"Will you excuse me a moment?" Reid placed his napkin on the table and headed to the elegant retiring room to use the pot and gather his thoughts. He caught a waiter and asked for the bill.

Upon his return, he found Turner's spirits oddly lifted.

"It's been months since we lounged in a mineral bath at Porretta's and put the world to rights." Turner reached for his wine, taking a long sip as he reminisced. "It will do us good to relax and make plans for the future."

Such was the improvement in his colleague's mood, one might think Turner had taken a swig of opium in Reid's absence.

"This last year has been hard for us both. Your father's passing left a void no man can fill." Reid had lost a friend and confidant. A brilliant teacher who had encouraged him where his own family had failed.

"I remember the day we met." Turner clinked his glass with Reid's, a cue for them to finish their beverages. "My father invited you to dinner, and I inherited an older brother overnight."

Reid smiled. "I dined with you every day for months."

He'd been eager to escape his grandfather's house. The arguments about choosing medicine as a career proved draining.

"I used to stand at the study door, straining to listen to your private conversations. They always sounded so fascinating."

Reid's heart softened at the memory. "Your father was the perfect mentor. I trusted his opinion and would not be the man I am today without his support."

Turner looked at Reid over the crystal rim. "He always said you had an insight most men lacked. It's why he trusted you with his scientific journals. Though I wish he'd mentioned *you* were to inherit them. I would have spent hours taking notes."

Reid thought it an odd thing to say. "He left them in my care, but they're for our mutual benefit. I expect you'll take them when you open your own practice."

The waiter came with the bill, and after a polite tussle with Turner over who should pay, Reid said, "It's the least I can do after the stress I've caused this week."

Turner thanked him and offered to pay next time. "I'll visit the retiring room while you finish your wine." He stood, lingering a second too long before striding out of the dining room.

The backward glance fed Reid's suspicions.

An odd feeling formed in his chest. It prickled the hairs on his nape, had his stomach performing somersaults.

He looked at Turner's empty wine glass and noted his

own was full when he was sure he'd taken more than a sip before leaving the table.

The tavern wench's words echoed in his mind.

O'Connor saw the devil adding something to his wife's wine.

Had Turner added something to Reid's wine?

The man had access to the patient list and the laudanum tinctures.

Was Turner the devious Mr Fellows?

He dismissed the notion, almost laughing to himself at the mere suggestion. Turner had no motive. They were friends and colleagues. And Mrs Ludgrove could identify him. She wouldn't have sent them on a wild goose chase.

Still, Reid reached for his wine and took the tiniest sip.

The slight bitter taste was barely noticeable.

Yet it was enough to have Reid reach for the hip flask in his pocket. He downed what was left of the brandy. With a surgeon's steady hand, he filled it with wine, accidentally spilling some on his dark trousers. Quickly replacing the stopper, he tucked the flask in his pocket just before Turner returned.

The man gestured to the mouthful of wine left in Reid's glass. "Are you drinking that, or shall we head to Porretta's?"

Reid stood, finishing the last drop and gesturing for Turner to lead the way. He drew his handkerchief from his pocket and dribbled the remnants of the wine into the cotton square.

On the short walk to the bathhouse, they discussed Hickman's betrayal, with Turner admitting he wasn't shocked.

"Hickman shakes less when you're out on calls."

"I'll admit, I pitied the man." Having Hickman act as Reid's secretary served a purpose. He'd seemed adept at administering medicines until Sofia took over the dispensary, and her skills put Hickman to shame.

Turner chuckled. "My father always said a soft heart carries a heavy burden. I suspect it's how you've found yourself lumbered with a wife."

Reid clenched his fists at his sides. "I love my wife," he snapped, regretting it instantly. Sofia deserved to be the first to hear his declaration. "She is by no means a burden."

He sensed Turner's animosity, but his colleague disguised it. "I meant no disrespect. It's just you were adamant you'd never marry."

"I said I would never marry for love after witnessing the disastrous end of my parents' marriage." He thought about Edmund's letters and his hint things were not as they seemed. Perhaps there was a clue amongst them that might explain what went wrong. "But we cannot help who we love."

"She's a remarkable woman."

"Yes." Reid wobbled a little. If Turner had drugged him, he would be showing symptoms by now. If Turner was innocent, he'd assume the wine had gone to Reid's head. "My mother would have loved Sofia. She had a good understanding of medicinal herbs, too."

While Reid fought a pang of regret, Turner made a surprising revelation. "I'm told her father thought dabbling in herbs was ungodly. A sin akin to witchcraft."

It was news to him.

"Sofia said her father supported her hobby." He deliberately tripped on the corner of a flagstone, blaming the potent wine.

"I was referring to your mother, Diana."

Time stilled for a moment.

"Has my grandfather been gossiping again?" he said,

feigning indifference but wanted to grab Turner by the throat and demand to know his game.

Turner's laugh lacked genuine mirth. "No, my father knew her through her charitable work at the hospital. They attended many of the same functions and became friends."

"He never mentioned it to me."

"Perhaps he wanted to avoid rousing sad memories."

They reached Porretta's Bathhouse, giving Reid time to cool his temper.

The entrance featured grand stone columns and a triangular pediment, evoking the elegance of Roman architecture. Hanson, the burly attendant, met them in the foyer. The smell of earthy minerals and exotic oils relaxed a man before he entered the bathing chamber.

Reid motioned for Turner to follow the attendant. "Undress and give Hanson your valuables while I pay and sign the register." He planned to write a note and send it to Rothley at The Jade.

Turner insisted on paying. "You bought dinner. Allow me to return the kindness."

Reid followed Hanson into the changing area—a place with pretty mosaic walls and stone benches. He was undressing when Turner entered and handed him a token for the storage chests.

They gave Hanson their tokens in exchange for plush cotton towels and use of the locked wooden boxes, then headed into the bathhouse.

The large pool—a labyrinth of stone and pale blue mosaic—twisted into secluded alcoves beneath an arched ceiling and the dim glow of candlelight.

Reid headed left, entering a hidden sanctuary. He sat on the edge of the mineral pool and lowered himself into the warm water. "I can't risk using the steps," he joked. "My head is so fuzzy, I'll likely slip and split my skull."

"At least there's a doctor at hand."

They settled into the rectangular-shaped pool occupied by two other men who passed pleasantries. When the men left, Reid returned to the topic of his mother. If Turner was framing him for murder, he had to know why.

"Did your father mention my mother often?" Reid slurred the odd word for effect. If laudanum had been added to the wine, he'd need to feign sleep soon. "I find it odd he never spoke about knowing her."

Turner relaxed back, spreading his arms out over the pool's edge. "Probably because he was in love with her and thought it might be awkward. My mother was still alive, and he never pursued the matter, even when your father was serving abroad. He hoped patience would reap the rewards. Then your mother died, and he spiralled into an odd melancholy that lasted a year."

Reid did not need to pretend to look stupefied.

He sat, mouth open, inhaling the steam.

"Why do you think my father pushed me out and took you under his wing?" Turner's laugh sounded hollow. "You were a gift from the gods. An idol he could worship in her absence."

Reid closed his eyes, absorbing the information.

Turner mistook his calm composure for drowsiness. All the horrid thoughts raging inside him burst forth in a torrent.

"I didn't know the extent of it until my father died and I read his private journal. You're the son he wanted. You're the son he pretended was his because, in his warped mind, it made him feel closer to your mother. I was tossed away like scraps in the gutter."

Reid breathed deeply. "Did my mother return his affections?"

He knew the answer like he knew his own name.

"No. But fate offered Father a boon. One that had disastrous consequences. That's the price one pays for meddling."

"You're not making sense." Reid closed his eyes again and let his head loll back. "Forgive me. I don't feel well. My mind is hazy. It must be the wine."

Turner chuckled. "We've got drunk together many times. It's never affected you this badly before."

"I downed the last glass too quickly," Reid mumbled. The best way to discover the truth was to pretend he was losing consciousness.

A lengthy silence ensued.

Turner sank deeper into the mineral bath, inhaling the steam and closing his eyes as the water soothed his limbs.

Reid pretended to sleep, too, but suddenly blinked as if waking from a stupor. "What's the price?" he garbled.

"The price?"

"For m-meddling."

Turner exhaled a long, weary breath. "When your father died, your mother took to her bed, distraught. She asked my father to collect his personal effects because she was too weak to take the strain."

Reid heard the statement clearly.

A sickening sense of dread roiled inside him.

Somehow he knew what was coming next.

A twisted grin flickered across Turner's face. "He slipped a letter into your father's belongings. If he could break their bond, he might win her affections. That's the pathetic comment written by your precious mentor. Then she died, and he spent the rest of his life ignoring me and pandering to you."

Reid slapped his hand to his mouth, nausea rising. His mother died of a broken heart, a symptom made worse by his father's betrayal. All these years, he'd despised his father and worshipped his mentor.

It was all a lie.

Believing the end was nigh, Turner made a damning statement. "It's a shock, I know, but it will all be over soon. I'll have the practice my father helped you build. I'll have your wife. And the debt you owe me will be repaid."

Sofia sat in Lord Rothley's imposing black carriage, wringing her hands as the vehicle charged along The Strand, heading for Pall Mall. Panic had her jigging her leg. Her heart galloped so fast it hammered against her ribcage.

Mr Dalton thumped the carriage roof and called to Lord Rothley's coachman. "Head for Porretta's, not the Clarendon. Hurry, man!" He remained perched on the edge of the seat, his rage evident in the ceaseless grinding of his teeth.

"What if they're still at the Clarendon?" she said.

"It's easier to kill a man in a mineral bath than a packed dining room. You're sure Turner is the devil who's trying to ruin Gentry, not that moron he calls a cousin?"

"I'm certain, though Mr Turner's motive is unclear." She'd spent many hours with the doctor and found him helpful and polite. He treated Reid like an elder brother. Thus his sudden hostility left her baffled.

"Nothing surprises me anymore." Lord Rothley spoke like a true cynic, his cold tone slicing the air. "If Turner has harmed a hair on Gentry's head, I'll kill him with my bare hands."

A sickening thought entered her mind. "He will have added something to Reid's wine during dinner." Criminals were creatures of habit. "A subdued man might easily drown in a bathhouse. Murder will look like an accident." She slapped her hand to her mouth, fearing they were already too late. "Convince me it won't end like this."

The marquess' dark, knowing eyes said to fear the worst. "I'm a doomsayer. Experience has led me to expect disaster."

"This time I pray you're wrong."

Sofia gripped the overhead strap as the vehicle swerved into St James' Street. It came to a crashing halt outside the Roman-inspired bathhouse.

Mr Dalton alighted first. He didn't offer his hand but gripped Sofia by the waist, lifting her to the pavement.

"We won't tear through Porretta's like crazed imbeciles," Lord Rothley instructed. "We'll use gentle persuasion to gain entrance. You'll have to wait in the foyer, Mrs Gentry."

"There's more chance of Lucifer appearing on a three-headed dragon."

Mr Dalton snorted. "I'll use my cravat to cover your eyes, Mrs Gentry."

"I'm a student of anatomy, sir. I'm not afraid to walk through a bathhouse full of naked men. Now please hurry."

Lord Rothley spoke to the gentleman behind the large marble desk, his tone firm and dangerously polite. "We have reason to believe a crime is in progress." He slapped his calling card and a few sovereigns on the counter and asked to see the register.

The man obliged. Not because greed had him eyeing the gold but because the marquess leaned over the desk and snarled like he might rip out the man's jugular with his teeth.

The marquess noted the entries before whirling around. "Gentry is here, but not with Turner. According to the register, he arrived with Algernon."

Sofia frowned. "How odd."

Mr Dalton approached the marble counter. "We're checking the bathhouse. Summon a constable."

After a brief argument with a burly attendant in the dressing room, with Mr Dalton warning he had knocked out men twice his size, the fellow let them pass.

"We won't charge into the bathhouse yelling at the top of our lungs," she said, creeping across the tiled floor. "We'll assess the situation and determine if Reid is in danger."

"I agree." Lord Rothley quickly slipped his hand over her eyes when they met two naked men drying themselves with towels. "Dalton, we proceed with caution."

The bathhouse looked empty, though the air was thick with mineral-scented steam. She heard the soft hum of conversation, but the stone pools ran through the underground cavern like a maze, and the dim candlelight made it impossible to locate the source.

Then she heard a voice she recognised.

She gestured towards a secluded pool on her left, partially hidden behind a bricked arch, and whispered, "I hear Mr Turner." He *was* the villain because he'd signed Algernon's name in the register.

They crept closer.

Sweat gathered on her brow, and the cavern felt suddenly smaller.

Her heart stuttered when she heard Reid's incoherent reply. Mr Turner must have drugged the wine to subdue him.

"Your father took everything from me," Reid mumbled. "I've paid my dues and owe you nothing."

"Do you know what it's like spending endless nights thinking how you might make your father proud?" Mr Turner countered. "You stole my family."

"And your father s-stole mine."

Reid sounded unwell.

"And so you thought to discredit me," Reid stated.

She raised her skirts, ready to race to her husband's aid, but the marquess caught her wrist. "Wait. Gentry means to drag the truth from Turner. We need to give him another minute."

Mr Dalton hid behind the stone wall, waiting for a cue to charge.

"I knew you'd begin to wonder if your tinctures were killing your patients." Mr Turner's arrogant tone sounded so unlike him. "When you started gathering evidence in the room upstairs, I knew it would drive you mad, and the coroner would eventually become suspicious."

Reid made no reply.

He had neglected the practice, helping Mr Turner to take control in his absence. Heavens, he'd even decided to make the man his partner.

Anger erupted in her veins. She wanted to air her disgust, but the marquess held her in his steely grip.

"Then you made a mistake." Reid sounded weak and drowsy. "O'Connor saw you drug Mrs Ludgrove and black-mailed you. You couldn't risk him telling anyone and saw another way to get rid of me."

Mr Turner's sinister chuckle chilled her blood.

"The fool didn't see me coming. I've always been good with a scalpel, not that my father noticed. Apparently, I lacked your steady hand."

"You poured laudanum into my wine." Reid's words were barely audible now. "The magistrate knows that someone … someone is trying to implicate me. If I drown here, he'll know you were with me."

"Will he? Algernon signed the register. His scorecard was at the murder scene. People recognised his boots. He bought laudanum, and we look alike. He wants Bretton Hall. You've told me so yourself."

Mr Turner had planned this with meticulous precision.

Sofia's chest tightened. Her thoughts spun wildly. She tugged the marquess' hand, urging him to act. They needed to keep Reid awake and administer a saltwater emetic.

"But we were like brothers," Reid said.

Tears filled her eyes. Her heart wept for him.

"You're the brother I didn't want," Mr Turner snapped. "Hickman told me about the wager at White's. It made it easier to cover my tracks."

"Not entirely," Lord Rothley said with an aristocrat's aplomb. He stepped out from the shadows, pulling Sofia with him. "You made the mistake of courting Mrs Ludgrove. She didn't die like you hoped."

Mr Turner stared, disbelief in his eyes. His mouth dropped open when Mr Dalton entered the chamber and threatened to gut him like a fish.

That's when Mr Turner launched himself at Reid, grabbing him around the throat, promising to choke him and drag him under.

Reid lacked the strength to fight.

"He's barely conscious. You'll do as I say if you want him to live." The wild dart of Mr Turner's eyes betrayed his desperation. "Get into the pool. All of you. Use the steps at the far end. Hurry before I drown him."

"Perhaps the steam has affected your eyesight," the marquess said darkly. "You're outnumbered, Turner. You'll leave this bathhouse in shackles. Assuming I don't kill you first."

Sofia stepped forward. "Please, Mr Turner. Whatever madness has seized you, the man I know wouldn't be so cold and callous."

Mr Turner blinked like he had grit in his eyes. "You should have told me about the Merricks. I would have married you. Then I might have been satisfied with ruining him."

Sofia sat on the side of the pool and lowered herself slowly into the water, which thankfully only came up to her waist. Her skirts ballooned.

"It wouldn't have mattered." She looked at Reid, not Mr Turner, a sob catching in her throat. Had he drunk too much laudanum? Was he seconds away from closing his eyes forever? Would this moment be their last? "I married Mr Gentry because I was in love with him. I am madly in love with him. There will never be another man for me."

"You hardly know him," Mr Turner countered.

"That's where you're wrong." She held Reid's gaze and took a few tentative steps. Fear for the future wrapped around her heart like a strangling vine. "I have known him forever. Every insignificant moment in my life has brought me closer to finding him."

"Let Gentry go," Lord Rothley cried.

"It's too late." Mr Turner's tight expression held a hint of regret. "When the tincture takes full effect, I doubt he'll wake."

Her anguish left her in a pained sob. "Why? He's never hurt anyone." She clutched her abdomen as she inched through the water. "Let him go. He doesn't deserve your wrath."

Reid stared at her like his heart was breaking, too. "There's no need to cry, Sofia. Fate has other plans for us." He slipped his fingers around Mr Turner's forearm. "Thank heavens for Annie. It's how I knew not to drink the wine."

As quick as she absorbed the information, Reid bit Mr Turner's arm and then elbowed him in the abdomen. "You'll hang for what you've done," he growled, grabbing the devil and forcing his head under the water.

A struggle ensued—a wild thrashing in the pool.

Reid punched Mr Turner on the nose, the spurt of blood streaking the water crimson. The men grappled, but Reid was the stronger of the two, delivering a sharp blow to Mr Turner's chin that sent him plunging to the bottom of the pool.

Being a man of action, Mr Dalton jumped into the water and hauled Mr Turner out. That's when the constable arrived with the attendant, and Lord Rothley eloquently explained what had occurred.

Reid didn't seem to care what happened outside the pool. He stared at Sofia as they raced towards each other in the water.

Her throat tightened. Tears welled again as she threw herself into his arms. "I thought I'd lost you." She clung to him, gripping his wet body and refusing to let go. "I thought it was the end of us."

He wrapped his arms around her waist, their bodies pressed so tightly together that their breaths rose and fell as one. "I owe Annie and Doyle my life. If they hadn't mentioned the wine ... I ..."

"It doesn't matter now." She clasped his cheeks in her hands, drawing his mouth to hers and kissing him wildly.

The man's lips were as potent as opium. The desire to feel pleasure, not pain, was a persistent pounding in her blood.

"My father never had a mistress." He spoke like the knowledge had restored his faith in life, in love. "One lie caused untold damage. Turner gave me no cause to doubt him, but jealousy is like a poison that rots a man's mind. Secrets destroy relationships."

She swallowed past the knot in her throat. She had to declare her feelings properly this time. "I've kept a secret from you."

A slow, sensual smile tugged his lips. "That you're madly in love with me? Or was that a ploy to distract Turner and buy some time?"

It was impossible to convey what she felt in her heart. "Everything I said was true. I'm so desperately in love with you, Reid. I was afraid to tell you. I know you want a convenient marriage, but—"

"I want you, Sofia. I wanted you before you begged me to hire you." He claimed her lips, the kiss a languorous mating. "I love you. I should have told you earlier at The Jade. God knows the words have danced on my tongue all day."

"They have?" She blinked back tears of happiness.

"I know what true love looks like. Now I know how it feels. I came close to losing everything tonight." He hung his head. The realisation of what might have been overwhelmed him.

She brushed her hand through his damp hair in soft, reassuring strokes. "We love each other, Reid. That's a blessing. A reason to celebrate. I never thought I'd marry a man I admire, let alone one I love to distraction."

Lord Rothley cleared his throat. "I'm accompanying Turner and the constable to Bow Street. You need to dress and meet us there. Dalton will return with my carriage. Might I suggest you find dry clothes, Mrs Gentry, before you catch a chill?"

"I'm sure the doctor has a cure for all her ailments," Mr Dalton joked as the men lingered at the poolside.

Reid thanked them for having the foresight to come to the bathhouse. "I'm the brother Turner didn't want. The grandson the viscount finds unworthy. Thank God you value my friendship."

"There's no time to wallow in self-pity," Lord Rothley said. "That's my domain. And as much as we love you, we came on your wife's insistence. I'm sure you'll thank her properly later. Now, get out of the pool. Public displays of affection should be outlawed."

The men left when the constable called them.

"We could spend a few more minutes here," Reid suggested. "We would both appreciate the healing power of the minerals."

She smiled. "Perhaps we might return and hire the private room you mentioned that caters to married couples."

Desire darkened his eyes. "I'll book a pool for a night next week. And now our problems are over, we should treat ourselves to a stay at the Adelphi."

"I can hardly wait."

Although an erotic vision of them making love raised her pulse, something else niggled deep in her gut. A disturbing feeling warning her their troubles were far from over.

Chapter Twenty

Hare and Hounds
Two weeks later

The lively crowd in the taproom clapped their hands to Pete the Piper's rendition of *The Irish Washerwoman* on his penny whistle. Some knew the words and sang along. Some, including Sofia, had pushed the tables aside to dance, laughing with every spirited turn and buoyant skip-step.

Doyle grabbed Annie around the waist and swept her into the tide of dancers. The wench didn't strike Doyle with a pewter tankard but linked arms and made merry.

The Countess of Berridge was Sofia's partner.

Reid watched the women laugh as they twirled with each other. Their eyes sparkled with exhilaration. Tendrils of hair tumbled from their pins, bobbing against their cheeks in time with the music.

Aaron Chance stood beside Reid, his posture stiff.

"There's nothing more attractive to a man than seeing his wife happy," Reid said, staring at Sofia with burning admiration. He'd never wanted her more than he did at that moment.

"I'm not afraid of anything, but love scares the hell out of me," Aaron admitted. "Even so, I wouldn't change a damn thing."

"Yes." Reid could not imagine his life without Sofia. Every day with her was a blessing. "Love strips us bare, yet makes us feel whole."

Aaron drank from his tankard, though his dark eyes remained fixed on his wife. Seconds passed before he changed the subject. "Daventry said the evidence against Turner is conclusive."

The searing ache left by his colleague's betrayal returned. "Mrs Ludgrove finally gave a statement, and the waiter at Antoine's identified him." A deep sadness swept through him, too. "His father's journal confirmed Turner's motive for wanting rid of me."

It had made difficult reading.

His heart and throat constricted as he imagined his mentor slipping the cruel letter in amongst his father's possessions. If only his mother had read the letters his Uncle Edmund had received. She might have realised how deeply she was loved.

"It must be a relief to know your cousin is innocent."

"He's still a fool. Trusting him will always be an issue."

He trusted Sofia, Rothley and his other friends.

He trusted Aaron Chance and Lucius Daventry.

No one else.

"People can only hide behind a mask for so long," came Aaron's wise observation. "My wife believes we should approach all relationships with an open heart. I prefer cautious optimism."

Their wives called to them, beckoning them to dance.

Aaron shook his head. "Joanna knows hell will freeze over before I prance about like a dandy. I'll make up for the disappointment later."

Reid laughed. He thought of a story he would tell his wife when they were alone. A detailed description of an erotic dance during a hot night in Madras.

"I hear Merrick moved out of the house in Dean Street and took the stage back to Scotland with his sister."

"Because he knows it's not his house," Reid said, clenching his teeth, though he was glad to see the back of Victor Merrick. "Daventry's probate lawyer is still investigating, but it looks like Sofia's grandmother owned the house. She left it in trust for Sofia, but Mr Moorland was permitted to live there until his death."

"It sounds complicated."

"It's more complicated because the lawyer suspects Judith's will is a forgery." It was undoubtedly why Merrick packed his belongings and fled to Scotland.

"Do you think Merrick killed her?"

"I'm convinced he did." The coroner cited death by hypothermia based on her wet clothes and the windy conditions.

While their wives sang and danced a country reel, the conversation turned to more pleasant topics: the recent birth of Aaron's nephew, born to his brother Aramis; the new properties he had acquired; and his spirited debates on reform in the House of Lords.

For a moment, life was perfect.

Then a young groom from the stables entered, bringing the smell of hay and horse sweat. He approached Reid, tugging off his dusty cap. "A cove came into the stall and asked me to give you this, gov'nor."

Reid took the folded note and gave the lad a shilling.

The lad shifted nervously. "He said it's for your eyes only. Said there'll be trouble if anyone sees what's written inside."

"Trouble?" Pulse rising, Reid scanned the taproom, searching for a man sitting quietly alone, but he knew most of the faces here tonight.

The lad wrung his cap with dirty fingers. "He said a pretty lady might get hurt." His bottom lip wobbled. "That no one will notice a blade in the back when everyone's dancing."

"What the devil?" Aaron growled.

"Don't react," Reid said, attempting to remain calm while his mind ran amok. "He may still be watching us." Or one of his cronies lurked in plain sight. "I'd better do as he says."

He drew back a few feet, peeled open the folds and read the terse message. Whoever sent the note held his grandfather hostage. A carriage awaited Reid on the Barking Road. No one would be harmed if he climbed into the vehicle and came alone.

There was no ransom request.

No demand for gold and silver.

Which meant Reid was the prize.

He glanced up, hunting for signs of an accomplice.

Sofia smiled and waved at him, her eyes gleaming like polished emeralds. She believed their problems were over and a future filled with love lay ahead.

He waved back at her, receiving the knowing grin that said she would devour him in bed tonight.

"I must leave," he whispered to Aaron. "Watch Sofia. Keep her safe. Don't concern yourself with me."

Sofia turned away, clapping and singing to a new song.

Reid needed to go now.

He pretended to tuck the note inside his coat but turned to Aaron, gave him a playful pat on the back and slid the letter into the man's trouser pocket.

He left the Hare and Hounds without alerting Sofia and strode through the darkness towards the Barking Road.

A veil of mist rolled off the surrounding fields, swirling and shifting around a lone black coach parked fifty yards ahead.

The jarvey didn't doff his cap or make conversation when Reid approached. He didn't clamber to open the door but sat as rigid as a stone effigy.

Reid climbed into the empty vehicle, which jolted forward and gained speed before he could settle into the worn leather seat. The jarvey drove as if pursued by a horde of axe-wielding heathens.

They turned off the main road ten minutes later and journeyed half a mile along a narrow dirt track. Branches whipped the window, the driver's curses mirroring Reid's anger at the situation.

An old barn loomed at the end of the misty lane, its ghostly timbers pale beneath the light of the waxing moon. All was quiet but for the distant hoot of an owl and the faint grumble of men's voices.

Reid alighted when the carriage stopped.

The coachman said nothing but pointed at the path leading to the barn.

Ivy covered half the roof, and the huge barn door hung askew. The faint glow of lamplight filtered through the gap.

He knew to expect Victor Merrick. Only a few men dared to kidnap an elderly viscount. Desperate men did desperate things and it wouldn't be long before the lawyer proved Victor was guilty of fraud and murder.

The punch came as soon as Reid opened the creaking door and stepped inside the old hay barn. Victor hit him squarely in the jaw, knocking him to the ground.

Reid spat out blood and wiggled his jaw, relieved nothing was broken.

"You said you wouldn't hurt him," came an eloquent voice Reid knew.

Reid scrambled to his feet to meet the barrel of Merrick's pistol.

"Move, lad, before I make your wife a widow." Merrick gestured to the musty hay seat, the once golden strands now grey and brittle. No doubt it was a home for mice. "Sit there."

Reid did as Merrick commanded.

His grandfather appeared from a darkened corner of the barn. His white hair was neatly combed, not sticking up in tufts. His hands and feet were unbound. There wasn't one crease in his coat. Not a scratch or blemish where he'd put up a fight.

"You weren't dragged from your fireside chair, then?" Reid said with dripping sarcasm. "You weren't made to change out of your banyan at gunpoint? You're here of your own volition."

With his eyes downcast, his grandfather's countenance carried the burden of guilt. "Merrick left me little choice in the matter."

It wasn't hard to imagine what the men had discussed. "You went to visit him when Hickman gave you the address. You will have presented your calling card, believing your title carries some sway."

The viscount shot Merrick a look as cold as ice. "He didn't care a whit. He wanted to trade information."

Merrick sniggered, though kept his pistol raised. "Tell him!" Merrick shouted. "Tell him what you offered if I got rid of Sofia."

"Tell him what you threatened if I didn't pay."

Reid studied both men, struggling to pick the most wicked.

Merrick made no excuses and was capable of killing in cold blood. His grandfather was Machiavellian, a cunning man always one step ahead in his calculated schemes—until now.

It proved no man was infallible.

"You're more alike than you realise," Reid said, wishing Uncle Edmund had mentioned the viscount's devious tactics before. "You both strive to control everyone and everything."

The viscount took umbrage. "I'm embroiled in this mess because of your poor choices. I've been forced to step in and fix your mistake."

"I love my wife. There's no mistake."

The viscount groaned and began pleading with Merrick. "He doesn't love her. He loves the idea of hurting me. If you take her, I'll ensure he raises no objection. Take her tonight. Take the money and leave. Was that not the plan?"

Merrick raised a thick, black brow, looking somewhat amused. "The plan was always to have Sofia. I spread the rumours about the auction. I left the letter suggesting Harrop would buy her. Knowing the fool was a degenerate, I made her serve him wine at card games."

"You underestimated her." A rush of pride filled Reid's chest. He admired his wife's strength and dedication. "Sofia wasn't waiting for you to save her when you returned from

Scotland with Judith conveniently dead." She'd left the only home she'd known and taken control of her own affairs.

Merrick's sinister smile made Reid's stomach squirm. "The girl has spirit. She almost ruined everything by marrying you, but then your grandfather gave me an idea to solve all our problems."

The viscount gestured to the small wooden chest on the ground beside Merrick. "Take the coins and jewels. You know where to find the girl. Go now, and you could be in France tomorrow."

Merrick laughed. "You aristocrats are all the same. You think money solves every problem, but you're missing a crucial part of the plan." He aimed the pistol at the viscount but barked instructions at Reid. "The noose on the floor. Drag it over your head, or I'll shoot the old man."

"Why put a noose around his neck?" The viscount's words tumbled out in a garbled rush. "You have my word we won't follow. How can we? My coachman is still waiting at the East India Docks."

"He won't leave until we're dead."

Merrick only had one shot and meant to hang Reid first.

"Why kill us?" the viscount said with a huff of superiority. "I've kept my end of the bargain."

It seemed money could not buy intelligence. "Judith Merrick didn't own the house in Dean Street. More than likely, Sofia does. To get the house and the money, Merrick needs to kill me so he can marry my wife."

Sofia knew something was wrong when she turned and saw Aaron Chance standing alone. A strange unease sent her heart sinking to her stomach, but still, she scanned the taproom, looking for Reid.

Mr Chance wore a deep frown of suspicion as he studied every face in the crowd. He met her gaze and marched towards her. "Would you care to dance, Mrs Gentry?" He didn't give her the option to accept or decline but gripped her arm.

Joanna's face brightened when Mr Chance took to the floor. She clapped with delight as he swung Sofia around until she was dizzy from all the whirling.

Sofia held her breath, waiting for the blow she'd been expecting.

"We have a problem," he whispered through a feigned smile.

"Where's Reid?"

"Just laugh and act like everything is fine." He twirled her under his arm three times. "But glance around the room and tell me if you notice anyone watching you."

"Where's my husband?"

"There's no time for questions."

She did as he asked. No one glanced her way. They were all singing or supping ale or nodding in time to the music. Two men debated putting another log on the fire. Another tried to get his whippet to hop on its hind legs.

"I see nothing untoward."

"Look again," Mr Chance demanded.

She linked arms with him, as did another woman, barging into their intimate circle and grabbing Sofia's arm, too.

"Dance," the woman said in a soft Scottish burr, her eyes pleading. "For heaven's sake, dinnae stop until I've told ye what I ken."

Mr Chance glared. "Start talking."

"Do ye remember me?" the woman asked Sofia. "I've red hair beneath this dark wig. I let ye into the house in Dean Street."

With her fiery hair concealed, she bore no resemblance to the woman who had ushered them into the drawing room. "You're Mr Merrick's sister?" The words carried curiosity, not certainty.

In the time she'd known him, Victor had never mentioned a sister. It was all rather suspect. Why bring her to London now? Had he needed a witness to confirm Judith's death was an accident? And why hadn't she returned to Scotland with Victor?

"I'm nae his sister," the Scotswoman confessed. "We've been friends since we were bairns, but I'd nae seen him in years. He offered me a chance to come to London, but he's nae the man I remember."

"We don't care about your life story," Mr Chance said, irritated. "Just tell us what the hell is going on. Did Merrick write the note? Did he take Viscount Hanberry hostage?"

"What?" Sofia blurted.

"Aye, but they've got an arrangement." The Scotswoman urged them to keep dancing. "I dinnae ken who's watching. Victor threatened me until I agreed to do his bidding. He said he needs money. I'm to remain here and make sure Mrs Gentry does nae leave the inn."

"Where is my husband?" Sofia demanded to know.

"Somewhere close, I suspect. I heard talk of a barn half a mile from the Barking Road. But ye cannae leave. His men might kill us all."

Mr Chance tugged his arm free. "No disrespect, but if Merrick trusted you to watch the target, he has no capable men." He faced Sofia. "Fetch Doyle and meet me outside.

Bring the Scotswoman, too, we'll need her statement. Be quick."

Mr Chance left the inn, taking his wife with him.

Through narrowed eyes, Sofia looked for Mr Doyle and saw him talking to Annie in a quieter corner of the taproom.

"Mr Gentry is in trouble and needs your help," she said, hoping her abrupt tone revealed her inner turmoil. "Your insight saved his life once. I need the same from you again."

The light-fingered fellow was reluctant to move. "What trouble? I saw him drinking with a friend a moment ago." Mr Doyle turned his attention to the lively throng, his eyes darting back and forth. "Well, he was there."

"Do you know of a barn nearby? Off the Barking Road? Somewhere secluded?" Losing patience, she gripped Mr Doyle's elbow and gave him a firm shake. "The Earl of Berridge wishes to speak to you outside." She deliberately used Mr Chance's title, knowing it carried more weight. "He'll ask the same question—and demand an answer."

"There's old man Frogart's place. Though it ain't been used in years. I've spent one or two nights there myself."

"Good." She pulled Mr Doyle towards the exit. "Direct the earl to the barn."

Mr Chance had summoned Reid's coachman, Nokes, complaining it was taking too long to hitch the horses. He saw Mr Doyle and fired a range of questions before the man mentioned the barn.

"Take me there."

"If you drive a coach down the narrow lane, milord, they'll hear you coming. Best approach through the woods and across the field."

"There's no time, and I promised not to leave Mrs Gentry." Mr Chance looked skyward as if appealing to the heavens. His whispered plea drifted on the still night air. "I'll go alone. Bring me a horse."

Mr Chance was right to place his trust in divine providence. Another vehicle came hurtling into the yard: an imposing carriage pulled by a team of muscled black Friesians.

The Marquess of Rothley vaulted to the ground as the vehicle rolled to a stop. "Where's Gentry? Fetch him!"

"He's not here. We need your carriage. I'll explain en route." Mr Chance gestured to his wife, Sofia and the Scotswoman. "Climb inside. Doyle, ride atop the box and direct the driver. Hurry."

A minute later, the vehicle charged out of the yard and headed towards Barking at breakneck speed. The padded leather cushions failed to absorb the shock as the carriage bounced through ruts in the road.

"Read this." Mr Chance gave the marquess the note.

Lord Rothley scanned the missive. "Recent events make sense now. Gentry asked me to have his grandfather followed but never gave the order to stop."

"Your man followed him tonight?" the countess asked.

"Yes, Gentry's grandfather left his carriage at the East India Docks. He carried a small wooden chest to an awaiting vehicle but was forced inside at gunpoint. When I learnt they were heading towards the Barking Road, and knew you were at the inn, I came at once."

"Thank heavens you did," Sofia said, her heart full of gratitude. She had never been so glad to see anyone. "Mr Merrick must need money and likely threatened the viscount."

"Indeed," the marquess replied, though the shadow in his dark eyes hinted at far more sinister suspicions.

"Aye, Victor has nae plans to return to Scotland but mentioned visiting France for a time. He intends to leave once he's gathered the funds."

"Who is this woman?" the marquess said.

Before anyone could reply, the carriage stopped at the end of a narrow lane.

Mr Doyle climbed down and came to the window. "This is the place. I can't say anyone's there for sure, but it's a half a mile to the barn."

Sofia moved to alight. "It will take ten minutes to walk, five if I run."

"I'll go," Mr Chance said. "Wait with Rothley."

"Must you go alone?" The countess ran her hand over her abdomen. "Can we not all go together?"

Fearing they were losing precious time, Sofia quickly devised a plan. "We'll go on ahead." She gripped the Scotswoman's arm. "We'll pretend I tried to leave the inn and was brought here. You follow behind. Handle any men who might cause trouble. Enter the barn if you think we're in danger."

Ignoring the men's protests, Sofia climbed from the vehicle, taking the Scotswoman with her. "If you want to escape gaol, you'll help me overthrow Victor."

"We'll be directly behind you," the marquess said, removing a walnut case from beneath his seat. "I'll take great pleasure in ridding the world of a man like Merrick."

The path was dark, narrow and thankfully dry. They covered the distance quickly, though slowed when a black conveyance loomed into view, blocking the track.

The burly man atop the box had his head bowed, the collar of his greatcoat raised to his chin. His snore rose and fell like the steady sawing of wood.

They edged sideways through the gap.

Sofia snagged her dress on a bramble and stifled a groan.

The men moved behind like wraiths in the darkness, the glint of moonlight on their raised pistols, alerting her to their presence.

Deep voices echoed inside the old barn.

"Do as I say, or I'll shoot the old man," Victor said coldly.

She would know his voice anywhere, but nothing terrified her more than the stare of those obsidian eyes at night.

"You've one shot," Reid countered. "If you fire at him, you'll have to kill me with your bare hands."

He was alive!

A relieved breath left her in a whoosh of air.

The coach wheels creaked as the driver shifted in his seat, but the fellow slept as deeply as a bear in winter.

"You'll say you caught me following my husband," Sofia whispered to the Scotswoman, who began edging back from the barn door when Victor cursed loudly.

"He'll kill me for betraying him."

"He'll kill you anyway. He can't afford loose ends."

"Put the damn noose around your neck, boy!" Victor yelled.

Afraid of what Victor might do next, Sofia burst through the barn door, stumbling over an imagined obstacle. "Stop pushing me," she called to the Scotswoman.

The woman had no choice but to act the part. "If ye had nae been so nosy, ye would nae be in this predicament."

Victor clenched his jaw, his eyes thunderclouds of fury. Yet he spoke calmly, every word laced with a veiled threat. "I told you to keep her at the inn."

"I could nae stop her." The woman heaved from exertion.

"She ran into the yard and followed the carriage for a mile. She was so fast I could nae catch her."

Sofia looked at Reid, sitting on a hay bale. The lit lantern hanging above gave a modicum of light. "Are you hurt?"

"You shouldn't have come." The tremor in his voice betrayed an inner chaos. "Merrick means to take you with him when he leaves."

She turned to Victor, knowing she could no longer remain silent. "I'll never leave with you." She noticed the wooden chest near his feet. "I suspect the viscount paid the ransom. Take your money. No one will stop you."

Except for the two peers outside, brandishing pistols.

Victor found her amusing. "You may have lost your virtue, but you still possess that innocent charm. A ransom signifies an exchange."

Though puzzled, she could not mention that she knew Victor had forced the viscount into the carriage at gunpoint.

"I doubt Viscount Hanberry came here of his own free will. Now he knows men of your ilk cannot be trusted. You mean to take his money and hurt someone he loves."

Victor chuckled like she was stupid. "If he loved his grandson, he wouldn't have paid me to kidnap you. The old devil is my partner."

Her world shifted.

"He paid you to kidnap me?" The words slipped through her like ice-cold water, chilling her veins and numbing every muscle. Tears built, stinging the backs of her eyes. "Why?"

She knew why.

She wasn't a suitable match for his grandson, but the measures he'd taken to get rid of her beggared belief.

"Don't waste your tears on him, Sofia," Reid said, his bitter contempt directed elsewhere. "If a decent, moral person finds you lacking, perhaps it's worth some reflection. But the opinion of a selfish devil is beneath notice."

"Marrying her was your biggest mistake," the viscount snapped.

"No, my only regret is trusting you."

"Doubtless both statements are true," Victor mused. "Ruining my plans will cost you your lives. You've complicated matters. Then again, I'm ten thousand pounds richer for the trouble."

"Only one of us will die here tonight." Reid stood, kicking away the noose. "Shoot. You're likely to hit a beam in this dim light and with your shaky aim."

Victor stamped his booted foot. "Don't test me, boy. Do you want to know what the local justice will find when he comes here? A doctor dangling from the beams. A grandfather so distraught he used a pistol to end his misery."

That's not how this night would end.

Upon her signal, their friends would charge into the barn and arrest Victor Merrick. Only one question remained: Would they arrest a viscount?

Keen to bring this matter to an end, she faced Victor. "Leave while you can. Being a wanted felon, I suggest you venture somewhere farther than France."

Victor lunged at her, seizing her elbow and yanking her to his side. Tightening his grip, he aimed the pistol at her and sneered at the hostages. "Kneel. Both of you."

Hands raised, Reid did as Victor asked. "Don't hurt her."

His grandfather refused. "I kneel for no man. I'll certainly not bow to a criminal. Go. Take the girl as planned. My grandson will come to his senses soon enough."

The cold, callous nature of the comment roused Victor's ire. "If you're still breathing when I leave here, I'll visit you in Cavendish Square and finish the job." He released Sofia and made the mistake of stepping forward. "I know a wicked devil when I see one. The only thing keeping you from Newgate is that silver spoon in your mouth."

The viscount looked down his snooty nose. "Is it wicked to protect one's heritage? Besides, I'm not the one waving a pistol."

No, but he was just as dangerous.

Sofia reached slowly into her hair, removing the pearl-topped hat pin she'd used as a decorative piece in her coiffure. Since the incident with Mr Turner, she felt safer knowing she had a weapon.

"You're a damnable heathen," the viscount added, his tone venomous.

Victor aimed at Reid, not the elderly fool. "I've been climbing the ranks since escaping the workhouse. I'll trample over anyone who stands in my way, including your grandson."

With tensions heightening by the second, she called for help.

"Now!" she cried, just as Victor cocked the pistol. She gripped the hat pin, plunging it through Victor's coat sleeve, deep into his arm.

"Argh!" The pistol tumbled from his grip as the beast howled and dropped to his knees, cursing her to Hades.

Everything happened in a blinding flash.

Lord Rothley and Mr Chance charged into the barn. A fight ensued, though Mr Chance delivered a powerful blow that sent Victor spinning to the ground.

Lord Rothley grabbed the noose and used it to secure Victor's feet. "The coachman is a hired thug. We tied him up and left him inside the vehicle until we can summon the local justice of the peace."

Reid didn't ask why the marquess wasn't lounging at home, reading morbid poetry and sipping cognac. He called to Sofia, opening his arms and sweeping her into a crushing embrace.

He lifted her off the ground, kissed her ten times on the temple and uttered, "Ignore my grandfather. I'll make sure he never bothers us again."

Aaron Chance grabbed Victor by the scruff of his coat, forcing him to his feet. "What should we do with Viscount Hanberry?"

Reid faced the viscount whose arrogant stance faltered. "Do you know what happens to those who poison families with their evil plots and schemes?"

"No, but I believe you're going to tell me."

"They spend endless days and nights alone. They dine alone. They die alone." Reid turned to Aaron Chance, his tone firm when he said, "My grandfather is an accessory to kidnapping. Take him and his chest of coffers back to London. Let him answer to Lord Melbourne."

Chapter Twenty-One

The vibrant hum of conversation and music swept through the corridors of the Earl and Countess of Berridge's opulent townhouse.

Hidden in the dark depths of the library, Reid vaguely recognised Beethoven's Minuet, but he was more engrossed in the feel of his wife's breast in his palm and the sensual glide of her mouth over his.

Someone rattled the doorknob again.

Sofia broke contact, her breath warm against his lips.

"It's locked," he reassured her.

"We've been here far too long. As the guests of honour, we should return to the ball before we're missed."

"I doubt the countess will notice. She's busy making sure her ladies are dancing." Poor Rothley had taken to hiding in the orangery on the pretence of smoking a cheroot. That was probably him trying the library door.

"Reid, if we don't stop now, it might spoil our time at the Adelphi tonight." She ran her hand over his chest. "In our story, we were mindless with need and falling over ourselves to undress."

"You're right." Despite a raging cockstand, he tucked his wife back into her gown and straightened the bodice. "Anticipation heightens desire."

"We need only stay for another hour," she said, watching him button his trousers. "We should keep Lord Rothley company before the man turns into the wolf and tells everyone what they can do with their Viennese Waltz."

Reid laughed. "The countess is determined to drag him from the doldrums and find him a suitable bride."

"Do you think Miss Bourne will ever return to London?"

Reid cupped Sofia's cheek. She was a hopeless romantic at heart. "I know you want Rothley to be as happy as we are, but Miss Bourne left London years ago. I doubt he will ever see her again."

"I hate to think of him all alone at Studland Park."

"He has Mrs Boswell for company and spends as much time at his townhouse in Hanover Square." He captured her hand. "Come, let's return to the ballroom. We'll think of a morbid topic to entertain Rothley for the next hour."

Upon their return, they stole an opportunity to dance a waltz.

Uncle Edmund drew them aside as they made to leave the floor, keen to have a private word, though they had dined with him last night.

"Is this where you tell me the viscount is dead?" Reid said

coldly. He would never forgive his grandfather for hurting Sofia.

Edmund shook his head. "He's confined to his bed with pneumonia. He's not expected to survive the week. As you know, I'm instructed to deal with all legal and financial affairs."

While they charged Merrick with kidnapping, murder and fraud, the King banished Viscount Hanberry to his country estate for a year. He attributed the viscount's deplorable actions to his failing health and a desire to protect his lineage.

"If you're going to ask me to manage Chatham Park, the answer is no." He had employed a new doctor. Sofia was his herbalist and secretary and tended to the poor at the practice on Thursdays.

"I'm giving you Bretton Hall," Edmund said, raising his hand to stifle an objection. "You don't have to live there permanently, but the house was always meant for your father, and I'm eager to mend past mistakes."

Edmund could not undo the damage done.

He couldn't retract the lie that saw Reid's father being sent to the prestigious University of Edinburgh in the dead of night. The lie that kept him there for seven months, resulting in Reid's illegitimacy. He couldn't erase the fake letters sent to his parents. More lies to tear two people in love apart.

But Edmund had helped to piece the puzzle together. He confirmed he'd discovered Reid's mother was with child and went to Edinburgh to inform Reid's father.

Edmund gripped Reid's shoulder. "I've made mistakes but want us to be a proper family. Algernon needs someone strong and moral who can help focus his mind. And I'd like to be a support to you and Sofia."

The warm words sounded genuine, but how could he trust

his instincts? He looked at Sofia. Her smile said he should accept the offer and embrace his family.

"I'll have nothing to do with Bretton Hall while my grandfather still draws breath. But my father spoke fondly of the time he spent there. Ask me again when you've succeeded to the title."

Mrs Reagan, a widow known to frequent The Jade, walked by and gave Edmund a look that carried more than a passing pleasantry.

Edmund bowed to Sofia. "If you will excuse me. The countess insisted I put my name on numerous ladies' cards. I would hate to neglect the wishes of my hostess."

Reid sighed as he watched his uncle follow Mrs Reagan to the terrace. "If only Edmund had spoken up sooner. If only I'd been made more aware of my grandfather's antics."

Sofia ran her gloved hand up his arm, a loving smile curling her lips. "Don't give it another thought. Life plays out exactly as it should. The Lord's master plan is beyond our understanding, but the truth always prevails."

"Had life been different, we might never have met." He felt the pain of that possibility as if he'd lived those lonely days.

"Then I am grateful for the times I cried myself to sleep, for the times I saw no end to the nightmare."

He brought her gloved hand to his lips, moving the silk aside to press a lingering kiss on her wrist. "Let's leave."

She laughed. "We agreed to stay for another hour."

He stroked her ring finger, preparing to tease her about her vow to obey him. "Did you not wear your ring tonight?"

They had an appointment to purchase a new ring at Woodcroft's tomorrow. Perhaps that's why she'd left it at home.

Sofia gasped. She snatched back her hand and tore off her glove. "Of course I wore it. This ball is in our honour. I've not taken my gloves off all evening, except when—"

"You touched me scandalously in the library."

Touch me. Touch me before I lose my damn mind.

"Reid, you must help me find it before Lord Rothley notices. I know it was a gift, but I feel he was entrusting it to my care." She rubbed her finger like she might make it magically reappear. "I should have secured it with thread."

"Don't worry." He kissed her forehead. "We'll not leave here until it's on your finger. But we should hurry before Rothley locks himself in the library to avoid dancing."

Rothley wasn't in the library. He was drinking champagne with Dalton, Aaron Chance and Lucius Daventry.

They would have avoided the men and headed to the hallway, but Miss Woolf approached the group, undeterred by their intimidating demeanour. She curtsied to Rothley, whose gaze remained fixed on her scarlet hair, not the plunging neckline of her gown.

Miss Woolf spoke, and the men turned to scan the ballroom. The lady pointed the moment she spotted Sofia in the crowd.

With no option but to join their friends, Reid whispered, "Wait a few minutes, then say you need air."

"Miss Woolf has been looking for you," Rothley said with some sarcasm. "Haven't we all?"

"We were dancing a waltz," Sofia replied.

"Yes, I'm sure you were." Rothley turned to Miss Woolf. "Well, now you've found Mrs Gentry, I imagine you're keen to retire to the ladies' room."

"Actually, no. I found her ring on the floor in the library." Miss Woolf produced the offending article, holding the treasure between her dainty fingers. "I knew it was yours, Sofia. We remarked the emeralds are the same shade as your eyes."

Despite Rothley's sharp intake of breath, Sofia laughed. "I believe the gems match the shade of your eyes more than mine."

Lucius Daventry studied the ring, then Miss Woolf. "Yes, they're remarkably similar. Almost as though the ring was made for you."

"Were you alone in the library, Miss Woolf?" The marquess seemed to scrutinise her face.

"Yes, of course."

"Doing what? The door was locked for some time."

"Lord Berridge has a fine selection of books. The countess said I could borrow one."

"What did you choose?" Rothley made it sound like she was on trial. "I don't see one in your hand."

Miss Woolf gave a bemused grin. "I'd barely browsed the first bookshelf when I noticed the ring. Is it a crime to loiter alone in a library? Am I under arrest, my lord?"

Rothley laughed like he'd meant to tease her, not pry into her personal affairs. "If it were, I'd have spent the last ten years in Newgate. As a repeat offender, they may have transported me to the colonies."

"They'd likely chain me alongside you, my lord, after arresting me for an insatiable appetite for melancholy rhymes."

Rothley smiled.

Good God!

Rothley never smiled.

"It's hard to break an addiction when I own the best selection of books in the country," he said, though wasn't boasting.

Miss Woolf's chest rose rapidly. "Then one might ask

what you're doing here." The lady caught herself, her cheeks turning as red as her hair. "Forgive me. A night spent with friends is preferable to a night spent alone with books."

"Indeed."

Miss Woolf excused herself, and Rothley watched her go.

"You do owe Miss Woolf a dance," Sofia told Rothley. "We agreed as much before we left The Jade to question Mrs Ludgrove."

"I'll not dance here. Not where gossipmongers reign supreme. Perhaps at The Jade. If I'm unfortunate enough to find myself there again."

Though they no longer needed to visit the library, Reid stood waiting for his wife to suggest a stroll outside to take the night air.

Then his uncle appeared, his cravat slightly askew, and asked Sofia to dance. Twenty minutes passed quickly, and she eventually returned, laughing and a little breathless.

Wanting her to himself, he slid his arm around her waist, drawing her close. "The countess will soon make a toast in our honour," he whispered in her ear. "Then we'll remind them we need to return to the Adelphi before the porter locks the doors."

"What do you plan to do with your family home in Dean Street, Mrs Gentry?" Daventry asked, and the conversation turned to the various possibilities.

"I might use it as a refuge for ladies down on their luck," Sofia said, her gaze drifting to a blonde woman cutting through the crowd. "A haven for ladies like Miss Tyler."

Miss Tyler came striding towards them, her unforgiving eyes fixed on Dalton. She looked like she wanted to murder him, not seek an introduction.

"Mother of all saints!" Dalton groaned.

"Do you know Miss Tyler?" Reid said.

Dalton shifted. "Her name isn't Miss Tyler."

Everyone in the group stared at Dalton, not the approaching Miss Heaven Knows Who. The man looked like he'd seen a ghost.

Sofia was quick to disagree. "You're mistaken, sir. Miss Tyler is a member of The Burnished Jade and lists axe throwing among her many accomplishments. The countess has taken her under her wing."

"Does *Miss Tyler* hail from Chippenham?" Dalton asked.

"Yes, though I believe she has Danish ancestry. A distant relative was amongst the Norsemen who settled in the area nine hundred years ago." Sofia tapped Rothley's arm. "We've had rather morbid conversations about blood pacts and firelit rituals. I could introduce you."

Rothley shook his head. "I prefer to go to bed at night confident I'll wake in the morning. Preferably without losing a pint of blood."

"Miss Tyler once—"

"Her name is not Miss Tyler," Dalton growled.

Sofia huffed. "What is it then?"

"Mrs Dalton."

Reid jerked in response. "A relation?"

"In a fashion. The lady is my wife."

A stunned silence ensued.

"Is this a joke?" Reid's heart skipped a beat as the woman with the questionable identity breached their group.

"I only wish it were."

"When the devil did you marry?"

Dalton didn't answer because his wife said, "Hello, Daniel."

"Elsa."

She stepped forward and kissed both his cheeks.

Dalton didn't move. He didn't breathe or blink.

Elsa removed two shillings from inside her glove. She gripped Dalton's hand and thrust the coins into his palm. "I believe that's what you paid for me. Now I've settled the debt I demand an annulment."

Despite his usual bravado, Dalton's face crumpled. He gripped his wife's elbow—the wife none of his friends knew existed. "Excuse us. This conversation calls for privacy."

Everyone stood in silence, watching the pair march through the crowd and onto the terrace.

Rothley sipped his champagne. "Who knew the night would take such an unexpected turn? Tell me I'm not the only one picking my chin up off the floor."

Reid wished he could make light of it and persuade them it was a joke, but Dalton was a private man, a serious man, and his shock had been genuine.

"I'm sure he'll explain everything in due course." Reid would learn the truth tomorrow and offer Dalton his support.

Tonight, he had a more important matter on his mind.

Tonight, he planned to ask his wife to marry him.

Adelphi Hotel
Adams Street, The Strand

The marble floors in the Adelphi's foyer gleamed amid the gaslight. Plush velvet curtains framed the tall windows, but Sofia focused on the sweeping staircase, eager to be alone with her husband.

Reid took her hand, and they mounted the stairs slowly, conserving their energy for the moment they stumbled into their room in a passionate frenzy. He drew her to a halt in a corridor lined with oil paintings and gilt mirrors.

"I thought we'd never escape the ballroom." He stood behind her, wrapping his strong arms around her waist and gazing at their reflection in the looking glass.

She rested her head on his chest and gave a contented sigh. "I had a wonderful time tonight, but I've been counting the hours until I have you to myself."

Reid kissed her hair. "I love you."

Her heart swelled. "I love you."

Tears threatened when she thought of the horrors they'd faced, but the past was behind them, the future uncertain. Nothing mattered but this perfect moment, where they were safe, happy, and in love.

"Can you see me without your spectacles?" he teased. "You might have come home with my friend Rutland by mistake."

"I could find you in a dark room packed with people. Your soul speaks to mine. Everything feels right when we're together."

"Which is why I'd like to ask you something privately." He took her hand, drawing her down the long corridor to the expensive Lancaster Suite.

Like their wedding night, the maid had turned down the bed and slipped a warming pan between the linens. A crystal decanter of burgundy and two matching glasses awaited them on the side table.

"No rose on the pillow?" she said, chuckling. "Perhaps we should have stayed at the Castle Inn. I'm told you can get one for a few pence there."

"I'm not sure I want to sleep in a bed made by Mrs Pugh or her congou-drinking sister."

Sofia kicked off her slippers. "Who said anything about sleeping?"

While Reid locked the door and shrugged out of his coat, she smelled the colourful array of hothouse flowers in the vase. The porter had remembered to light the fire at ten o'clock as instructed, but it wasn't the gentle heat of the flames that warmed her.

"Will you continue to keep me in suspense?" She watched him slowly slip off his shoes. "In our fantasy, you tore off my clothes and ravaged me senseless on that bed."

He drank her in, his gaze sweeping over her like a caress, sending a wave of heat through her body. His lips curved into a sensual smile. He looked handsome and so irresistible.

"It's a miracle we're still dressed and not a tangle of limbs in bed." He prowled towards her. "But before I ravish every inch of your naked body, there's something I must do."

"You have me intrigued, Mr Gentry."

He cupped her nape, the action affectionate yet possessive. "There's something I want to ask you. I'd get down on one knee, but I want you to see the truth burning in my eyes when I open my heart."

The world faded away. The opulent room could have been an alley in Whitechapel for all she cared.

She'd never thought a man would look at her like this, like she was the air he breathed, like she was a goddess amongst mortals.

She held his intense blue gaze. "What do you want to ask me?"

"Will you marry me, Sofia? Will you be my wife?"

She swallowed past a lump in her throat, a little overwhelmed and a tad confused. "We're already married."

"We agreed to marry. I never proposed."

He drew her closer, his mouth slanting over hers. The kiss was a deep yet silent proclamation, a promise to love her for eternity.

"I married you because I craved you, Sofia. As time passed, I knew I could never let you go. But I stand here as a man desperately in love, wanting to marry you for all the right reasons. I promise to be the one person you can depend on. The man you will come to respect and admire."

"You are the man I respect and admire most in this world."

She kissed *him* this time, pouring everything of herself into every slow stroke of her tongue, clinging to him because whatever existed between them was nothing short of sublime.

"You saved me," he said against her mouth.

"No, you saved me, Reid."

He grinned. "As a doctor, I'm trained to cure all ailments."

"I'm quite proficient when it comes to remedies myself."

"Perhaps I should put you to the test." He reached for her hand, drawing it over the rigid length in his trousers. "What will you do when your touch arouses your patient?"

The comment echoed what he'd said when she'd first begged him to hire her, when kissing him had been but a late-night fantasy.

"That depends on the patient," she hummed, firming her fingers around his solid manhood. "If *you* sought my help, I would unbutton your trousers."

He quickly saw to the task himself. "Then what?"

"Remove them and lie on the bed, sir."

Mouth dry, she watched him undress and climb onto the bed, the air pulsing wildly, the thrum of sexual tension tugging deep in her core.

She stripped down to her chemise and corset and moved to examine and caress every throbbing inch of him. "Does it hurt here?"

"Lower," he growled as she trailed her fingers over his abdomen and wrapped her hand around his solid shaft. One stroke, and he was urging her to straddle him. "Climb on top of me, Sofia. Get on top of me. Get on top of me now."

She didn't wait. Why would she? Having Reid Gentry inside her was a pleasure beyond words.

The feel of him filling her, of her stretching to accommodate him, had her closing her eyes and moaning aloud. "Love is the cure for every ailment."

He gripped her hips, thrusting upwards. "When our mouths and bodies meet, all our troubles disappear."

"Ours was not merely a lesson in scandal." She met his gaze, bent her head and kissed him softly. "We triumphed over treachery, survived the worst betrayals, and emerged stronger."

He cupped her cheek, his smile dazzling. "Darling, ours was a lesson in love."

I hope you enjoyed reading *A Lesson in Scandal.*

Did Mr Dalton purchase a bride for two shillings? How is it his friends know nothing about his marital status? Why would he marry his neighbour's sister and abandon her the same night?
Find out in …

One Wicked Secret
Tales from The Burnished Jade - Book 2

More titles by Adele Clee

Gentlemen of the Order

Dauntless

Raven

Valiant

Dark Angel

Ladies of the Order

The Devereaux Affair

More than a Masquerade

Mine at Midnight

Your Scarred Heart

No Life for a Lady

Scandal Sheet Survivors

More than Tempted

Not so Wicked

Never a Duchess

No One's Bride

Rogues of Fortune's Den

A Little Bit Dangerous

Temptress in Disguise

Lady Gambit

My Kind of Scoundrel

The Last Chance

www.ingramcontent.com/pod-product-compliance
Lightning Source LLC
Chambersburg PA
CBHW030540190726
48283CB00006B/1954